AF505620

Contents

1. Jyothi

My name is Vijay. I am 18 years of age. I was born in Tamil nadu. Now I am living with my parents in pune. I was a bit hesitant in writing this in the beginning. But I wanted to share my feelings, deeds and thoughts to like minded.

Since this is a long story extracted from my "secret diary" you will get the clear picture of my feeling and dreams with regard to a neighbor aunty, even though it is common for a boy generating erotic thoughts about neighboring ladies, but no one ever tried to put in diary.

Here I am trying to publish it with the hope that you will find it for an enjoyable reading and will be a change of `hardcore story emotional sex".

At first I felt it really awkward to publish it. This is an extract from my `secret dairy' with regard to sex with her. It all started two years ago when a boy named Arun Kumar from our neighboring street admitted in our school as a new student named in a junior class. We came close each other gradually.

From him I came to know that they are new to our place and staying in the next street. So friends, after a couple of days, he invited me to his house. Up to that time I don't like having visit to other's houses because that makes me feel very uncomfortable there.

Anyway, I went there that day along with my junior friend. I still remember the day like it happened yesterday. As we reached his house a very beautiful lady opened the door. My friend introduced each other. She was Jyothi his mummy.

She was so hot in physical appearance and in dress that I could feel my erect penis bulging in my jeans. She was 38-28-36. I was shocked when he introduced her as his mom. I was heartbroken. She was a cute girl like- just I felt like that. I couldn't hear also what she spoke at first sight.

From that night and every night, I used to think about her. She was the heroine of my dreams every night. Gradually I used to masturbate thinking about her. Not even in my wildest dreams I ever and always dreamt that this beautiful lady would fall in love with me.

Yes, within three months she and I are so madly in love. We cannot take our hands off each other, constantly talking to her on the phone whenever her husband leaves for work. Talking about how we love each other. Having fights for silly matters.

I used to go her house at least once a week. The sex I have with her still excites me especially I did the first time with her. I always think of making this lady my wife and having kids but I know that would never happen. I still remember the first time I touched her body, we kissed.

My first sex attempt with her, the first bath with her, the tricks I applied to get her in line, and more and more. We had together many times and her seductive moves towards me and the naughty games we played each other- I wrote in my secret diary at that time. How it happened!

I think you are also curious to know about it. At first, I didn't have the courage to speak to her in the beginning. In fact, the first time she saw me, she even asked "you don't speak right and why are you so shy?" I couldn't even answer her question.

But as days passed, I got the courage to speak with her frankly. In fact, I even took interest in her son's studies. He was only an average student. And I was one of the toppers of my class at that time. I helped him out in test papers. I didn't do it with the intention of impressing his mom.

Once I was invited to my friend's house for lunch on a weekend evening for the first time. She was wearing a pink sleeveless maxi. She looked damn sweet in that dress. She left her hair untied – just after evening bath. Her face was really glowing that day.

Following her to the hall I got a view of her wonderful and well shaped ass and how I wished if I could hug her from behind and kiss her. That day I saw my friend's father for the first time. How jealous I was at that man for marrying this lady of my dreams, I know it was childish to think.

But I already accepted her in my mind as my own. But his husband in fact was good natured man. I couldn't eat the food properly because she was sitting right in front of me. The dining table was quite small. So, a slight movement by my toe would touch hers. After dinner we sat down for watching a movie.

My friend already went in to his room for sleep. She sat near her hubby and their bodies touching each other. And as the movie progressed, I noticed his hands feeling her stomach. She was neither too fat nor slim. She was a bit plum, yummy!

Anyway, as we were watching the movie in between the movie I noticed her hubby talking to her some thing with his eyes and he excused to their bed room. There me and Jyothi aunty remained there. When she turned towards my side to explain something with regard to the movie, I noticed her maxi revealing her thighs.

I pretended not to notice, but it was impossible for me to divert my eyes from viewing those thighs. How I wished to touch those marvelous thighs of hers. When the movie was over, I decided to go home. Both her hubby and my best friend were already slept, so I thought of not waking them up.

She accompanied me to the door step I said good night to her and left. Gradually I was getting really comfortable talking to her. Her eyes and smile virtually attracted my attention. During my next week visit – then she said something that made my heart jump up in joy.

Both I and Arun (her son) can go for tuition together. Our tuition timings are from 10:30 to 12pm. "why doesn't u come to our house in the morning, so that you and arun can go together for tuition if u doesn't mind". She said her hubby's office starts at 9. I told her I would come at around 10. She agreed.

The front door was closed. I pressed the calling bell within few seconds she appeared in the door step as I was entering, she started to tie her hair up. Her hands were up to tie her hair her shaved armpits were visible through her maxi hand side. She looked hot even with her hair up.

When she said the final bye to me how I wished to lift her up and grab and hug her. From that day onwards I was a regular visitor to their house. Some times I was alone with her for just 15 minutes but those 15 minutes was enough to admire her beauty.

As I longed for the next day to come and so I can be alone with her. Somedays I would see her fresh after a bath. I would sit there and chat with her not concentrating on what she said. I would just stare at her as she would dry her hair. It was amazing to see her do it.

Somedays she would sit on the dining table and read the newspaper, and I would join her. One day our tuition was suddenly cancelled. So, I and my friend decided to hangout at their home. We three sat to play caroms.

She was sitting near me, and sometimes unknowingly her leg would brush mine, though it was incidental bit it giving me an electric shock. After a game she excused herself, saying she wanted to take a bath. As she went, I was in no mood to play.

I could feel my erect penis hitting against my pants, and how I longed to go and see her naked. I imagined, how she must look naked during her bath, how she would be applying soap to those marvelous breasts of hers, how she positions for soaping and washing her pooru(pussy) etc.

Also I wished to wash off the soap off her body. But that time it remained only sweet dreams to me. After a couple of weeks, when me and Jyothi aunty really got to talking, I started to come early by half an hour or so. Now I had 45 minutes of precious time with her.

Now I had the full freedom in their house. I usually accompanied her in kitchen and talking. She had a hobby of cooking new dishes weekly. I remember the first time she asked me to taste her new dish. She took a small teaspoon of the curry and came near me. I could really smell her.

She used shower gel while taking a shower. She usually kept her mangalsutra outside. I never knew that this hubby loving lady had a really wild side in her. Our tuition was shifted to a weekend one day. My friend still had another subject's tuition at 7:30. So I thought of going at regular time to his house.

As I rang the bell excited to see her no one was opening the door. After about 5 minutes she opened the door. Her top two buttons of her maxi were open, her hair was not combed and she was kinda gasping. I got the feeling confused and eager as to what she was doing there in privacy.

What made her to reach near door step so late? After some time when her hubby came out to take some water from the fridge my doubts were confirmed. She and her hubby were having sex in privacy as their son was left to tuition just half an hour ago.

In my inner heart I felt so angry at him for having sex with my beloved. One day we both went out together to a shop to buy her son a birthday gift. She wore a lovely yellow colored salwar, which was really tight. As we were resting, I really had the feeling that she was my wife.

She would often see how the watch fit on my hand. We were getting really comfortable with each other. After our shopping I asked her if she could come with me to my house as I had forgotten to take my tuition book. She agreed. I then was playing host, showing my house.

Both my parents were working personal so we were alone. I grabbed her by the hand to show some of my childhood photos. She was surprised to see how I looked when I was young. She was so close to me that time, sitting together some times our body touching, I could just kiss her rosy lips.

We were so comfortable now we would hold our hands together quite often. Jyothi aunty usually wore an underskirt beneath her maxi. It didn't give me a picture of her butt would look like. I was so curious about. But one day I noticed she wore this blue maxi and no underskirt.

I was very excited to see the outline of her panties. Wow that was a sight! We were sipping tea in her kitchen. I cracked jokes that made her laugh really laugh. It was amazing to see her laugh. She offered me breakfast. She told me to complete the breakfast which I left in plate.

I bluntly refused. But she kept on telling me to finish it. She sat really close to me and started feeding me the bread and egg. I tried so hard not to show any reaction to it. I felt like holding her cheeks and giving her a hot wet kiss. But I couldn't do it. What would she think?

I would be dead if her son- my friend- knew I had this feeling to his mom. I quickly got rid of that feeling from my mind for that time only. As I followed her to the drawing room I noticed she was wearing a black bra. From there I started to enjoy every moment of life while with her.

I was now a part of their family. I could go to their house any time of the day and there would be no complaint on their part.

I was very careful in my flirting with her. When her husband and son were in the house, I would try not to speak much with her. I learned to control my temptations as per prevailing conditions.

When we were alone I would openly flirt with her. I know that ladies want to hear praising words from others, telling her how beautiful she was and all. And she liked the attention she got. I knew she carved for the attention. I would just keep staring at her. We became really close now.

We would discuss various things in our regular chats at the kitchen. Some time I tried tactics as to not going to their house for weeks. And then when I would turn up at their house after a gap she would be angry at me for the long absence. But I was still not ready to take the drastic step.

It often crosses my mind but I would resist it. I liked it the way it was going at that time and I want to know how she consider and care me. Neither her husband nor her son liked to go shopping. So, we both would go out together someday to different shopping.

Once while we were just looking at clothes, I saw some nice night dresses for ladies. It was a colorful loose shirt and loose pants. I suggested it for her. She was skeptic in the beginning but when I told her she would look pretty in these, she agreed in the end. I accompanied her to every section.

But she avoided me by saying "you wait here" I understood that she was going to purchase bra, panty etc. I felt hurt. Why she avoided me? What is wrong in it? At first, I though I must convey my grievance. But at last, I though it was awkward to talk to her about.

I couldn't understand why she is keeping barrier lines in our relation.

Once when me and jyothi aunty was discussing various things, I noticed a big photo album. And when I asked what it was she told it was her cousin sister's wedding reception photos. She then opened it and showed me all the photos in the album.

I saw aunty in saree in well make up, she looked very hot in the saree. An orange colored saree in make up with nice lipstick. She looked hot. No one would say even she looked like a mother of a 12 yr. Old. The next day, when I and she were alone, I brought up her beauty in discussion.

I told her she looked very beautiful in saree. She immediately blushed. She tried to change the topic, but I kept on getting back to the topic of saree and I even complained as to why she wasn't wearing it. She kept quiet and just kept on looking at me.

Sometimes giving me a smile always and then at last she spoke. "Ok, you know what lets make a deal you promise to attend the diwali function at our house and I promise to wear a saree that day. I readily agreed. I really wanted to know what Jyothi aunty thought of me really.

Did she think of me as a friend? What was my status in her mind? Just her son's friend or some thing other But I was too afraid to ask her direct about it also. What would she think if I asked her this question and how odd it would be if she had no feelings towards me?

She definitely was behaving very freely towards me. But I really wanted to be sure. Every day the thought as to how would she look naked made me feel really excited. I would masturbate often whenever I had that thought. Was it lust or was it love? Whatever it was I loved it.

One day I got the chance. We both were alone in the house. She was going to take a bath. I was pretending to read the newspaper. After she had gone in to the bathroom and locked the door I waited for about 5 minutes. Then I made my move, If she found out what I was about to do it would be my end then and there.

I looked through the key hole. It was filled with dirt. I couldn't see anything. So I thought of cleaning it. I decided to hold on to my desire for one more day. The next day I made sure the key hole was cleaned before she went for a bath. This time I waited only for two minutes.

I had no patience at all. I looked through the key hole and the sight I saw was amazing. I was able to see Jyothi aunt's butt only and a curve of her left breast. My heart was pounding. I was very excited that day. I started to masturbate with the new images of her in my mind, her milky white body really amazing.

Her husband might be really enjoying her daily. As she got out of bath and came to me, I was a bit scared as to whether she might have suspected as to what I might have done, her smiling at me, gave me the relief. I love it when she wears a maxi. She looks really sexy in it.

She looks sexy in everything, her beautiful butt, high profile boobs. But that day I could see her nipples through the maxi even. She had really big breasts. And I longed to see them my penis shot up at the thought of that. While she was bathing I had stolen one of the photos from their photo album.

I wanted to see the photo of my lovely aunty in a saree every night. I thought me and she were getting really close now. All is left to grab at the first opportunity to have sex with her. Wild thoughts entering in mind but when would that opportunity come was the question in mind.

A few days later her hubby bought her a new mobile. I was thrilled on hearing that. Now I can console myself, that on days when there is no tuition I can hear her voice at least. She and I would talk to each other now everyday. We were like really close friends now.

During Fridays, we would talk in the afternoon, as soon as her son and husband would go for a nap. I was her confidant now. Whenever she would get angry at her hubby, her son, the neighbors, she would tell me and I would defend her or oppose her.

Soon that started to happen so frequently that; as soon as she would quarrel with anyone she would call me. So, one day I decided to ask the big question. While we were discussing something over the phone, I planted this question, "I mean who am I to say this, I am just your son's best friend".

To which she angrily responded, "If you were just that, I wouldn't say this to you even. You are more than that to me now. You are my best friend." I was jumping in joy. Now I confirm that I have a special place in her heart. She even said, "You know many things that my hubby also doesn't know."

To which I jokingly said, "Why don't you marry me". She started to laugh, thinking I said a joke. To which she responded trying to participate in the joke, "you don't want to marry me, you are young and handsome and I am an old married lady".

To which I replied, "I don't find you old, I find you irresistible, our body is still like that of a young girl" to which she laughed even more loudly. I quickly changed the topic. But now I was sure I could bring in these topics as a joke even. I even started to touch her, whenever we would be alone.

Touching her in the sense, scare her from behind. During those times, I would get really try to control my penis from erecting. I tried to feel her butt against my penis many times. All I wanted to do was to lift her maxi and feel her butt with my penis.

She would also take the initiative in touching me some days. Whenever I would not shave she would touch my cheeks and tell me to shave and advice me be neat and clean. My big moment almost came one day. That day I went an hour early. She was busy watching a movie.

She was seriously watching it, and told me not to disturb her, as it was the last part. I thought of disturbing her, by coming in her view. Sitting near her, and blocking her view with my hand. She got annoyed by it. Suddenly I just decided to lay my head on her lap. She seemed not to mind.

I decided to make sure and tried again blocking her view with my hand. She took my hand and kept it on my chest and didn't remove her hand. I was in heaven. Here I was in the lap of my dream woman. I tried, to move my head trying to show, that I want to break free but actually I was feeling her wonderful thighs.

It was a great feeling. I removed my hand from its fixed place and first tried to feel her palms of her left hand which was placed on my chest. Slowly I went up her hand, and I reached her shoulders. I once again tried to block her view to make this as naïve as possible.

And then I started to feel her face. Wow, here I was, feeling her face, my fingers just caressing her cheeks, touching her ears, hair. I thought, this could be the green signal. This could be the moment, which I had dreamt for the past 4 months.

The movie got over, and I decided, to stop it, other wise she would get suspicious of my intentions. I pretended nothing just happened. And she caught my neck as she was in a playful mood, Jyothi aunty said "you stupid, didn't allow me to see the movie," pushing me to the other side of the sofa.

Now I was lying down on the sofa and she was almost on me. I separated her hands, pretending she was strong trying to feel her on me. Suddenly she slipped and she fell on top of me. That was a magical feeling. For two seconds she was in a position I could wrap my hands around her. But didn't.

She got up. Suddenly her hubby came. I thought she would lie, as to what we were doing, but she told him the truth. She seemed to have to no sexual feeling towards me. After her husband left, I changed the topic and asked about her marriage.

She got married at the age of 18. She was very naïve then, and was not ready to marry even. But then she said something that broke my heart. She said, "But over the years I realized what a wonderful husband I have. I love him very much." I was speechless.

All my dreams weren't going to be true. I was about to cry then. I was kinda mood less the rest of the time I was there. She seemed to notice it, and kept on asking what the problem was. But I said it was nothing. She called on my phone, and asked me to meet her downstairs.

This was the first time, I actually waited for him to call me, and say it was time to go for our ecomomics tuition. She tried to stop me, and demanded the reason of my sulkiness. She asked if I would come the next day, I told her that I couldn't come as I had to study.

She then caught my hand and asked me whether it was her fault I was sulky. I told her it wasn't. But kinda got the sense that it was something that she said that made me sulk. She asked me if it was because of what she said of me disturbing her. I said yes to that, so that I could get out of there.

She pulled me towards her, held my cheeks by her hands and looked me in the eye and said "for your info, Mr. moody boy, you didn't disturb me. I was joking yaar, I can't joke with my jaan also?" Now I felt I was not out of the race, and I was back on track when she said the word "my beloved" to me.

I know that she didn't actually mean to say this in the literary sense, but however naïve her thoughts might have been, I was feeling very happy. If she didn't have any feelings now for me, I could build it easily, because of the foundation I had built.

I was overjoyed that day, of the special relationship we were having. The next day I was not feeling very well. I was having high temperature. My mom and dad, were out of city with my cousin sister, and would be coming in the evening only, and I didn't want to stay home. I wanted to see my prince.

So I went to her house. She was surprised to see me kinda tired. When I told her, I was not feeling well; she touched my forehead, and started to worry, as I had fever. She told me to lie on the bed.

I refused at first, but she refused to hear me even. She took me to her bedroom, and made me lay in her bed.

At first I told her, that I wanted to go home, but she refused, she told "no one is at your home right now, its better u sleep here; I am here at least to take care of you." She called his son, and told him that I wouldn't be coming for tuition and school even.

He even called me and told me, to take rest in his house, and that, he would give his notes to me to copy when he comes back. I was feeling excited. Wow, now I could spend a lot of time with my princess. She gave me medicine and sat by my side.

I dozed off for a while, and woke up when her hubby came by; I pretended to be still asleep. He was kinda worried, when she called him and told him about my fever. He touched my forehead, and agreed with her, that I should be here only, at least I get better.

He even told her, he wouldn't be home for lunch and would come home in the evening. I was so happy. After he had gone, she came, and sat by my side. I was all the time smelling her. I slept for a while and when I woke up, my God, she was lying in the other side of same bed.

Lying in bed by her stomach she was watching a movie. I can see very near her butt, maxi was tight, the curve of her panty is visible even though it was under her skirt, and her bra in side of maxi I thought of having fun, I went really close to her side and placed my thighs on her butt, she smiled at me.

"How are you feeling?" I told I was feeling better then. I was really feeling better, now I could smell her body, whatever be the reason, I was enjoying it. Never in my wildest dreams, would I ever imagine this. I noticed my leg was on her maxi.

Instead of touching her leg with mine, I thought of pulling her maxi up, pretending that I was doing it unknowingly. A few turns of my body to my right and left, alas, I was able to lift the back side of her maxi to upper side. She seemed to watch the movie, and in between saw how I was feeling.

She had no idea, that her maxi little up to her upper thigh only. But the problem was I couldn't see her inner thighs. I even thought of running my hand through her butt and thighs innocently and gently touching her panties. But I knew that was dangerous. But I desperately wanted to see it. I couldn't think of a way.

Suddenly someone rang the bell, I pretended to sleep, and Jyothi aunty got up my leg which was on top of a portion of the maxi, kinda pulled her back. I opened my eyes a bit, to see my dream come true. Even if it was just for a second, I saw her butts and thighs with my body.

Now all I needed to think of for a way to get a chance to remove those panties. It was her neighbor. The moment was gone. Now she wouldn't come in that same position, as she was two minutes before. I lost my chance. But I was excited of the progress I made.

After an hour I told her I was feeling better and I wanted to go home. I was excited to go and masturbate thinking of that day's events. She accompanied me to the lift. I decided to do something big. It even took her by surprise. Before entering into the lift, I turned and hugged her just for a second.

Before she could say anything I told her "thank you for looking after me." She smiled and said, "Anything for a friend." I was excited by her not getting angry by my hugging her. I didn't go the next day.

I could now ask frankly as to what she was wearing, what color is her panties and all. These types of talks always made me feel very erotic. And she enjoyed answering to my queries. She even revealed her inner most secrets, as to how she desperately waited everyday to see me.

How attracted she felt to my body features. How young she felt in when she was in my company. And she also told me that she kinda figured that I was attracted to her. I decided to visit her less now, since I wouldn't be able to resist the temptation of tearing off her clothes, and making love to her.

In fact was the one who told her, it will be kinda risky to have sex, when there are chances of her husband coming into the house at any time since he works in nearby, which is just opposite to their building. We used to talk for hours on the phone.

I wanted to talk with her 24 hrs a day. One day our topic of discussion was sex. Once I asked about their lovemaking, about her view of second child, what is the contraceptive applying during love making etc how many times per week etc About weakness and hangover after love making etc.

She was not so frank in answering to any of my direct questions but responded with hints. We got into real dirty talking from then onwards. I was waiting for the right time to do it with her. I told her I was getting desperate to do it with her.

She maturely said, now you are not a matured for it "let's wait for the right time... I don't want to abruptly stop our love making." So one day I just went without the intention of love making with her. She was wearing that sexy sleeveless pink maxi that time.

She was talking over the phone at that time. I just sat there and stared at her beautiful eyes and boobs. She couldn't concentrate to what the person was telling her over phone. I thought of playing naughty tricks. Standing just back to her I first started to rub her butt with my front aside little budged due to erected penis.

My hands tied her from back and touched her high profile boobs on top of her maxi and bra. I pressed hard her butt crack side with my penis bumped jeans. She felt tingling sensation; she gave me that wicked look. Then I surprised her, when I started slowly lifting her hem of maxi. She tried to resist me.

But I refused to stop. She was in talks on phone and my hands now, in full force, ventured into her maxi. She stopped resisting now. She was wearing underskirt, and now I was royally massaging her heavy whitish thighs and inner thighs. She tried not to moan. My fingers slowly moved upwards.

She gave me the look trying to say "no". I pretended not to understand, and continued. My fingers got in touch with her panties. I rubbed her triangle over her panties. I pulled her closer. She suddenly told the person whom she was talking on phone that that she would call later. She cut the phone.

Then she came closer to me, and kissed me. Her hand was on my face, and my hands, now my hands got into her panties. But she was standing with tighter thighs; I was now feeling her pubic hair, very thick and curled hair there and played with her pubic hair.

Then down below, my face on shoulder and ear side, I touched her vagina lips, first I could not understand what this skin piece was. I pulled her pooru(pussy) lips fingered her pooru(pussy) canal, but I can't understand the shape of it, continued rubbing and fingering there.

She moaned very loudly. "Lets not do it now, he (her husband) will be coming soon. Please…….please! She said "my husband is planning for a tour along with son then day after tomorrow. I don't want to go, and I will be here. Then we can have the entire afternoon to ourselves."

I agreed to stop, but not before give her a long kiss. She noticed I was not happy with this abrupt stop to once again what could have been a hot wild sex. "Wait, before we stop, here's one sample for you what I will do to you on Friday." She got on her knees, unzipped my pants, and took out my penis from shuddy(underwear) for sight of my penis.

Her right hand held to bottom of my erect penis, and she started kissing my kunna(penis). I moaned in excitement. She then gave it a big kiss, and then said, "The rest in next" and she guided my penis inside of my shuddy (underwear) and locked the sib. I smiled at her. I then pulled up my pants.

I couldn't bear with the wait. The wait was exactly killing me. I wanted her now. I cannot take her out of my mind. The magnificent moment that we had, was in my head, and I would think about the entire incident again and again. I couldn't even sleep in night thinking about it.

I was waiting for the next day to come, not to make anyone suspicious. My hand kinda shivered when I rang the bell. It was she who opened the door. Jyothi aunty gave me that million dollar smile. She was wearing a red t-shirt and her husband's jeans.

Oh, how close I was that day to see those enormous breasts of hers. Her butt, tightly covered in jeans, when she started to walk I have a view of her tight panty line through her butt, I thought; now she would really be close to me. But surprisingly she seemed to act normal.

My studies started, and I was back to my daily routine. I was surprised to see her act normal. I wanted to bring up that topic, but I was scared. What if she refuses to continue from where we stopped? Then one day, I took the courage to bring up that topic during our conversation.

My fears were true. She said what happened that evening between us was wrong. "I kinda acted stupid that day. I don't know what got over me. But it has to stop. You are my son's friend..." I didn't let her finish, "don't say that. You even once said you considered me more than that I love you, please don't ditch me like that," we argued for quite sometime.

At last I had to agree with her. I was disappointed. But I knew, nothing would convince her of my love. The next few days, I was very reluctant to go to her house even. Some days, I purposefully didn't go. But she neither called, nor enquired when I would go to their house the next day.

I began to believe it was all over. One day when I went their house, I saw playing with a very cute baby. It was her neighbor's baby. The neighbor had gone out for shopping, and she volunteered to take care of the baby. I also got to playing with the babies.

After that uncomfortable conversation, this is the first time; we were comfortable with each other. I would take the baby, and make all sorts of funny faces to make it laugh. She would come close to the baby who is in my arms, and sometimes kiss it. I got really excited at that sight.

At one instance, the baby happened to catch her mangal sutra, and refused to leave in an attempt to release the baby's hold, she bends over, and that gave me a chance to see the inside part of her maxi. The baby and I got a glance of her enormous breasts.

The baby some times tried to pull her maxi buttons to suck her breast. She sighed. It was a wonderful sight. We had a lot of fun that day. The baby in fact was a blessing in disguise for us to get back close to each other. On another day, I noticed aunty was sitting and writing some things in her diary.

I sat opposite to her and started chatting with her. I thought of playing with her, by disturbing her concentration. She would ask me to stop it, but her smile showed that she was not serious about it and she was enjoying it. Slowly, my toe started to rub her toe. From rubbing her toe, it went to her ankle.

She didn't say anything. My toe started its journey in to her maxi feeling her legs. Then she gave me the stare but with the smile, telling me to stop it. I was enjoying it. Then she got up to make coffee. I followed her. I stood right behind her, and started playing with her hips.

She was definitely enjoying my silly gestures at her. I would also make sure her butt had the feel of my aroused penis. My hands were feeling her stomach and boobs over her maxi. She stopped making coffee and decided to go to the bedroom.

I ran up to her, wrapped my hands around her stomach from behind, lifted her a little, and took her to the bedroom. She started to laugh all the way into the bedroom. We stood in front of the mirror. She took her talcum powder and pretended to ignore me.

My hands started exploring under her stomach on top of maxi. I got to her triangle area and Started to press and rub there. I started to really feel it now. She kept on telling me to stop it, but I couldn't stop it anymore. She turned around, and began to kiss me slowly, we did the French kiss.

Aaahhhh, it was a magical feeling. I began rubbing her breasts more, and started pinching her nipples through her maxi. Suddenly she stopped. "He will come any minute, we can't do this now." I got really angry. "We can do it tomorrow, I promise." But I was not in the mood for waiting for the next day to come.

She began to plead me. "I haven't enjoyed you properly, what if tomorrow u change your mind?" "No, dear" while she was saying this slid her hands into my shuddy, and got hold of my dick… "I was desperate. Please show me your breasts, and I will agree."

"You promise!" She said, and I agreed. She removed her t-shirt, and now she was in her bra. I quickly removed her bra hooks at back. Yes, at last I got to see her breasts. Little sagged, it was really huge. Her nipples like grapes were standing erect out. It was damn sexy.

She was feeling nervous, standing topless in front of me. I began touching it, and started to kiss it. "No, dear, not today please" I didn't listen to her; I began licking her beasts, kissing, and small bite of her nipple. She moaned simply. She tried hard to push me.

But at last I stopped. "tomorrow, I am not going to take no for an answer," she looked into my eyes and started to massage my penis as well, shaking my penis with her hand, pulled out my foreskin fully, shaking faster and faster I ejaculated in open, my shuklam (semen) made a long jump.

Then she said "next time, I won't say no. I have begun to love you. I know this is extremely wrong. But let's keep it as top secret strictly between ourselves." My exams were getting really close, so I thought of not visiting Jyothi aunty anymore. I was now waiting for the exams to get over.

We would talk on the phone. Our talks would last for hours. I would sometimes ask naughtily as to what she was wearing today and she would jokingly say "a bra and shuddy (underwear)". What is the color of your shuddy (underwear) today? Do you wear it in night, do you sleep nude at night?

She responded my every question with yes or no. Answer. Another question to her "did you do it yesterday with your husband?" I asked! She said `no I am on my period' how may days it will take? I asked. She said 4 to 5 days. I said "that means now your flower is packed in extra cloth isn't it?

She said, no, "Now days I am using pads in place of cloth piece. Then she asked to me what about you yesterday night? Did u masturbate yesterday thinking of me? I said "yes, imagining your pooru(pussy)". Then she told "till you didn't see that then how can you imagine it?

I said "once I touched your pooru(pussy) lips and the crack there. Then I smelled my fingers. Still, I can feel your pooru(pussy) smell on my fingers". She laughed and said "you naughty, you like that smell"? "Yes very much, it felt very erotic" I said in return. "Do you shave your pubic hair?" I asked. She said "some times".

You do it daily? She said "2-3 days per week. "May I help you in shaving your flower" "please" I requested on the phone. Will you give me your panties to feel it in my thing? She said "wait" then I asked the most embarrassing question to her "how do you feel your hubby's kunna (penis) entering in your flower"?

She said after some seconds "feel something fitted extra in the abdomen". My kunna (penis) started to leak. After completing our talks on phone I had done a speedy masturbation. I was getting really excited as the exams were slowly one by one getting over. On the last day of the exam, that night was crucial for me.

I made many plans how to seduce her and how to work with her body and how to talk to her more erotically in order to build in her crave for full nudity and intercourse. I wanted her to know that I loved her, and how I want to have sex with her. How I wanted to love her passionately.

I would imagine myself getting married to her. About our passionate wild sex, she is getting pregnant by my penis. Even if none of those dreams get fulfilled, just I wanted to see her naked, and make love to her. I wanted to see her desperately. I was getting really excited.

After completing the last paper of my exam I reached her house. There I saw small crowd, I enquired about it from people standing there what happened. I came to know that her grand father-in law expired at his native place. Her husband and son were leaving for funeral.

After they left I thought of leaving her alone, and go home, but she asked me to stay for a while. She explained me the sad demise of her grand father (in-law). I couldn't even watch my princess crying. I told her it's all right, and hugged her. She placed her head on my shoulders.

We were in hugging each other for some minutes. I couldn't control it anymore. I desperately wanted to kiss her, and I knew, since her hubby and son are going on leave, this was my only and best chance for it. I kissed her cheek. At first she thought, I was doing it to console her.

But as I began to kiss her again, she slowly started lifting her head, and feel suspicious. "What are you doing?" She asked angrily.

"I love you dear. I know this is not right, but I couldn't hold it anymore. Ever since I laid my eyes on you I fell in love with you. Every night I thought of you. I cannot live without you. I know this is not right. But the fact is I am really in love with you, and there hasn't been a day where I would pray to god and ask as to why he is torturing me."

She was trying to push me. "No, this is wrong, you are my son's age, and you are like a son to me." I was got angry when she said that, "no, but I love you. You can do whatever you want. If you tell me to get out of this house and to never see you again, and then fine, I will do as you say. But I just say you that I love you"

I didn't complete the sentence and I planted a big kiss on her rosy lips. Suddenly to my reply, she kissed back. Yes. My big dream was coming into a reality. I was living my fantasy. My tongue began to go inside and explore her mouth. I pushed her, and was kissing her against the wall.

She was now passionately kissing. We stopped smooching for a while and began kissing each other's neck, cheeks, ahhh, it was a wonderful feeling. We were kissing each other passionately. I began to caress those big breasts of her. At last I got to feel those lovely breasts of hers. I was feeling her nipples.

Then my hands slid down and I slowly started pulling her maxi up, with one finger feeling her legs as I was pulling her maxi up. She was starting to slow down realizing as to what I was doing. She stopped kissing. "No, dear please, this is wrong, please" she began pushing me away, but I was not ready to quit.

Her maxi and underskirt were up to her panties now. I without thinking more slide my hands inside her panties, and in one swift motion felt her hairy pussy. I pulled down her panty; the spot of her panty covering her pooru(pussy) was dammed… She resisted at first, but then at last I put a kiss on it. She started to moan.

She took me to the bed room. She laid herself on the bed. I helped her out of her panty, a big panty having colorful flowers on it. I had a first time view of her pussy and the first sight of a pussy in my life. We kissed for a while. Her black bra was somewhat visible through her maxi.

My dick was getting impatient then she stopped to remove her maxi, then underskirt. Then I came out of my jeans, now I was laying with her in a shuddy (underwear) only. She inserted her hand in my shuddy (underwear). Freed my kunna (penis) out of shuddy (underwear), she tried to pull out my shuddy (underwear).

But it was so tight that I helped her to through it out. So at last she got to see my erect penis. She placed her right hand on it. Then she removed her maxi. I pushed her to the bed, as I wanted to take the opportunity of removing her panties and bra. I teasingly went on kissing her legs, thighs.

I stopped for a second to watch that wonderful hairy pussy of hers. I quickly then unhooked her bra. Now we were completely naked. We got to kissing. We kissed and kissed more. I was getting all too excited. This was a dream that come true for me.

I started to explore her other parts of the body, while I was doing that I decided to finger her pussy, but I was not enough knowledge of pooru(pussy) parts. I began by licking her neck going down, till I reached those huge breasts of her. I started licking her breasts, nipples.

I pretended to be a baby sucking milk from his mom. I then gave her right breast nipple a bite to increase her moaning. I went down, kissing her stomach, her belly button. I stopped fingering. Used my two hands to separate her two legs waited for a second, and then gave her pussy a big kiss and lick.

I continued licking it. And she was enjoying it, by running her fingers through my hair pressing my head to her pussy. I waited for a long long time for this. While we kissed, I massaged her big breasts. Then the naughty girl, got on me. She was sitting on my dick. I was enjoying her weight on me.

Her hands were feeling my hairless chest. Then she got into the exploring act. She was doing it slowly and in a very hot and sexy way kissing with her tongue slowly coming out and feeling the surface of my chest. Allowing a mature woman exploring our body with her tongue is a special thing to be experienced.

Slowly she got to my dick. With one hand holding it upwards, she invited it into her mouth. Starting it all off with the tongue playing with the tip of my kunna (penis) she took it fully in her mouth. She then took out a condom from her handbag. She was well prepared. She fixed and rolled down it in my kunna(penis).

Then came the insertion part, I started awkwardly. I don't know where to fit in her flower. I tried here and there. She started to laugh. Then I let Jyothi aunty to guide me. With her hands on my butt cheeks, she was showing me the right motion.

Just like sitting for pee position the full view of her pooru (pussy) was an ever remembering experience for me. Pooru (pussy) mouth opened widely, hair all around it, the inner part of her pooru (pussy) was in full view to me, the pink clit, she positioned herself in my kunna (penis), holding it with her one hand she guided it in to her pooru (pussy).

Then she slowly pressing her pooru (pussy) on it allowing it to go deep into her pooru (pussy), she let me do the motion. Her moaning started getting loud. Her boobs were dancing in accordance with her hip movement. I started to increase the motion. Her moaning was starting to get loud.

She was directing the speed of the insertion. I kissed her then to lower her moaning, just incase. We continued with our exploration. Then she whispered in my ear. "Let's do it while bathing." Holding hands naked we walked into the bathroom, we continued our kissing.

I always fantasized screwing her under the shower. We applied soap over each other's naked body. Her butt caught my attention while I was washing her backside; I went down and bit her butt cheek. She gave me a funny stare as to what I was doing.

I was on my knees, and I continued my exploration over the

lower part of her body. She parted her thighs for enough space for my mouth in her pooru (pussy), I pulled out her pooru (pussy) lips to sides and started to suck her kanth (clit) more and more.

I felt wetness in her pooru (pussy), smelled differently, inserted my tongue into her hole, now her hole was more visible, fully pinkish inside of it , as she pressed my face more and more to her pooru, she got on four legs like dog and cow, now I can see her big butt and cracks, and her black little as hole.

I kneeled down back of her positioned my kunna (penis) into her pooru(pussy) with a big thrust, she started to move back and forth against my thrust, at that time I was rubbing with my finger her ass hole mouth but she didn't care what I was doing with her ass.

At last my movement increased, speeded my thrust, her breasts were hanging and swinging like that of a church bell. At last, I started to spit my shuklam(semen) in her pooru(pussy) but in the condom. She was breathing heavily, she moves forward to release my kunna (penis) from her pooru, my kunna (penis) was freed from her pooru (pussy).

But still in condom, started to hang down, she turned around, caught my kunna (penis) rolled the condom and freed kunna (penis) from the condom, she started to shake it, took some time to re-charge it, then she guided my kunna (penis) to her mouth, started to suck it, her mouth move back and forth she was standing on her kneels.

She cupped my balls, and little hair all over there, when it got hardness she laid herself back opened her thighs and knees high in the air, now her pooru (pussy) is more opened, then she used her fingers to widen her pooru (pussy) lips to sides, her swollen clit (kanth) was more erect condition, reddish in color.

Her pooru (pussy) hole is more visible and can see the inner side of her pooru (pussy) hole, she invited me to insert my kunna (penis) into her pooru (pussy), by kneeling in between her thighs and she placed her thighs on my shoulders and tightened her pooru (pussy) muscles, and ordered me to thrust harder and faster.

I started to thrust, fully pulled back my penis and re-entered fully with hard thrust to pleasure her. She guided my hands into her boobs started to press my hand on her boobs with her hands along with my movement of kunna (penis) in her pooru (pussy).

Within seconds she climaxed, one big aaaaah sound from her along with heavy breathing happened to hear from her. But I continued it up to my second orgasm and finished fastly ejaculated in her pooru (pussy), but this time directly without condom support.

Laying on top of her body my face in between her boobs waited to return back to normal breathing of both then I open the shove and helped each other to wash every area of our body with the help of soap and water, I felt some grinning pain on my kunna (penis) when she soaped in the ring portion.

She also said about some slight pain in her kanth, I quickly wiped myself with towel, ran out of bath room and selected her maxi, shuddy(underwear) and bra from her fresh cloth line and positioned her shuddy(underwear) to enter her legs into it then I pulled it up – a hard job- heavy thighs.

I fitted her pooru (pussy) in it neatly and rightly, fixed the elastic band of her buttock v shape line clearly, then helped her to accommodate her boob in bra cups, so hard to lock it in. Then I placed a loving kiss in to her check and said many thanks.

This was the wonderful sex adventure and thereby the experiences cultivated by hardship and cleverness, ended in a pleasantest. It was my first-time sex experience also the ever remembering one.

2. Nagma

I am Nagma. I am from a big joint family. I have completed my 12th science from a good college. My family consists of 17 members. This is my first time to express my experience with my big brother "the night on the next day of my marriage". I am writing my experience after 11 months of my marriage. I have been married on 10th august 2005 with a fine doctor. Okay here is my story…

I was working in MNP BPO Company as a live supporter agent in Pune, xxx technology. Our Team members were satisfied on my skills, because I was expert touch typist and having good communication skills. I was just 24 years old.

Last year I was 23 and they handled the subscribed job to work from home, providing me a PC and connection with studio, cause of some of my family restriction….

I was engaged on July 10th and on my engagement ceremony, marriage date was fixed right after 1 month. I was too excited and frightened to get to see any male's penis in my life, but I was unsuccessful. I had just seen it on the internet. I just wanted to see the real penis of any guy, boy, anyone and that was my target in the life.

I was unsatisfied that maybe I will die without seeing a real penis… And when my marriage was fixed, I was totally distressed that the days have come in my life, but was so frightened about having sex firstly in my life with an unknown partner.

I was totally, fully, sad that what will happen on the first day of my night. Questioning myself from the date of engagement over my home from morning to evening and full night, anytime, anywhere, while working, while eating, even while sleeping.

I can't mention in words my thoughts. The day was coming near and near.

My big brother Bunty was a male beautician was well qualified and used to fulfill all my needs in my life from school to college. He was married to a young dance teacher who was from our city too. He got her pregnant so she had gone to her parents' home for rest.

She will come on the marriage date and my brother had a salon attached to our native residence place, where no ladies were allowed. He was nearly 6" tall with good personality and was a national player of hockey and he was athletic.

Many of my colonies' girls were trying to make love(sex) with him, but he was too good and faithful and used to think not to play with anybody's life (especially girls). In short to tell he was totally physically fit for any women.

Any actress would also give her life for him, that much good he was through externally as well as internally.

Coming to my story…. the day came which was 8th of august 2005 two day before my marriage. My facial and scrubbing and the other things which are done before marriage was going to be done by my brother on that day, because he was good beautician.

He suggested to my parents that it is better to get those all sorts of pre wedding care in his shop but after shop closing time that is after 10 o clock. The whole day I stayed with my relatives who were here from many places for my marriage ceremony.

After getting mehndi and all other things, at late night, nearly 11 o clock after dinner my brother and I were at the shop for my pre wedding care. As I have told you that I was thinking of all the things that what will happen on the first day.

Because I was virgin and it will be more painful to me to manage that night with that new guy, but I ignored. Me and my brother only were in the shop late at night. After entering inside he shut down the shutter.

We were on the step that when I was wearing my haldi's saree my brother told me to take off my upper folds of the saree from my shoulder so the beauty care may not affect the saree. I was on the chair for the same. My brother started the process on my face, hands, legs and lumbar region.

While doing all sorts of face wash and every type of scrubbing and massaging, I became too hot. My body was feeling things I can't even mention, not even in words. One important thing was my brother's wife was not with him for last one and a half month. He was also somewhat impressed by my sweetness.

But he was unable to express himself because was his innocent thinking and I was going to get married. While all sorts of experiments were going on my body, he was totally free while doing all the experiments with those herbal products on me.

First, he started up on my face and he strictly told me not to open my eyes, cause it may affect the eyes. He cut two pieces of one cucumber and placed upon my eyes. After that he massaged my neck with that specific mixture, next he massaged it to my hands as well as legs till my knees.

While he was doing this all I was too hot and I started moaning. He was able to determine that what is wrong with me. He told me Nagma stops those feeling, I am your big Brother and it is not good that we should make any wrong relation here.

You are my dearest and nearest and sweetest small sister getting married in a few days. But I was unable to control myself, I pleaded to my Bunty brother and let him know all the things troubling me since the engagement date. My Brother became red hearing all these things.

He too couldn't control himself, that he also did not know that he too is in the same temptation upon me many times, but cause of innocent mind he hasn't troubled me or any other virgins before. But today he let loose and the moment came in my life.

Bunty bhaiya (brother) started massaging my breasts from top of my blouse and said that I had been masturbating every night thinking of you since last one and half month (cause his wife was not here) and waiting for this wonderful night, but could not try anything (cause of big family)

"Now please don't stop.... Let it go.... Please", he now too pleaded me the same. Then he started. I was happy to hear all this from my own brother's mouth. He washed my face, legs, upper hands, lumbar as well as my mehndi, completing everything in a few minutes. He smooched me.

Our tongues met and started playing. I had never expected all this so easily but now he was all mine. I slowly removed his t-shirt and was amazed to see his hairy chest, cuts, arms all and everything. I was exhausted. He said Nagma you are too sexy, and though you are my own sister.

I like you too much too much, more than my wife also. Then I asked" Bunty brother, can I ask you something? I never had sex earlier?" He said "Nagma, since this is the first time any guy has touched you. I always wanted me to be the one." he was blushing. This was making me wild.

He asked "Nagma, would you like to give me a blow job the way those girls give in the movie" he knew where I was working, that I have seen those xxx pointing towards dick. I wanted it badly but was still hesitating, as he was my brother and we were from one family.

I said, "Bunty, I surely want it if you don't mind". He said "oh come on Nagma... Thanks". There is no need to hesitate, so what if I am your brother. Now we are from one family and now we are friends and though you are getting married day after tomorrow, it is good to know something before your first night.

I will seduce you and you help me with it, that way there will be no pain while you are with your hubby. And he told in sweet language that my little sister will be burdened by that doctor and he will give her pain too. So, a friend in need is a friend indeed as like my brother understood.

Just forget our relation and let's enjoy this moment". I held his cock in my soft hands and started moving it up and down. He was looking in my eyes and my eyes were fucking her body. I slowly moved my tongue on the tip of his 9" dick. Wow…. It was like a dream.

This is my first time……… and we both were unable to expect this situation because of my first time…. I asked brother how does your wife mean my sister in law take this huge cook, she is too cute than me, how does she bears….. He shyly knocked me and said, ask her only after she meets you….

Okay… I said I will definitely….

I covered his dick with my lips and started playing with his balls with my one hand. It was amazing…. The head of the penis was quickly moving up and down giving me the best of life, for which I was waiting from many years. I was finding myself uncomfortable taking his big dick in my mouth.

But he still continues. I was trying to take it completely. He started moving hard too and fro. Aaaaaa……. Aaaahhhhhh…… Aaahhahhhh he was feeling that he was about to cum……aaahhhhh…. Nagma… Aahhh… Faster… Faster Nagma…..don't stop please….. Nagma …

He was moaning…. He was about to cum but I did not want to eat his cum though he wanted me too. Next, he didn't inform me and I didn't get to know as it was my first time. He was doing it faster and faster to make me enjoy….. Aaahhhh… Aaahhh….

And in just another one minute he shot it all in my mouth...

Catching my hair tight he choked me and pulled my mouth... He was still shooting his cum and it spread all inside mouth and throat and coming out. I was totally exhausted...... I was feeling bad at that time... that gummy gummy chicky cum.... So bad.... I took a wash quickly.

Now he was opening the buttons of my blouse and my round small & firm tits were erect. His hands were now fondling my soft boobs. He kissed my boobs and pressed my pink nipples with his lips and there came a loud moan out of me.

He slowly removed my saree along with my panty. Wooowww.... It was a wonderful view of well shaven pink fresh pussy of mine to him. He was now again kissing me and also moving his hands all over my body. I had never imagined that things will go so easy.

All my luck. He moved his hand on my pussy and started rubbing it. My pussy was all wet. He stopped me and said I want you to kiss all over your body "he said innocently". I smiled at him and he started kissing me from toes to ankle and legs and then thighs.

As he reached between my thighs to kiss my pussy, I held his head with his hairs and pressed it towards my pussy. It was giving me pleasure and though it was new for me.

"Lick me dear...lick me...lick me hard...". He started eating my pussy like a dog. He thought of doing it with his sweet sister was making him hard. He continued licking me. "aaaaahhh.... Aaahhhh ahhhh.... Ooooohhh... Uffffff" my moans were making me wild.

Suddenly I came all over his mouth pulling his hairs with that wonderful pain. I had never seen such a big orgasm in my life coming from me first time as I am peeing. His face was completely wet with my perfumed sweet juice. Then he asked me if I was sure to fuck.

I said I wanted it to be you to break my cherry. I said please do it I love you so much while pulling me into his arms, he started kissing me and raised my legs and opened them more to receive his large cock into my tight virgin pussy as he was entering my pussy.

I said, "its hurts so bad"

He said that now I am at your hymen and that's what's hurting you.

I said ok I am ready as I raised my hips forward and pushed toward his cook and we came together in the middle as over hips met while French kissing he was moaning and I was moaning as well.

It felt so good inside me my brothers cock just knowing he was deep within me, my body was feeling his depths and having his arms around me and his legs around my back. My pussy was full of blood, but I don't care, because he was my own brother, no one else. I was crying, when my brother asked can I stop. But didn't allow him to stop. We continued.... He was very sensitive and was much careful, as we were slowly thrusting one another for at least 30 mins I felt his balls tighten, I must have felt his cock swell and started to kiss my pelvis, he then said can I cum inside of me I said you can, but.....

Nothing happens if I gets pregnant and I started to tighten his legs around my back looking in his eyes saying fill my pussy with your seed and make me your women for these remaining days as he was feeling his balls to the point of no return he started to unload deep within me.

Pumping load after load deep inside me and were kissing I said uff my god I can feel your cum shooting in me, while laying there after unloading the biggest load of my life from my big brother, his cock was deep in me and still hard, now I started to cum again and could not stop

He was so wet and then he fucked me and seduced me greatly on that wonderful beautiful night. Well that night was the best of many nights to come.

Next morning when we woke up I found that he was unaware of what happened last night. But then the guilty feeling was still there in his as well as my mind. The whole day we went with that feeling. At night I went to sleep in my room. As I slipped into my bed that incident started hitting my thoughts.

My eye was close and was again feeling that softness in my thoughts. Those thoughts were coming again and again to my mind and in few minutes I found my pussy getting wet. My hand was pumping it gently. I was surprised of this sudden change in me.

From guilty I had started fantasizing my own brother. But it was all so beautiful. His big dick and his soft skin.... I had never ever determined anything like that about my brother's pleasure given me that night. Today I realized that he is so hot and beautiful with innocence, my sister-in-law is lucky.

Lastly one thing I want to tell you that I gave birth to a small child. When we counted it was after our marriage date 9 months and 7th day only. (usually, baby delivers after 9 months and 9 days) and I determined that that baby is not of anyone but my own brothers....

3. Shilpa

This happened when I was teaching in the local college at Sujanpur. I had my own house at Sujanpur and for most of the year I used to be alone at my home because my parents had gone to stay with my brother abroad.

Since I was alone at home, my house became a place for parties and fucking of prostitutes. Often, my friends used to bring their girlfriends to my place and used to fuck them all night and sometimes even I got lucky in fucking them.

I had this huge drawer full of panties with me due to stealing of my friend's girlfriends' panties. There were all kinds of them, in every possible color and every design, from the cheap cotton ones to the designers; I had all in my collection. Sometimes I even used to put them on for the night.

I even remember that I even went to teach in the college with one of the panties inside my jeans. Well, I was just so horny all the time. The incident which I am going to narrate happened between me and another female teacher of history in the college.

Her name was Shilpa and her husband used to work in the local bank. They had rented out an apartment here and they had two small kids too. She used to teach history and was not very open in the beginning. She only talked to the point and nothing irrelevant.

To add to this shyness, she even wore such clothes which didn't reveal even an inch of her body. Her sleeves were covered to the wrist and she would keep the dupatta over her tits and she wore heavy cotton suits and thus initially it was difficult to make out how big her tits really were.

It was only when she opened the almirah to keep her books; I could make out the size of her globes. They must have been 36dd and she had a bumper ass too. I wondered what kind of panties she wore. The strangest thing about her was that she belonged to Bihar, a very rural and rustic part of India.

Though she had a dusky complexion but it was more to the fairer side. It took a lot of time for me to get her to talk but I had the advantage of a free period when only she and I used to be there in the small staff room. It was in the afternoon before lunch when both of us waited together for our lecture.

She didn't talk much initially but soon my jokes and funny nature was helping me out and she became a little more open with me. It was the summer after monsoon, and one day she took me by my horns as she came to college.

I clearly remember that it was nearly 9'o clock in the morning when I reached the staff room. It was very early in the college and a few students were waiting in the classes while the staff room was just empty. Only the peon was there but she was doing some other chores outside.

I was just looking over the book and preparing for my lecture when Shilpa came inside and said "Good morning Ankit sir". She was dressed in a very light-yellow suit and I could clearly make out her flowery bra underneath it. A little bit of her tummy could be seen and it was fat, had flab around it which looked so kinky.

Her bellybutton was in fact another pussy of hers as she had gathered some flesh around her third closed hole but it looked so much inviting. I was only making out from the outsides of her suit. As she came towards me, her dupatta slipped and for the first time I saw her breasts looking so big from the front.

Then, we started to talk and we kept talking so much that we missed our class. In the afternoon too, we kept talking and slowly she asking me questions of all types. She even told me that she didn't feel much strange for extra-marital affairs as it is between a male and female to do it.

She even told me that she liked the doggy position more than the missionary but her husband was not keen and enthusiastic about it. She said that she wished she had more spice in her sexual life. O my God! My fellow lecturer talking this stuff to me and my pole had already risen.

I was stupefied but soon the bell rang and off to class, she went. Besides this little horny chat, she often started calling me up in the afternoon at times and she used to talk for hours. Slowly I was also developing a liking for her. I started masturbating on the name of her unseen cunt every night.

Her huge mammary used to hang from the sky at night in my dreams and I used to suck them and chew on the rubbery nipples which I had not yet seen. Gradually, she was changing in her attitudes too.

Now, she started wearing short sleeved suits and sometimes she even went to the extent of putting on sleeveless suits in such a conservative Indian college. By and by she was becoming attractive each day. One evening, I saw her strolling right in front of my house with her 3-year-old kid.

I went out and asked her to come in for a cup of tea. I played cartoons on the TV and the kid was busy watching them. Then I went to the kitchen and Shilpa followed me. She was wearing a similar cotton suit of revealing nature, this time her arms were very short. I poured water and kept in on gas in a tumbler.

But as I turned back to get some sugar, Shilpa was right behind me, her big breasts moved on my chest and back. I got an instant hard-on as I turned towards her, "Oh Shilpa madam! Aap (You)", she didn't look surprised by the uneasy situation we were in.

Her breasts were crushing my chest and her face was so close to me. She had a mole on her neck which looked like a third nipple, it was so nice and I wanted to suck that mole on the dusky fat neck. She had three nipples including her mole and three holes including her bellybutton.

All this was so kinky.

"maine socha pata nahin Ankit sir ko chai banana bhi aati hai ya nahin?" (I thought I don't know if Ankit sir does know how to make tea or not) And then saying this she put her arms on my back and pushed me to kitchen sink sandwiching me almost while my prick almost felt her big supple thighs. "Madam, main bana lunga na" (Madam, I will make it)

I stammered as I felt my heart in my mouth feeling her nipples stiffen on my chest under the bra. "kaun se doodh se banaoge chai." (Which milk will you use to make the tea) As she laughed pressing me even more and winking her eye. I was getting so horny by all of this and now I became bold to put my hands over her bumper ass.

I squeezed it a little. "mere doodh ki chai to nahin peeni hai sir?" (You won't the drink the tea of my milk, Sir) Oh my God what was happening, I couldn't believe it. She was inviting me for a cup of tea with her breasts milk. I was gone for reason now. As I bent her face and kissed on her neck right on her mole.

I stretched my palm fully to cup her humongous buttocks which felt so spongy. "Shilpa madam, ek chumma to de do. Hai kya sexy body hai tumari" (Give me a kiss, what a sexy body you have) now she was also turned on and she put her hand on my cock over my pajama and started rubbing it.

"chuma kyun meri jaan, jo chahe who le lo aaj mujh se" (Why just a kiss honey, take what you want from me today) she said in a filthy bihari accent now, "hamar badan main aag lagae rahe, ab kuano chumma magnat ho" (My body is on fire, now why are you asking for a kiss) I looked at her face and she appeared like a cheap bihari slut for a second and then a housewife slut for another.

Within a second I just raised her arms to get her shirt out. Her beautiful breasts swung to me in full glory encased like an antique in a cream flowery bra. The bra was making nice contrast with her bubbly brown flesh. It was probably a half cup bra since I could make out almost half of the areolas peeking outside it.

I looked down at her flabby tummy and my cock rose like a demon from slumber, her bellybutton was too inciting for me and I quickly bent down and kissed her madly on her tummy taking full and sumptuous bites of that soft brown flesh while she started moaning too.

My hands had instinctively gone to her huge mountains of flesh on her back as I kept my face in the valley of her flabby tummy. I was tweezing her big buttocks like I m kneading the flour and soon my face traveled upwards to her breasts. I was surprised to find the bra gone now.

She had taken it off for me, how nice of her. Her huge bounteous breasts were staring me in the face and her beautiful bean like nipples were standing like pencil erasers on their ends as I moved my hands to support them from below. As I lifted her big boobs in my hands.

They beamed perfect rotundity and were so round that they could make a circle look square in front of them. Here I was holding her hidden treasures in my hands. Her areolas must have been more than the size of a small c d and were deep brown covering almost half of her breasts.

At the center of them erect those proud nipples who knew no shame now. I softly caressed them with my hands just to feel how huge they were. I put my face in the valley of her breasts now and I kissed on the sliding gorge lapping up with my tongue.

Slowly my mouth was moving over to her areolas and I lapped

them up, licked them hard like a dog drinking water with his tongue, and finally when I reached the nipples, I stopped to have a full look at this heavenly lusted breast now. The moment my lips touched her nipple.

A flurry of uncontrollable passion rose within me and countless sparks emitted together from her nipple as if there has been a short circuit somewhere in her body. I was eating the nipple now as if it was a chewing gum. I was trying to milk her but the milk wouldn't come.

Soon, she understood what I was trying and disengaged me and said, "Ankit sir, main abhi aayi, aap bedroom main chalo." (Ankit sir I will just come; you go to the bedroom) She went in my drawing room near the TV where her child was sitting. She took him in her lap and thrust her nipple into his mouth.

The child even protested as he was probably not in the mood for some milk. But she forced her big breast in his mouth and soon milk started flowing. Now she came over to me in the bedroom and lay on the bed offering me her huge breasts. A drop of milk had formed on her right breast now.

I lapped it up with my tongue and then started to suck on her nipple. O my god, milk was flowing into my mouth. There were streams and wild torrents of milk inside my mouth now. "doodh chai ke liye hai Ankit sir, aapke liye nahin" (Milk is for the tea Ankit sire, not for you) she asked me to spit that milk in a tumbler.

Thus, we started collecting milk for the cup of tea. The taste of her milk was a little salty but it was so nice to have it in my mouth. Slowly I emptied both her big boobies. She disengaged me from her boobs and kept the tumbler on the side. I got up and locked the bedroom door and blew the fan at full speed.

When I turned back, I saw that Shilpa was removing her salwar and now her beautiful black ass came out clad in the flimsiest of all panties. I couldn't imagine in my dreams that beneath this conservative college teacher lays a sexy woman who has a drive for sexy underwear too.

Her panty was nearly transparent and it was just a strip connecting and covering in a manner of revealing more and concealing less. Her pubic hair was dense and there were some around her asshole too.

I couldn't wait for her so I jumped on her in the bed. She spread her legs for me and then pulled the panty to a side and moaned in a husky voice, "Ankit sir, I have never tried alternate sexuality. Will you help me? No one has licked my pussy before. Ankit sir, will you do it please"

Well, here she was so horny and inviting me to suck her pussy. I got so excited that I tore the panty with my teeth and then chewed on her large's pubic hair for sometime before finally giving French kiss on her vaginal lips. She writhed and moaned in ecstasy as I lapped up her jelly like clitoris between my teeth.

I thrust two fingers now in her cunt and started to pump them while my lips were nibbling at her fiery brown clit. I increased the motion of my fingers in and out and my hands went out to her huge sag less tits.

I squeezed them to my delight while she writhed like a snake and bumped her ass on my face, grinding her juicy well fucked pussy on my lips. She was jumping on my mouth now and I felt that she could come any time now.

I shifted and took my cock out, masturbated it a bit for complete erection and then quickly slid it in her glory hole. Her pussy was so large that I had no problem in accommodating my boner in the very first go. I seized this opportunity for complete fun as I could slide in and out completely now.

As it was loose, so I would take my cock out fully and then insert it again with a thud. Every time it entered her pussy it made a huge sound of pouch...Oh god I loved this sex play. I asked her,

"Shilpa teri choot bahut khulli hai ..." (Shilpa your pussy is wide open)

"haan haan college ki ladkiyon se to khuli hi hogi na" (Yes yes compared to college girls it will be wide open) she laughed indicating that I fucked college girls too, which indeed I did at times. Now I lifted her in the air while standing and fucked her while she locked her legs at the back of my waist and with her arms on my neck.

She bounced like an expert on my cock. It was going up inside her like a piston now. I increased the speed too while my mouth natural found her well milked and breastfeeding motherly tits. My hands rested on her bumper ass as I fucked her in abandon.

She then, pushed me back on the bed and came over me, thus controlling the game of love. She pushed my face back and then she started to dance in front of my face with her tits. She started to swing her huge melons on my face and slapping them in between.

She also slapped her ass as she swung her tits on my face. My face was being slapped by two huge mountains of flesh and it was ecstasy. I couldn't hold on longer and bit them again and again. I bit her titties so hard that my tooth marks were there on all over her flesh.

She was moaning loudly all this time. I was surprised to hear that now her language was getting filthier, "hai hai hai Ankit sir…le mere mummon ko kha lo, hai. Mar gayi …daanton se mat kato na, mere pati ko pata chal jayega… Hai le meri chuchy, lel le mere mumme…kha mere mummon ko…tumhari liye hi to itne bade kiye hain…kha… mere yaar. Bana mujhe apni randi, apni rakheal…chaat jee bhar ke…" (oh my oh my Ankit sir…. Take and eat my boobies…Oh my… I am dying…don't bite with your teeth, my husband will come to know…. Oh, my pussy…take my boobies…I have made it big for you only…eat…my friend…. Make me your whore, your keep… Lick me till your heart content)

She was thrusting her full tit in my mouth. I could feel my cheeks swelling. Oh my god her whole huge breast was inside my mouth. I looked at the adjacent mirror and I saw my mouth swelling with her complete tit as if my body was glued to her. My mouth was a hole where she plugged her tits.

I was getting completely crazy now and I could feel her stroking my erect cock now. "chodoge Ankit sir, meri phudi maroge kya.... itne bade laude say" (Will you fuck my pussy.... with this big cock) Ankit Sir, she implored while shaking my cock and I was too dumbfounded to hear her use these filthy words.

I didn't give any reply with my mouth as she had already taken my cock to her dripping wet pussy. She kept it on her pussy lips and rubbed there. My cock was already throbbing and it rubbed and slapped against her vaginal lips. Then she pushed me back thereby removing her boob from my mouth.

She adjusted my cock with her hands and then with me lying down she started to jump on me. My cock was going like a knife in the butter. The sensation of hitting her pussy walls was too much for me, and I also started to pump from below. "hai, chodo mujhe, phaad do meri phuddy ...hai...mere raja... uuuuiiii". (hai.... Fuck me, tear up my pussy.... hai... my King... uuuuiiii)

She was ranting and raving a bitch on heat. I inserted my finger in her asshole now and continued to hump her with my cock. I slapped her ass and tits a number of times sometimes even slapping her face. Finally, I couldn't hold it no more while she was moaning so much.

I'm sure neighbors must have heard. I smooched her for one last time as I felt the storm rising in me. I asked her, "Shilpa madam! Mera chuutne wala hai...hai...uuuff...kya bahar nikalun" (I am about to cum... ohh ...ohhh uuuff.... Should I remove it outside) I was pretty relieved when she said that she is in her safer days so that I can ejaculate inside.

I cum with a bucket of semen inside her and I almost passed out as I cum. We lay there intertwined for sometime with my limp cock still in her juicy pussy. We were woken by her little son who woke her up by sucking her well used tits.

She just smiled and set her clothes right and left after a cup of tea I made from her breasts milk. Damn, it was tasty I must say. After that, we had many sex sessions and we made the full use of her free period, in both senses of the word.

I even had a miss timed shot with her at the temple in the evening when no one was there and she conceived due to that. Our baby is due in three months while her Bihari husband thinks it is his seed. Life has never been more adventurous. I would love to suck more milk when the child is born.

Till, then let me just masturbate on the sight of her protruded belly which is due to me. I m so proud and never been happy.

4. Maddy

My name is Aaditya Prasanna. My parents used to call me Maddy at home. My father is a senior IAS officer posted at Shimla. I basically belong to Banaras in Uttar Pradesh but I was born and studied in Shimla until I went to Punjab University Chandigarh for my higher education. I used to come home a lot of times.

The reason was that my mother used to have some fits problem. Once she even fainted in the toilet. Even though with all the care, she was getting better and better. Being a government servant, my father didn't have much time so I had to attend to her needs. My mother was not like the other Indian Brahmin mothers.

She had married my father early and my dad was 10 yrs older than her. So, she bore me in her teens only and now when I was 17, she was hardly 35. Later on, she went on to do a PhD in Sanskrit literature but she could pass for any college going girl in her looks.

In fact, when we moved on the mall in the evening, many mistook her for being my girlfriend. Not many people knew that we are mother and son. As she was the wife of a bureaucrat, she used to pay a lot of attention to her fitness and beauty. She visited parlor every third day. She was truly very beautiful.

She very fair, with her 36dd breasts jutting out; she could excite many men around and at home. She was given to traditional an outfit at home which was normally a sari with a full blouse and bangles, bindi and all. I never had any sexual urges towards her. I always thought of her as my loving mother.

She was also very religious and spent a lot of time in meditation and religious offerings. She used to dress up like a new bride with full jewelry and bangles and traditional bordered saris. It was strange that she still wore designer colorful bras and panties which I saw often drying in the sun at the back of the bathroom balcony.

I often picked them up and smelt them and only put them down after masturbation. I think that was when I picked up this panty fetish. I loved each and every panty in the world. I also used to look at drying panties of my neighbor's wife who wasn't attractive but had nice torn panties.

She also attended a lot of religious communions and spent a large part of her time in working with charities and other religious functions. Every morning, she used to bathe early and then after properly decorating herself, she did prayer and often woke me up by offering the prasadam of the prayer.

She was just like my friend and with her I used to spend a lot of my time. And now when she was having fits, I knew it's the loving care of her son which she needs. I used to take care of her medication and all. We were going smooth and happy and she was getting better all the time. Maybe I was in love with my own mother!

After a few days, father told us on the dining table that he had arranged a vacation tour for us and he had to stay back for some official work and could join us only after 2 weeks. Mother looked at me and said that she would be so happy to go out and asked father about the tour details.

Well, it was an amazing tour of snowcapped mountains dad had decided for us. At every stop we could find rest houses so stay won't be a problem and we also had a driver and a servant more to take care of us. Dad had arranged it to perfection. I was only too happy to say that I was more than willing to take mother out.

We started early in the morning and mother came dressed in a floral white sari with a pink blouse. I had seen her for the first time in such exciting colors but there were more surprises later which I would tell. We sat at the back seat of the white ambassador car and it had dark windshields.

There was also a partition between us and the driver. He could not see us. His name is Suryakantam Prasanna. He kept our luggage and we started our journey. Initially we talked about general things and then my mother, started asking me about my love life.

I was hesitant as I didn't have any girlfriends and I was still a virgin. Mother kept breaking the ice and soon she was talking naughty stuff with me. Then she told me how she used to tame boys in college with her looks. She said that she had brought a couple of her old college day jeans to wear in the tour and asked whether I would mind if she wants to dress in jeans for the tour.

Obviously, I said yes and to my utter surprise she pulled out a bag and started looking for them. She then took them out and I saw that they were really old and mom said that she will put them on later. After a long journey, we reached a forest guest house at the height of 4000mts.

It was the only building to be seen in the jungle. The huge mountains were towering from behind. There was also a small outhouse located at some distance from the big bungalow. The servants quickly got down with luggage and kept it in a room. There were a few officials of the guest house too but since my father was an IAS.

They all received us on their palms. They told us that in the evening no one stays here and we have the whole bungalow to ourselves. One of them was a friend of our driver so he also asked to go to village with them. Now we had only one servant left. Mother told him that if he wanted to go with them, he should do only after the food is ready and all the basic work is done. The servant then left us at about 8 in the evening after the food smelled well. We were very hungry from the travel and quickly had our fill. Then, mom got up and went to the room and came after changing into her nightgown. Then she asked me to change too.

I went inside the room and found that the bed was laid down with at least some 20 panties on it. I was spellbound to find even Victoria's secret and Roberto Cavalli in them. My mother's luggage was open and there was no hint of any much clothing in them but for a pair of jeans and some woolens. God so many panties but why?

I was about to smell their aroma when mom called me and I went out. She was standing in the center of the hall with a book on her hands. I went up to her and asked what it is about. She asked me to sit down and not to tell anyone about what is going to happen tonight. I was excited as I was unsure what is going to happen.

I quickly glimpse the book and found the photos of gods and goddesses on it. Oh god, maybe another religious lecture tonight! But it was not to be. Mother then asked me if I knew anything about tantra. I obviously said no. Well, she went on to explain the mysterious powers associated with tantra and how it could finally bring about the best of spirituality in anybody.

She said that this tantra has got many parts but the best is the part where lord Shiva has conveyed some mysterious powers to Goddess Parvati and this is called ' yoni tantra'. She went to explain that since it was very sacred and mysterious, not many people knew about it and this book that she was holding was given to her long back by some sadhu who knew about it.

She said that she was only waiting for the right time to use this magical book. I took a look at the book. It had some handwritten Sanskrit text and various drawings of mandalas besides numerous illustrations of the pudenda. I tried to understand the meaning of the words but they were in Sanskrit so obviously I couldn't do it.

I asked mother that I was still unclear what it was about and why had she brought the book on our tour. She told me that she has read the book completely and she wanted to use this tantra in tour only and for that she needed my help. Then she told me that it is written in the book that one who worships the yoni of his mother will attain some secret power in the dream and the mother will become a goddess.

Of course, I was ready and a little excited too since I had no idea what all this is going to be. My mother told me that after performing the yoni tantra she will get mysterious powers and might even become a Shakti (goddess). I was surprised by her belief in these old Indian texts.

Then she asked me if could cooperate with her for this tantric journey with her. I said yes that I would be happy to do anything for my mother. In fact, she surprised me by saying that I will also reap some secret reward by doing this. It might come to me in a dream. I just said to go ahead with it and see what happens.

Then, my mother, the traditional devout Hindu Brahmin married lady with me as her alibi started out to test the ancient wisdom of sacred and mysterious oriental texts. She went out of the room and appeared with a block of marble shaped as a shiva-Linga (phallus) and decorated it with flowers and then made some tantric figures with grains of rice and lit two candles by the side.

Then she took out a chart from her handbag, unfolded it and threw some flowers on it. It was a mandala with a lot of erotic postures of copulation. Then she asked me to get dressed in a dhoti. My chest was nude and now I was just dressed in a cloth wrapped on my thighs.

Then to my utter surprise she removed the gown and dressed in beads of exquisite marigold flowers. Her nipples were covered by a natural bra of flowers and she had the same at her waist. She even wore bangles made of those and had a bunch on the head too. She looked like a goddess.

For the first time in my life, I felt my lund (cock) hardening seeing my mother in all her glory. Her luscious chuchies (breasts) were so inviting and her waist was so slim and I could see a bit of her fur through the flowers too. She smiled at me and asked me to sit down and perform the rites for the ritual.

She asked me to recite "om kamdevaya namah, om shivaya namah, om ratidevi namah, om vyabhichaar namah, om asaya kamkrida shishuna drishyante, om matriyoni namah, om matrivakhsha namah, om matribhaga namah, om asaya sangamasya kaami putra putrid prajanante, om kamdevaya namah" (Hindi mantra prayer that is chanted)

The whole room was resounded with the chants I and my mother made. By now, my mother had removed the flowers panty she had. Then she asked me to smear some indoor (vermillion) on her soft shiny black little tuft. I put some on it. Then she started me to work on it with my fingers.

I started finger fucking my mother and she kept chanting with even more aggressiveness. Then in a moment she collapsed and cum was running from her thighs. She quickly collected some and smeared it on the marble Linga. Then, she told me to go to sleep as it was complete.

The next morning, she was normal and we didn't talk about it. The driver took us to sight-seeing and we were home by evening. This went on for a few days while my nightly tantric escapades with my mother continued unabated. Now I started having fantasies about my mother.

I used to imagine her as a mother taking care of me and then kissing me with the same mouth that had given me guidance. She had a body of ivory and her smile with her nicely loosened hair always made me fall love with her. I used to imagine her shapely breasts being suckled by my lips as a child while breast-feeding and now as a grown up sucking those lovely mountains of lust.

I used to see them every day but had never gotten to see the nipple, though her areola was pretty bigger and even a few flowers couldn't even hide it. Her breasts were unusually tight and very shapely that even they could make a round circle look square. Then, she had a maddening bellybutton on the top of her silky-smooth tummy.

There was a line a small black hair running from her belly-button to her crotch making her look sexier. I started beating my cock thinking of my mother. I got up and went to her room one morning while she was out doing some exercises; I searched her bathroom and found the pair of her freshly used panties.

I brought them with me to my room. I wrapped them on my face and jacked off bathed in the heavenly aroma of my mother's pussy and rich ammonia smell of her urine. Once I had done it, I started to feel guilty about the whole thing. Hell, she was my own mother. How could I be a pervert to do a thing like this?

I cursed myself and struggled with these feelings all the time. After all, she was letting me make her cum just for religious purpose, and what a pervert I have been thinking incest with my own mother. That night, it was the eighth day of the ritual.

She started the usual chants and then told me that it is written in the book that after one week she must do the Linga pooja. She asked me to open my dhoti and my cock was all erect there. She rubbed some turmeric on it and washed my lund(cock) with gangajal (the water of holy ganga). Then she started to stroke it. It was overwhelming.

My own mother jacking me off, I couldn't hold on for long and ejaculated soon. She took my semen and smeared it over the Linga. Then, she said that the ritual is complete and she thanked me for helping her. I went to my room and slept. I had a strange dream at night.

A half-naked woman resembling my mother came into my dream and said "I'm Rati, the goddess of incestual love. Now you can ask for a wish since you have completed the yoni tantra"

I asked for the power of making love to any woman I want and she granted it and disappeared saying that I just had to call her name while using this spell but I can use it for limited chances only. She said that when I called her name again the spell would stop.

I woke up in the morning and thought about the dream. My mother was up in the kitchen making some breakfast. I walked to the door and saw her in her flimsy nightgown. She still had those flowery bra and panty inside. I went up to her and hugged her in my arms from behind.

"Good morning beta! Kya baat hai aaj bada pyaar aa raha hai"(What happen today you are showing me a lot of love) she said as i hugged her close.

"Oh ma! You know I love you so much" I said while my hand rubbed her little fleshy tummy over her gown.

"Acha beta. (Alright son) Tell me how much you love me" she said with a distinct horniness in her voice.

"maami, (Mummy) I think you are the woman of my dreams. I would do anything to have you by my side" as I said this my hands were rubbing her tummy up to her milky melons brushing them from below.

"You always have my love since you are my son. My lovely beta(son), I love you too Maddy" my body had now aligned with the backside of mother making our touch very intimate. I had never in my past run my hand over her body for so long. I was just enjoying the feel while my head nuzzled through the smell of shampoo in my mother's hair.

I could also smell the marigold flowers and it was just making me feel so secure with my mother. I loved her so much. Suddenly I was reminded of my dream and I thought of giving it a try. I just thought of sex with my mother and said "Rati" into her ear.

Well, it worked. My mother just turned around and pulled the hem of the gown ever so slowly raising it to her humongous chuchies and then flipped over her head. Now, she was exactly in the ritual dress but it was something else we wanted to do. She then undressed me quickly without saying a word and kissed me right on my mouth.

I was thinking in my mind if it was really happening. Was it my own blood mother who was kissing me with her tongue entwined with me? I couldn't hold any longer and tore her flowery bra. The sight of her amazing chuchies in full was a heaven in itself. I needed nothing else. My essence seemed to melt by their fullness and ripeness.

Before I could think of anything, I straightaway took them in my mouth and started sucking the nipples. Maybe the son's instincts but her nipples were becoming absolutely harder and bigger. Then I stopped sucking and for a moment saw my mother in just her flowery panties.

God she was looking like one 18-year-old but for her big jugs and a little flab on the waist. Nevertheless, it added that extra charm to her fleshy chutar (bum). Then I started lapping up her wide pinkish brown areola. She was moaning with ecstasy but didn't say a word.

Then I took the other nipple in my fingers and started nibbling it lightly while my teeth were literally chewing the other nipple in my mouth. My other hand reached to her bottom and I spanked her there. I spanked her again and again. My mother's hands were on my hand and gently caressing my hair.

Then I switched her big boobies and gave them pleasure alternately. After having my fill for half an hour, I proceeded down to her silky belly. I licked every part, back and front of her middle before smelling my birthplace. The hairline was exciting me and I finally tore the flower panty and she was for the first time in my life, fully nude.

By heavens my holy mother full nude in front of me, her boobies all red by my endless mauling and her pussy juices dripping a bit and that unshaven choot(cunt) begged me to suck it. I was in a fix what to do when she took hold of my 7-inch lund(cock) and pushed me on the sink. She came atop me and straddled me.

I picked her up with our genitals locked and carried her to her bed. There she humped me for multiple orgasms. It was an ecstasy to see her beautiful motherly breast jiggling and slapping in air while she jumped on my cock. Soon, it was difficult to hold back and I came inside her many times.

Then, we slept with our bodies hugged together and in a kind of trance. That morning, I fucked my mother three times before the driver gave a knock at the door. I quickly said "Rati" into her so as to break her spell. She was surprised by her condition and quickly wore clothes when the driver came. I knew she would ask me later about it.

5. Nymphomaniac Goddess

It is an incident of my life which has changed the world for me. Yes, bless me for I am married to my son. We live as husband and wife in the suburbs of Punjab where I attend to his children and he goes to the office.

Well, to know how it started and got to the present day, read on. I belong to a very conservative family of Brahmins. My father being a priest, and this has been the family occupation for generations, was a very pious man and so was my mother.

Thus, my upbringing was very religious and I learnt Sanskrit from my father and became very good at it. My father had a huge library of ancient Sanskrit texts where I used to read sometimes. Slowly my grasp over language became so good that I could understand difficult and cryptic texts with a slight of my hand.

Other than all this reading my routine was fairly conservative and very devotional. There used to be some religious function almost everyday around our house and I used to sing praises of God in them. I used to wear saffron robes at times. I was the outcome of generations of the purity of Brahmins. Normally I wore ghagra choli at home.

That was until I reached puberty. My mother told me about the periods and all and I was told to wear a rag on those days beneath my panties. Even my panties were of religious saffron color. Then, it went on and I started developing flesh on my breast and my nipples would sometime poke from the dress but since we lived in a very religious atmosphere, I guess no one noticed it.

I might have been 18 when I discovered a huge pile of ancient Sanskrit texts labeled as " kama-yoga", " rati- swaad rahasya" , " matri bhagah hi moksha" and even a copy of vastyayan' kamasutra. I think that was the time, I had become mature enough to understand them so I sat there and started to study them.

That was my first encounter to sex as I read, I could feel my body arousing. Perhaps, for the first time in my life, I was wet. I went on reading them and I will briefly tell here what those books were about. At first Kama yoga book was related to the feelings of sex in male and female.

Then there were chapters detailed on anatomy of each and it helped me understand my clitoris. There were postures of sex which were hand-drawn and apart from missionary position there were many other difficult postures for sex. Then there was a detailed discussion on morality and purity during sex and faithfulness to the other partner.

The second book was a Sanskrit stories collection of incest among gods and goddesses and how they were the sons and daughters of each other and yet they mated for sex. There was one particular erotic story of Ganesha bathing Parvati nude and one other of Kamadeva having sex with his mother Rati.

But besides these books and Kamasutra, the third book caught my attention. It was called "matribhagah hi moksha". I read the chapters with great enthusiasm as they were meant for someone pure like me in body and mind as I flipped through the pages.

I got to know that this was a book meant for conceiving a child who will then have ritual intercourse with his mother's vagina when he attains puberty. I kept on reading it and finished it in a few hours. The book inspired me to build my desires for having a boy and then mating with him, as Gods did in heavens.

The book also had a detailed procedure of how to do it. I was required to chant kamadava's and rati's name everyday for about 10000 times. This was huge but me being a very religious girl, found it pretty easy. Then, there were the sixteen fasts for lord Shiva on Monday which I duly adhered to.

There was also one ceremony or worshipping nude which I did at night. I stripped myself and then chanted in front of the phallus of lord Shiva. I kept it doing for about 4-5 years and then my parents married me to a renowned priest of the neighboring village in Punjab.

My married life was not an exciting one as my husband was also very religious and he had sex with me once a week or at the most two and that too in a very non-sexual kind of manner. In fact, he considered sex to be a bad ingredient of human beings as it blinds them to God. But as far as I was concerned, I craved for longer sex sessions.

This went on for some time and then I gave birth to our beloved son, Kamam. I was still immersed in my devotional routine when my son grew up. When he was about 3-4 years old I used to bathe him nude with me. I was so fascinated by his small prick that I sucked it for hours together. Soon, he grew up and reached puberty.

He must have been 19 years old when I spotted an erection on him. I was bathing him as usual, I was naked too and I started cleaning his pubic area with curd and sandalwood paste. We were pretty rich to bathe in sandalwood paste and curd when my hand continuously brushed against his groin. His little rod probably stiffened as I touched it a number of times.

Then after bathing him, I lunged on his semi-erect prick and sucked it like a lollypop. I was, more than sure that I was going to get my reward in a matter of weeks. I was more than happy now. My bathing sessions with him continued unabated and at night now I was sleeping with him on the pretext on my teaching.

My husband used to be away most of the time for one or other religious function and I had good enough time free with my son. There were only two of us in that huge house which had 10 rooms and it had a very tastefully decorated garden. The garden had in fact many hibiscus flowers in it which symbolized female fertility.

It also had a huge marble phallus of Lord Shiva at the center of it. Every morning I used to get up early and then collect those hibiscus flowers and then used to lay them down on phallus and meditate sitting nude besides offering the ritual chants for consummation with my son and attainment of moksha.

In fact, over the years I had read many esoteric and cryptic Sanskrit books over this subject that I was convinced without doubt that holy and pious women like me who has conserved her purity for generations and is so religious, will definitely attain nirvana once her son takes her, for better or worse.

After that I used to bathe him and suck on his prick and it had started getting harder and bigger day by day. I could also notice the appearance of pubic hair around his testicles and his testicles also appeared to be getting heavy and full of spunk everyday.

After bathing him, we would have breakfast and then I would go into the library and study while my son will do some other work. He had his schooling at home only so he was aloof from all social influences and it was only his mother which he knew as a friend and teacher.

Now, at 12 he was standing at my shoulders height and he was growing handsome day by day. He used to do a lot of yogic exercises which kept his body fully toned and his delicate hips were wonderful. I thought it was time that he had grown up and so I told him to sleep naked in my bed.

As my husband was away, so I had no problem in implementing my ideas. I had now completed 16 years of my regular chanting and now it was the time for the final ritual that of consummation with my beloved son. As he had attained that age, I felt horny day by day.

Sometimes, I even felt the pangs of horniness that I hugged him tight to my body at night while sleeping nude. I would lift him in my arms, place his head on my cushiony unmolested breasts and wrap my legs around him. Sometimes I could feel his prick growing against my tummy but most of the times he was sleeping.

Sometimes, I would even take his limp and small prick to my vagina and rub it on top for hours. At times I tried to push my entire breast in his mouth when he opened it in sleep. But, this was just the fun as I was yet to ritually mate with my son.

According to the book, the full moon night was the ideal time and the son should mate with his mother in a special posture at the earliest hour of the morning after observing fast for the previous day and engaging the whole day in religious activities. My husband was going away for a week and the full moon was just three days away.

I jumped in joy as I calculated the entire setting. Finally, it is going to happen. I am going to complete the cycle with my son. I started going hornier day by day and it became difficult for me to control them. So, I started to stay nude at home in day also so that my son could have a feast and prepare himself well for the final day which was just three days away.

When somebody would knock at the door, I would quickly change into my saffron robes. My son was there in just his saffron lungi. We hugged all the time as I had not yet exposed him to the joy of kissing. Most of the times, his prick would rub on the outer lips of my vagina as if trying to knock and get permission for access.

I would hold my huge buttery breasts unto his face and would hide his face in them. It was, all a part of mother in me, by letting his have play at home so what if his doll is his mother. After having good time for three days finally my destiny knocked on my doors.

On the full moon day, I gathered all my neighbors and friend of religious circle and hand a full kirtan and jaap there of Rama-yana first and then I also told them to read some shiva purana from the portion where rati mated with kamadeva.

All the gathering was surprised as this was for the first time perhaps somebody read any portion from that sexually explicit encounter of kamadeva and his mother rati. Since there weren't many people who could understand Sanskrit so there never caught the air of what it actually was.

Those who understood it, were old enough and they could never doubt the reputation of my family. So no one guessed that the chanting they were doing was the prelude to mother son union at night. In the afternoon, the function was over and I went to the kitchen and milked by boobs over a cup.

I mixed the milk from my breast with the Prasad am and soon it was distributed to all. Little did they know that this was a sin for them? Soon, they all went to their homes leaving me and my son. So far, I was tastefully adorned in a saffron sari and match-ing blouse but since now everybody had gone, I could take it off.

But then I thought of my son and went to him. I asked him to ac-company me to the prayer room. We went there and sat on the floor while there were images of Gods and Goddess copulating in front of us, which I had drawn flawlessly. I told my son to seek their blessings and then I started to chant. My son also joined me.

This went on for a few hours and now it was evening. I asked him to sleep early as we had to get up at midnight for the ultimate ceremony which he didn't know. Finally, I got up at midnight and took bath with him but this time very quickly. Then I asked him to dress in traditional dress. I too, wore a, lot of ornaments but no clothes.

Yes, there were the beads of jacaranda, marigold and hibiscus flowers all over my body. I was adorned as a sacrificial lamb on the alter of incest. My large heaving breasts were covered by the flowers so nicely that a small portion of my unusually large areola was only visible.

Similarly, my son could see my bush but yet couldn't spot my wet cunt lips. We both sat down on the floor and started chanting. I checked up and the muhuratum was for 3: 15 a. m. when the son's penis should enter mother's vagina in order to make her a goddess. Somehow, the time was spent in prayer and it was three in the morning.

I looked at my son and asked him, "beta! aaj main tumhe swarg ke taraf le jaa rahi hun. Kya tum taiyaar ho." (son today I am going to take you to heaven. Are you ready) I moved towards him and lit a lamp of oil and clarified butter on my left, and right? Then I took out some yantras and spread them on the floor. Then I told him to remove his clothes and I also positioned myself over the yantra carefully.

I took off my flowery bra and asked him again. "Beta! Is ghadi ka main shaadi se pehle se intezaar kar rahi hun. Kya tu taiyaar hai swarg ki yatra ke liye beta... kuch poochna to nahin" (Son! For this seat I am waiting before I got married. Are you ready to the trip to heaven...don't you want to ask something) I took his hands and placed them on my velvety boobs now and he said, "maa! tum meri janani ho. main kaise tumhara karza utaar sakta hun? Tum jo kaho main taiyaar hun." (Mother! You have given birth to me. How can I repay your debt? Whatever you say I am ready)

I could sense the heat building up in his body as his cock had grown now. I took his cock in my hands and rubbed its foreskin to expose its shining pink glans perhaps for the first time in open air and smeared vermillion on it and then I took some turmeric paste and applied it all over his groin.

Then I asked him to snap my flowery panty and see for the first time, the place where he came from. He didn't know anything about it so he wasn't stimulated sexually much but I was already so wet there. I looked at the clock. It was 3: 14. I positioned his cock over my vagina lips and rubbed his glans over my lips.

This had an immediate effect as his cock grew by an inch almost. I looked at the clock again and as it struck 3:15 I pushed myself over his cock and asked him to push it again and again. I started chanting loudly, "om kamadevaya namah, om rati devih namah om matriyoni namah om matri bhaga hi namah ev moksha om kama krida namah om vyabhichaar namah om matrimaithun namah om namah shivaya" (Hindu prayer chanting)

He started to push it with vigor now. Earlier I was shaking my hips to accommodate him and now he was going on his own, as if he knew how to copulate with his mother, from ages. I looked at his face, glowing with pride as he humped me to another level of ecstasy.

As soon as he got into a rhythm, I could hear strange sounds coming both from our genitals and from outside. I heard the sound of conches blowing together and I heard temple bells ringing many at a time and then I heard veena and flute too. I was floating into heaven now as my son deflowered me.

I felt that I had completed the cycle of being a mother to my son. All mothers give everything to their son but for the body and here I had given my body and soul to my son for his use. I took his hands to my breasts and started to press and then he began to caress my motherly treasures on his own.

My son found ecstasy in my huge cushiony breasts and he wanted to be there always as he kept his head in the center of the valley of my breasts. Then I changed position and went to the second yantra where I was stay like a doggie for sometime. Now my son came behind me, and he started to hump me from behind.

As his cock entered my forbidden yoni, I could hear thousand of conches blown together as if the heavens welcomed this unholy embrace. This time he was more self-driven in hitting his mother's vagina and I could sense my juices building up. But there was one more yantra to be performed.

I asked him to come to the third yantra and stand on it. Then I asked him to worship my vagina and apply kumkum over it. Then as per yantra, I lied on the floor on my back raising my legs to my breasts. I asked him to penetrate me while standing. Now he humped me while I was lying on the floor.

I could feel his cock going right through my pussy from top to bottom as he drove through my cunt like a driller. His every stroke was getting powerful now. I was expecting him to come any second now. As I sensed him coming, my excitement grew and my pussy started to shed juices.

He came with an explosion. I thought as if a bucket has been spilled in my womb. This was his first cum and it was huge. After that he drew his cock out and there was his spunk coming out of my wide-open pussy lips. I asked him to collect all the honey on my cunt and then I poured it in a glass and gave him to drink it.

He drank it and that was the end of ceremony. We went to bed after that and I told him not to tell anything to anyone. That night, I had a very strange dream. I was in heaven sitting on a huge golden chair studded with precious stones.

My body was dressed in the clothes of Hindu goddesses as they show on TV but the only thing different was that my clothes were made of exquisite jewelry and pearls were covering my white flesh. There was perfume in the air and there were a lot of people standing around me and bowing their heads to me.

Perhaps I was some kind of queen or something. Then I saw that Gods were also standing above in the air and throwing flowers at me. I was thinking what I could be when my son entered with a mukut on his head and he wore no clothes but a lot of beads of pearls as if he was some king but strangely there was no throne for him.

He came towards me and touched my feet and then he did the kinkiest thing in the world. He bent forward and smelt my pussy before worshipping it with hands. Then he slapped my cunt a few times. I was feeling as kinky as it was happening in public. Then, as he was caressing my mound, I turned my attention to the people who were standing.

Who were they? I was asking to myself as I noticed that all the women were mature when all the men were young and some were even boys. It took me no time to understand that they were all mothers and sons and each son was standing behind his mother.

Then, another strange thing happened. My husband entered carrying a mangal-sutra and two garlands. He came near us and my son disengaged from my vagina. He quickly started chanting some Vedic mantra which he has been chatting for years at marriages but this time it was his son marrying his wife.

My son then put his mangal-sutra on my neck and we exchanged garlands and everyone including gods showered flowers on us. Then, my husband turned away and went out while my son signaled everyone to move out but for the royal musicians. They were playing soft classical music as my son came near me.

We were all alone. "Do you know why there is only one throne here, mother" he asked me kissing my jewel studded nude body.

He continued, "It is because when we sit here, we sit being one. Mother, gods have designed a special posture for sitting here. You will sit in my lap while my lingam is immersed with your yoni. That will make the union complete, and then we will start our court mother. I shall address them in this posture while having some bite of your motherly mummeries. Only when we get down from the throne, shall our genitals disengage. Is that right mother, now, as that, I have wed you; you are my sweet wife too. You are my kamayani… You are my rati and rambha. It is here that the people will pay their oblations treating it as a Shiva lingam and a pavitra sthala. It will become teeth for anybody who wants to mate with his mother. Mother, you must build a secret temple to remember our union."

I felt soft music engulfing my soul as my son cum husband took me in that posture. His prick was quite bigger in the dream and it fully fitted his birth hole. Soon, I opened my eyes and I was shocked. In front me on every tall chair, all mothers and sons were copulating in that posture. I saw above and I saw Gods in frenzy too.

Then, I saw that Lord Shiva threw some hibiscus flowers on me. I woke up in the morning and it was quite a pleasant shock to find those flowers on my breasts. Later, in the day I figured out that probably I was blessed by God in some way. Those flowers were a symbol of fertility but why had God thrown them on me

He wanted me to have a child again. With my son…I felt overly overjoyed. I woke up and went to my son still without clothes. He was just getting up and I could spot his morning erection. His cock looked real and bigger just like as it was in the dream. I could not believe my eyes. Just one humping of his mother's pussy was doing wonders to his cock.

How could I resist it from growing as I cupped it in my hands and directed it to its creator's love tunnel? He swelled like a python in my vagina. It was growing all the more and I could feel it inside my womb getting even bigger. I was climbing on him on the bed and he was under me.

Slowly his mouth reached instinctively under my heavy breast and started to chew on the nipple of motherly flesh. Ah! What a relief to have my son back at the nesting place. I pressed myself more on his cock and it was entering my pussy as if it was tailor-made for my son.

After having him full in my glory mother whole, I looked at his face, so innocent yet so loving. I released his mouth from my nipples and asked him, "beta!(Son) Do you know what we are doing?"

"No maiya! (mother) But it seems we are playing some highly pleasurable game. I like it very much" he replied cupping my breasts and my waist." beta!(Son) What we were doing is called chudai(fucking)." I hugged his closer to my breasts and once again thrust my other nipple into his mouth and started humming a doggerel song from movie judai but replaced the words.

I was singing, "chudai re chudai. Beta kare maa ki chudai. Hai yeh chudai. Mera bete ki chudai." (fucking oh fucking. Son is fucking his mother. Oh fucking. My son's fucking) I kept singing and it was having an erotic effect on my son as I was hissing a lot while singing. He started to grow even more and I felt that the prick of a donkey must have been smaller in my pussy. I could not believe it so I took it out to verify.

The pinkish purple head was glistening with my juices and my God; the cock had become a real monster just in a day. I looked at him and asked, "Beta(son) this is your lingam(cock) or lund(cock) as u calls it besides urinating it has other functions also. You can use it in a woman to make her pregnant as your father did to make you in my womb."

"Beta(son) this intercourse is forbidden between a mother and a son. But I have initiated you into all this so that we attain heaven. Forgive me my son, for no one fucks that pussy where he came from. Since I have spent all my life in prayers and now, I have done the ultimate deed I want to spend the remaining days with you as a chuddakad(nymphomaniac)."

"My son as now you are also my new and second husband, you must use your mother as your wife and fill her besides fulfilling her other needs. I shall behave both as a mother and wife to you now. I shall be your mother when your father is around and I shall be your wife when we are alone."

"You must copulate and procreate with me my son, my husband and when my yoni is full of your lingam Prasad, it will give birth to an unholy incestuous child who will fuck his mother or her father and this cycle will continue and we both will have and incestuous generation my son. Now take me and make the woman of your lingam take me, my child."

As I was imploring him with my sermon, he was getting eroticized beyond measure. I don't know what came over him, he spat on my cunt and thrust his organ in one go. I felt as if someone hit my pussy with an iron dildo. He took me in arms standing while I wrapped my legs on his back for better penetration.

He started to fuck me now like a bull in heat. He said," maa gaana gao na. gaana sunte hue aisa karne ka bada maja aata hai." (Mother sing a song. Listening to a song and doing it gives me a lot of pleasure) And as if I heard him say, I started to hum again "Chudai re chudai mera beta kare chudai(Fucking oh fucking, My song is fucking) , hai...heeeeeeeee...ooooooooo... uuuuuuuu....uiiiii....haan...kar maa ki chudai(Do mother's fucking)...bhar de uski maang(apply a betrothal sendur (vermillion) to the middle line of the head where the hair is parted) ... aur(and)...choot(pussy)....kar maa ki chudai(Do mother's fucking)" , as soon as I spoke obscenities, I felt greatly overjoyed .

I had never used a filthy word in my life and I was really surprised how they came out of my mouth. But now I wanted to go on, I was enjoying it; there was a particular expression of joy in those words. I was breaking many taboos simultaneously; one was of mating with my son and the other was of language and there was also the taboo of religion which I was breaking.

He kept humping me and his cock was reaching to my inner depths now. It appeared, as if his cock was trying to unite with my vagina forever. It was a mother in me who let him do all he wanted. After about 10-15 minutes of strong and bullish humps, he spat his cream in my pussy. I liked it this time since all he did was on his own. I enjoyed it more when he did things on his own. I felt satisfied as a teacher. I had done my job.

6. Bharti

I am Viren completed my 12th. Till my high school, my family was in Hyderabad and my life was rocking during my school life. But when I got into higher secondary, my dad got transferred to Tirupati and we had to shift to there.

My life got jammed there and was extremely boring, I did not like it and I forcefully completed my school there. Then I insisted my parents to join me in Hyderabad and they agreed. I was to stay with my grandparents and joined a posh school nearby because the school I studied before was far away.

I got enough knowledge of sex through friends, internet and other sources. And a lust was growing inside me to have sex with a woman. And I was waiting for the right time. My new school was a good one. The total strength of my class was just 35 and half of them were just girls. They were beautiful.

But they have nothing to do with this story. That new school was very posh outside but inside (strictness, education) it was just ok. I planned to woo and fuck my class girls and made friendship with them. Soon almost all of them became my friends but I was afraid to start the topic of sex with them.

Our junior class also had some sexy babes and they too became my friends. But one girl named Bharti was closer to me. She was tall, fair, slim and beautiful. So, I decided to fuck her to control my hunger because I was not able to concentrate on studies because of sexual thoughts.

Soon the golden chance came. Both ours and juniors' classes

were on the fourth floor as the fifth one was being renovated. Once, some students from our class and our juniors had to stay back to decorate the school in the eve of a special day.

The whole school was empty except for some students and some auxiliary staff and some workers on the 5th floor. Some students were busy on the 1st floor; some on 2nd floor' some on 3rd and 4 of us were on 4th floor. Two of them were junior boys and the remaining were me and Bharti.

After some time, the other boys went down to canteen for snacks and I judged this was the right time to seduce her (coz the guys spend a lot time at canteen and moreover they may not return). We decorated the walls and were about to paste the colored ribbons on the top of the walls.

But in order to do that, I had to stand on a big stool or table to do that, even the benches were not sufficient in height. There was a long stool but I said that it was old and creaking, and I may fall from that. And I hit upon an idea and told her that I will stand on a bench and shell sit on my shoulders and paste them.

She did not agree fearing that she will fall down and moreover if someone sees them it may look bad. But I assured that no one will come I will hold her tightly. She agreed and first I stood on the bench and kneeled. Then she sat on my shoulders and that was so arousing that my dick stood up but it was covered by my full shirt.

Her pubic area was at the back of my head and her legs were on my shoulders! What a feeling it was! She wore a chudidar for some reason and she was exotic. I tried standing up but I was not able to stand due to her weight. I told her to get down and then I took her in my arms and told her to climb on my shoulders. She did and now I was standing and she was on my shoulders.

I gave her the ribbons and she asked me to hold her tight and immediately took my arms and kept them on her waist. Man! What a feeling! I was holding her tight and she was busy sticking. She completed some part and we had to move the bench to cover the remaining part of the wall.

I lifted her from my shoulders and was getting her down, when my hands touched her boobs. She did not say a word and I just got slipped and held her tight around her waist. My left hand was on her breast area and my right hand around her waist and my dick was on her ass.

I was still holding her and suddenly she started staring in my eyes. Her eyes were shining and there was lust in them. I wasted no time and grabbed her lips and started sucking them. She broke the kiss and said that someone may see us. She took me secretly to the 5th floor and without getting into any of the workers notice we went into the unused toilets and slipped into one of the latrines.

They were extremely clean and she hugged me tight and sucked my lips and then our tongues met. We kissed for sometime and started fondling her boobs and, a sexy back is my weakness and I started licking her back. Fortunately, she wore a low back dress and I got hold of her boobs and licked her back.

She asked for the real thing and I did not like to fuck her in a standing position. We did some hugging, fondling, kissing in the bathroom and soon it was 5:30. The workers leave at 5:30.

And I peeped out. There I saw the workers leaving and when all of them left, we came out and went inside a clean room. I bolted the door and started the action. She climbed on me with her legs crossed around my waist and started french kissing me. I removed her chunni and threw it aside.

She was wearing a dark fabric green Punjabi dress. I started removing and lo! Soon she was in a white bra. I pressed her tits thru the bra and kissed her cleavage and licked there. Then I removed her pajama and noticed her wearing a white silky panty. Wow! A beauty in white panty and white bra!

I removed my uniform and I was standing in my underwear

and my 7 inch dick standing still. She anxiously removed my undi and started playing with my dick. She fondled with it, she played with my balls. I asked her to give me a blow job. She replied innocently, hats that?

I opened her mouth and shoved my tool inside and asked her to suck and lick it as if it were a lollipop. She started doing it and soon increased the speed. I removed my dick from inside as I may climax, it may take time to regain. I freed her boobs and for first time I was seeing a girls tits!

I made her lie on the floor and started kissing her lips. Then I went down and started sucking her right tit and circled left one. Then I went down and licked her sexy navel. Her body started shaking and was enjoying it. Not to waste much time, I went down and removed panty.

What a sight! A naked pussy for the first time, that too a hairy one! It was my lucky day. I started licking it and she was shivering in ecstasy, and her pussy was dripping her love juices. I licked them and they were tasty. I inserted my index finger inside and started finger fucking and she started moaning.

Soon I inserted second finger and she started moaning more. Soon she climaxed and cummed on my face. I drank her juices and told her to get ready for the big one. I asked her, are you ready? Why are you asking for? Go on was the reply. I kept the tip of my dick and her entry and tried to shove in...But it was tight.

I forcefully inserted the tip inside and she started feeling pain... Of course, she was a virgin and had a tight cunt. I applied full force and entire 7" went inside along with a scream which escaped her mouth. I started fucking and soon gained speed and started giving her hard strokes.

Soon, pain vanished on her face and started enjoying it. The room was filled with her moaning and soon I was about to climax. But before that, her cunt muscles became tight and knew she came. I too came and shot my entire load inside. And fell on her, exhausted.

I removed my dick outside and shoved it inside her mouth. She started licking my sperm and licked it completely dry and started sucking it. Soon it regained its size and we were ready for another session. This time we did it in doggy session. Soon we climaxed and took some rest. Then we wore our clothes and left out silently.

This was my first experience. You might be wondering if this may ever happen. Nothing is impossible. Seducing this kind of college girls is very easy. Everyone can give a try

7. Piya

I met Piya on chat. We chatted about our interests and our life in US. Piya was in mid-30s, married with 2 sons. She had been in US for a long time and worked as a volunteer at a local library. After our first few chats, she would come on chat during afternoons and wait for me to login.

After the first week, I took a chance and asked her phone number, and to my surprise, she readily gave it to me. My home was very near to my work, and I would go home during lunch and call her from there. Our conversation on phone slowly turned a little naughty.

Once when I was telling her my favorite sexual positions, the conversation got really heated and I asked her if she was wet. Very wet, her voice was hoarse. I asked her to take off her clothes and we masturbated on phone for the first time. This became a routine for us.

I would come home for lunch, call her up, and we would masturbate. She was shy and did not talk much while masturbating. She just moaned and said yes, yes. In spite of all this, she was quite reluctant to meet me. "I don't know, Nikil. I have never done this before," was her argument.

Well, I want you to be comfortable with this idea. If you think you will feel bad or guilty after doing it, don't do it. I know I would love to. Moreover, we will do only what you are comfortable with. I knew she wanted to and she was trying to justify herself. Finally she relented.

"OK. If we meet, you have to use condoms always. And no oral sex please."

"Anything you want," I quickly agreed.

Although she did not mention anal sex, I knew that was out too. So around three weeks after I first met her on chat, I took a day off and booked a room in her city. I reached her city the night before. The next morning, I got ready and waited eagerly for her arrival. She came to my hotel around 10 AM and I was downstairs to receive her.

The first time I saw her, I was struck by how much in shape she was. She wasn't particularly very beautiful, but she was petite around 5'4" and fair. She was wearing a black Lycra pant which showed the lining of her panties and a red and blue top.

We came up and sat in the office room of the suite. Both of us sat on the same sofa. She was looking down and we both were a little nervous. I took the initiative and held her hand.

"I am glad we could finally meet," I said.

"Yes," she was quiet and a little shy. I started gently rubbing her hands with my other hand. I touched her cheek and she pressed her cheeks on my palm. "Do you want to go in?" I indicated towards the bed room. She nodded and I led her in the bedroom. The bedroom was dark with only the side lamps on.

She climbed up and lied down on the bed and looked at me. I climbed over her top to the other side and started caressing her cheek. Her eyes were closed and I moved my hand down gently caressing her breasts and tummy.

It was hard for me to control myself any longer and I started pushing my hands inside her pants. She shut her eyes tightly. I moved up and started kissing her neck while trying to take my hands inside her pants. I touched her panties and kept moving down. My hand grazed her shaved mound as she had earlier told me she would be.

I finally found her protruding clitoris. I gently touched it and pushed on between her pussy lips with my middle finger. It was already wet and sticky. I started gently rubbing her pussy and kissed her hard on her neck at the same time. I was now rubbing her pussy wildly and she was moaning.

I started sucking on her breasts over her top and continued to play with her pussy while my feet were rubbing on her feet. I finally slipped my middle finger inside her. As soon I pushed my finger inside, she pulled my head hard on her breasts seemingly out of control.

My hard-on was pressed on her thighs while I continued fingering her. I pressed my cock harder on her thighs rubbing myself on them. Very soon she started shuddering and I knew she had reached her first orgasm. She opened her eyes, smiled, and looked at me. I smiled back.

"How you liked it?" I asked.

"Wow," that's all she said and proceeded to hold my cock over my pants.

She smiled and I climbed on top of her placing myself between her legs. I was very hard and I started humping her over her clothes, my hard-on poking on her crotch. She bit her lip and started moving her hips to match me. My hands were grabbing her breasts, mauling them while I was dry-fucking this hot married woman.

I kissed her hard on her neck, and held her tight. Her hands were clenching my butts. I knew I was going to cum and I buried myself in her neck and let myself go, feeling my cock pulsating as it shot load after load in my pants.

8. *Pammi*

This story is about a 25 yrs old married lady with whom I have already spent a lot of time together, enjoying her beautiful body and fucking and making beautiful love to her. Her name is Pammi & she is a housewife. Her husband is neither impotent nor old but is more interested in making money than fucking his wife.

So, he is away from home about 20 days in a month making money & poor Pammi is left all by herself to manage everything. I simply wonder why such 'money minded' people care to get married, especially with a sexy & beautiful girl like Pammi as their wife! We came to know each other through the Internet & began to mail to each other.

This slowly turned into friendship and we began to share our feelings. We kept on exchanging mails for a few days & then, one day I asked her to describe her figure and herself. Her very next reply turned me on, completely. She said she was 5'6" tall, long hair-thick & black in color, silky smooth, good figure; 37D-28-38, slim waist with long legs.

I wanted to meet her & pay my respects to her beauty & enjoy her voluptuous body & expressed my desire of the same. She was hesitant initially but agreed after I convinced her that our meeting would be strictly confidential, there was nothing to worry about, as I am an honorable person she could trust & depend upon.

She was shy & afraid as this was the first time, she was meeting a guy after getting married, who was not her husband. We decided to meet on a cool Wednesday morning, as people would leave for their jobs and the people in her neighborhood would not notice a stranger going to her building.

I reached there before time & rang the bell. There was no answer. My heart sank! My love affair was over before it started!!! After sometime I rang again. I heard someone move behind the door & it opened. Pammi welcomed me with a smile. Boy! She was gorgeous, stunning, pretty, inviting & totally SEXY!!!

Her face was oval, hair was open, just as I like, was wearing a blue chiffon saree with black sandals. I could smell the lovely perfume & the whole thing was a big & grand affair for me. Boy, she is real class!!! I went in & she closed the door behind me. She asked me to sit on a couch. I couldn't take my eyes off her.

She laughed and asked me what the matter was. I praised her beauty with all the words I knew. By then my cock had hardened & she noticed it. She blushed!!! God in heaven! If her husband could ignore such a beauty then I doubt his masculinity. Or may be, it was the case of "ghar ki murgi dal baraabar" (Domestic chicken is equivalent to pulses).

We spoke for a few minutes & had some wine. Pammi loves red-wine. I found it very hard to control myself for long. So, did she. She told me frankly that her husband was a very good lover when they had married, about two years ago. But, now after about 14 months of marriage the romance had gone out their marriage.

The husband would come home drunk, indulge in a few moments of foreplay and in about 5 mins. The whole love-making & sex would be over. 'He is finished even before I have started', she said. While talking, absent mindedly she arranged and tied her hair in a bun-style. Each and every movement of hers denoted class.

Boy, she is really gorgeous!!! In her earlier mails she had told me about her husband who would also quarrel with her everyday for no reasons at all, due to the excessive drinking. I slowly came & sat beside her & put my hand on her shoulder to console her.

This was the beginning. She placed her head on my shoulder & the whole scene was romantic, good music, intoxicating perfume & above all a gorgeous sexy & hot woman beside me. I touched her cheeks & slowly moved my hands down to her neck. She pulled my face towards her & placed her lips over mine.

We French kissed & sucked each other's lips for about 10 mins and she pulled back and shook her hair. Her long waist-length hair fell & spread like a waterfall. And she looked even fairer, more sexy and more beautiful; her eyes were saying 'come take me quick.... I am all yours'.

I started unbuttoning her blouse & she blushed, smiled & closed her eyes & I continued to kiss her deeply. I opened her bra & saw the most wonderful pair of breasts I've ever seen. Her tits are big, yet very proportionate to her sexy figure. Her nipples were about an inch long & inviting. I could not hold any longer, I started sucking them.

Like a man who is hungry for a long time, I started to eat both her nipples, alternatively, while my free hands continued to press her tits & explore her sexy body. Her big tits reacted immediately. They stiffened and became even bigger. Her boobs became erect & she placed both her hands below her two tits.

By lifting her tits, she began to tease me & enjoying herself. One thing I am particular about is that my partner should enjoy the sexual foreplay to the fullest. So, in full earnest, I took it upon me to carry on sucking, kissing and biting her sexy soft tits.

My fingers meanwhile were busy exploring her back, neck and the armpit areas, the sensuous movements enhancing her pleasure.

Aaaahhhhh hhhhhhhh oooohhhhhh..........aahh aaaaaaaaahhhhhhhhhhhh she opened her beautiful mouth and began to make the sounds women like to make when they are aroused. I had already eaten her lipstick while French-kissing her but still her sexy lips were equally red and inviting.

I was sucking one while kneading the other. I was in heaven.... & so was she. Slowly I made her lie on her back & moved towards her belly button. I inserted my tongue into it & she arched her body & said 'love me... yes that's it, keep going on, I love you doing this to me.... boy you are really good.... just do this.... Yes.... ooohhh.... suck it.... fuck it.... yes... for the whole day'.

My hands were busy in removing her sari and the petticoat. As I have some good experience in this, I did it without her even knowing about it. 'Oh, when did you remove my sari & petticoat? I just did not come to know', she said. She was getting hot, now. She was arching her back & I could feel the heat coming from between her legs.

This made me interested in her sexy black panties. These were the latest fashion-type, thin types, just the elastic & then a thin soft cloth that did not even cover her hot & sexy cunt-lips. Her pussy was clean-shaven, smooth without ant blemish. I was in heaven!!! Without wasting time, I shifted my mouth to her hot and exciting pussy.

Like it is customary, I kissed & licked her soft inner thighs, the area around her lovely cunt that made her more excited. 'Yes, I love it...... yes more.... aaahhhh more.... Suck it deeply.... take my clit.... suck my clit...I love you when you suck my clit' she commanded. So, hungrily I began to suck her.

I opened her beautiful cunt-lips licked her love-hole and with a big thrust, I pushed my tongue in her hot & juicy hole. She gave out a loud scream, arched her back, spread her legs wider & offered her pussy to me to suck. I began, like an obedient pupil, opening my mouth & sucking her cunt-lips with the thin panty in between.

From the side of her panties, I kept on tongue-fucking her & alternatively, sucking her clit. This gave her immense pleasure. She asked me to stop so that she may remove her bra & panties. She quickly removed hers & I removed mine; we were now past the half-stage of our foreplay.

We were both naked, just, as we had planned to be, to explore, feel, enjoy, reach out & hold, to cherish the happiness that we get while we are naked with our sexy partner, our bodies touching, totally pressed against each other, in each others company, fully enjoying the foreplay of sex before launching the final attack.

Her eyes were shut. She was in heaven; enjoying to the maximum. I thought of giving here some more fun before getting into the final round. I bent & with my left hand slowly & gently opened her cunt-lips, once again. I simply love the sight of a hot, yielding and open pussy; it is the best sight in the world!!!!

There is no greater wonder in this world than the sight of a hot juicy pussy waiting to be licked and fucked!!!! I began to slowly lick her clitoris, her cherry with my tongue and my hand came up & begun to massage her inner-thighs. Now, Pammi is a vocal love maker.

She loves to speak, some times even scream as & when she desires, and while foreplay and fucking. 'Yes, that's greaaaattt..... I love the expert way you are treating my pussy..... I am in heaven!!! Yes, come on give it to me faster & deeper, yes… Now… suck my cunt… suck my cherry' and I obliged.

That's the duty of us men when we are in bed; especially with a gorgeous babe like Pammi.... We men have to oblige & deliver. She maneuvered herself in a manner that her face was at my crotch & she expertly took my 8" long fully erect cock and began sucking it. Boy, I was in heaven….just like her!!!!

What great pleasure, both of us slowly shifted into a 69 position, sucking and tongue sucking-fucking each other. We must have carried on for about 20mins. During which time Pammi kept on sucking and kept on her dirty talk. ' yes give it to me… suck me… take me … I love the way you suck my clit… yes keep going…'

By this time, we both were ready for the ultimate bout!!!! My cock was deliberately waiting to be freed from her mouth. I stopped & asked her to move on to her bed. We moved to her bedroom & on the way I was holding her boobs & tweaking her nipples from behind. She was laughing & enjoying herself.

'I love to walk naked in my house' she said. We sat on the bed & she said 'I want to suck you, some more now; my husband never allows me to even touch her cock' & bent over me to suck my manhood, once again, her long silky hairs fell on my stomach & covered the sucking scene from me.

I pushed her hair towards a side & enjoyed the scene of my cock being sucked by a real sexy beauty. She seemed to be a natural expert at blowjob & I was getting harder & stiffer. My balls were completely filled-up with my sperm and fully swollen. After about 15 mins, I was about to cum. I didn't want to cum before her.

So I slowly pulled her away from my cock & she looked at me in anger. I made her lay on her back, her clean shaved pussy, which I like was looking invitingly at me. She caught my hair & pulled my face closer to her pussy. I started licking her pussy again, as if I was starving from months & she started yelling aaaahhhhh-hhh…. deeeeeeper pleaseeeeeeeeeee.

I looked her face & it had a makeup of lust on it. Her juices were flowing continuously & it was only then I realized that the more beautiful a woman is, the tastier her juices are. Her juices tasted like nectar of the Gods. I inserted my middle finger in her pussy & started finger fucking her.

With my other hand, I started slowly smearing her lips, tickling her on her neck & moved a little down to cup one of her breasts.

Meanwhile I inserted my second finger also in her pussy and her moans turned into cries. Along with finger fucking I started spreading my fingers apart inside her pussy & rubbing the tender walls of her pussy.

At the same time, I was taking due care of both of her big sexy tits by squeezing one & sucking the other. She was wriggling as a fish out of water & her cries touched the skies. She said aaa-aaa… Aaaaaaammmmmmmmm……. ccccccccuuuummmmmmm iiiiiii nnnnnnnnn gggggggg & before she could finish her words she came violently.

Her pussy dripping with her perfumed nectar-juices…. She then relaxed with a satisfied look on her cute face. But I didn't stop fingering, sucking & tweaking her. She seemed to be regaining her strength & I immediately stopped as my hungry hard cock was craving for her pussy.

I once again kissed her on her hungry mouth, which she gladly reciprocated & just by deep kissing we were then ready for each other.

I spread her legs & surprisingly she was ready within no time. I put her legs on my shoulder & slowly inserted my cock in directly in her pussy. She screamed nnnnnnnnn oooooooo…. Aaa-aaaaa hhhhhhhhhhh as though she was a virgin. But she was so cute that I felt I was really hurting her.

But I love her so I pulled my cock out of her pussy & kissed her passionately on her lips, chin & neck. She hugged me tightly, kissed me all over my face, and said 'don't stop now… fuck me hard…. I want your big cock in my wet juicy pussy… yes. Aaaa …. Don't stop now'.

She then took my big throbbing cock in her hand & guided me into her love hole. I made slow pushes & she was moaning mmmm…. Yes… mmmmmmmm… Oooooooooohhhhhhh & at the same time pulling me inside her by putting her hands around my waist & ass and pulling me towards herself.

I had just entered her when with a hard push from behind she took my full 8" long, thick & pulsating cock right up her juicy pussy. I arched my back, thrusting my great big cock completely into her cunt. Then, with my big cock fully implanted in her hot & juicy love hole, I began to rock to and fro, without moving my pelvis.

She pushed herself upwards, & began to match my rhythm. We remained like that for about 5 mins. During which time Pammi had closed her eyes and was enjoying herself to the maximum. 'Faster.... please fuck me hard and quick... yes.... Faster....' and then I slowly I increased my pace of pumping my big throbbing cock in her pussy.

In & out, in & out my cock went & so did the volume of her moans and screams. The whole room was filled with her moans with the rhythm and speed at which my balls slapping her ass. Both of us were sweating & her hairs were spread on the white pillow.

While fucking her faster, I straighten up and caught hold of her thighs, which were on my shoulders. I gave love-bites & nibbled at her milky white thighs giving her more pleasure & taking her to even a higher heaven. After about 20 mins of fast and furious fucking, once she had no more words to scream.

She came again & again for about three times in a row. Her screams were so high-pitched, strong and great, just like her orgasm that I am certain the watchman in the next building must have also heard them! I was also about to come.

Suddenly, as she regained partial sense...She took my cock in her right hand, took it out of her love-hole & expertly began to suck me once again. I wanted to control myself & carry on till eternity. I wanted to hold her tight and keep going forever. But, as they say, all things must pass and that all great things have to come to a natural end.

The dam's floodgates were opening, yes, they wanted to open

but I did not want it to end. But alas I was at the crescendo of my orgasm & finally I came. She gulped the first spurt of my orgasm and she took my cock and made me cover her neck, face, moth and finally her hairs.

I collapsed on her naked body with my cum all over her mouth & face & hugged her tightly. 'I have always wanted to feel the hot juices of a man coming on my face, my ears, mouth and my body' she said 'but my husband does not oblige me'.

After about 30 mins. Of sleeping in each other's arms, we finally awoke. I don't know about you all, but for me, this short sleep after a good fucking is the best thing that can happen to me. She was really enjoying the pleasure with her eyes closed & had a satisfied look on her pretty face, and she told me so.

She was laughing with joy & told me that she had never enjoyed sex to this extent with her hubby. I was the first person to fuck her, other than her husband. She kissed me passionately all over my body & wish I was her husband. We slept in each other's arms for about an hour.

Later we had 4 rounds of mind-blowing, physically exciting and orgasm- tic sex, completely with her cries and screams and good music in the background, till the evening. It was one of the best days in my life & I told her so. She let me go only after I promised her that I satisfy her whenever she needs me.

She said 'You are the only person in this world that can fuck me and make me so high with desire. I wish I could marry you. I trust and depend on you. Don't ever break my trust in you'. Till this day, I have not broken it. I have been doing it with her for a long time with Pammi now, for over 20 months & she is completely happy & satisfied.

She is on pills or would have been pregnant by now! She calls me when her family members go to meet relatives locally in Mumbai or they go to Baroda, their home town.

9. Savita

I am Savita and married for five years. My husband Suraj and I have very active sex life and we enjoyed ourselves like anything. We shared our fantasies with each other and tried it in our bed room, but we don't have enough chances to try it out side.

Our fantasy will involve lesbian sex and threesome sex with Anita who is our relative and living next to us. She is a widow and has one son working in Chennai as software engineer. I always pretend Suraj as woman and treat him like a woman in private.

He wears only women out fits and inns while he is in home, I shaved his body hair completely and always lick and suck his cock and have strap on sex with him. He too enjoyed this very much and we tried whenever we get chance. Whenever we did this we fantasized about Anita.

She is in her mid forties and still very pretty and sexy, with firm 36c breasts and a perfectly shaped body. She is a typical south Indian middle-aged woman having large and bulgy hip and sexy ass. One Sunday we all together and talked about each other then she enquires about the chatting through net.

Her son wants to see her once in a while. I told her that it is not a problem I have computer with net connection so whenever she wants to talk to her son come and use it. She told me that I don't know how to use it so assist me in this regard and I willingly agreed to teach her.

From that day onwards often, she came to me and both surf through the net and chat with her son, this will give me a chance to be closer with her and I really enjoyed her company she too like it. We discussed everything and whenever I get a chance to be with her in alone, I started to talk about sex and about my personal experience.

First, she was very embarrassed and didn't ready to talk with me about sex and try to avoid those types of talks. But I never gave up the effort and slowly she shows interest in it and reciprocates with me. Slowly I developed a good rapport with her and her too very open to me and revealing her sexual encounter with her late husband.

We spent our day time mostly in surfing net or some dirty talk. Slowly I revealed our fantasy about her and want to have sex with her. First, she is shocked and afraid about the consequences, but Suraj and I convinced her and she half heartedly accepted our fantasy.

We never show any hurry to get her to our bed we leave the things in their own speed and allowed her enough time to decide how to carry out these things. But we never hide our fantasy in front of her so Suraj always wears his usual woman's inns in home, first she was very shy by seeing this but she never showed any disrespect to this and accepted it as it is.

Slowly the things started to develop from one phase to another now, we sat together and enjoy porn movies and discussed about the actions and the positions. Often, I put lesbian movies and threesome movies whenever she watched this type of movies she is nerves and often went to bath room.

One day as usual while we watching the porn movie, she was ready to leave for the bath room but I suddenly stopped her and said "Don't worry if you want to relive your self do it here, we never bother about it so don't be shy and discomfort, it will hurt us". I spoke.

First, she is very rigid but started to melt slowly, to give her company and make her comfort we too started to masturbate while we seeing the movie. One thing leads to other, over a period of time she ready for everything. I slowly started to undress her and Suraj was already nude and he undressed me.

Now three of us were naked and enjoyed the movie. I just stared at her.... God she is beautiful for sex in her shape. Her breast were hanging and swaying, her nipples are erect and looks like a rock and she has huge, saucer shaped areola around her both breasts.

It attracts me, she has an ample hip and ass and her thighs are in cream color and invite me to suck them. Her pussy hairs are neatly trimmed and she has patch of curly thick black hairs on her mound. It contrasts her body color and her pussy is wet and has bulgy and live outer lips.

God, I lost myself and Suraj had rock like erection and he too had an insatiable lust over her. Slowly I hugged her from the front and gave my ever first kiss to a real female, she too responds it with a huge moan and started to tighten the grip. Suraj come behind her and he to start hugs her and kisses her back, and her shoulder and all over her back.

She couldn't withstand this double assault and screamed with wild lust. I still explore her mouth and drink her juice from her mouth, while Suraj will bend over her body and kiss and lick, suck her ass, inner thighs he travels up to her feet and started to lick and suck her foot.

This will make her wriggled and she gave long breath and moans and screams often. Our breath will become erotic and I smelled her neck and brushed her long black hair to smell behind her ear. "God, mmm, it is nice", I breathed hotly.

"God, Savita, she is ever wet!" he panted.

"Well, Suraj, if you think she smelled great, you'll love how she tastes," I groaned as I suck her breasts all way into my mouth.

With that Suraj incentive I brought his fingers to my lips to taste her juices.

"Suraj, she does taste great!" I exclaimed." if you don't mind, aunty, I think I'd like to get a fuller taste of your sweet pussy".

Aunty gave great moan and she groaned and hissed me "Mmm, please do it, let me have your service, Mmmm, please go for It." she moaned and groaned continually.

Suraj and I slowly move aunty to our king size bed and make lay down on her back. God is looks like an angel, Suraj slowly switched over his place to her breasts and I sat on bed between her legs and licked her bald, swollen cunt lips from one end to the other, then stuck my tongue between them.

I kept darting it in and out and all around, and she was just going insane with lust. I fucked her with my tongue like a mini-penis. By fucking her with my tongue I too get horny and a few more minutes and I know I would be exploding in orgasm, only by fucking and sucking her cunt.

"Oh, God, Mmm, I love this, just love this", and want to get explode with her so I speed up my licks and started to suck her lips and darting her pink clit with wild lust.

Aunty begged Suraj "squeeze my tits, Suraj" she screamed and Suraj do it with full lust and he suck her nipples like a baby.

"Oh, God, Savi, yeah, give me more, lick me, God, please suck me, yeah there, there, please lick me, God, make me come, Mmm. Aunty grunted.

It makes me wild and I rub her clit with my tongue and suck her pussy, both will leak our honey like a stream and we reached our peak, so both will twist our body and she screamed, "Fuck me hard! Oh God! I love this! Harder baby!" she grunted.

Suraj placed aunt's body over his lap and grabbed hold go her quivering melons, covering her large black nipples with his hands.

Again, she screamed" Squeeze my tits, Suraj, oh god, oh yeah, I'm coming!"

She gave loud groan and shivered.

"Oh shit, me too!" I panted, and held on her and pushed my slick pussy back upon her body. Are groaned, moaned and screamed, I sure we would wake the neighbors. We hugged very tightly and twisted our body to have more and more intimacy.

It took us a while to stop shaking with post orgasmic bliss.

Once we slowly recovered from our haven, I searched for Suraj and he was jerking his dick with lust, I slowly turn over to him and took his dick in my mouth and started to sucking slowly on his long thick cock licking his big balls and devouring him. I was enjoying myself.

Soon aunty too joined with this party and she gave him a wonderful lick and suck. We both suck and lick his cock with lust after a while he started coming without warning, and I swallowed as much as I could and shared it with aunty, she to loved this and we French kissed and share his juice. We both licking him clean and enjoying every last drop.

This experience really changed our sex life. And now whenever we want to have sex with each other we don't have any hesitation and we all enjoyed our life with its full glory. When Suraj is not there, Savita and Anita Aunty enjoy their daily sex life with 69 positions and with some strap on things.

10. Raminder

I am 22 yrs aged Punjabi guy from Chandigarh. The story is of the period when I used to study at Punjabi university in Patiala and where I used to stay in Patiala, there was a Punjabi family in my neighborhood that family had one old lady and a son and daughter in law. Son was 27 years and working in some MNC and daughter in law was 24 years house wife.

Son was Hanit, and her wife name Raminder (Rami) I used to call her as Rami bhabhi. Let me tell you Rami bhabi is pure punjaban, with killing stats and white colors skin, I always used to admire her beauty and was dying to capture a chance to sleep with her.

I know her husband is a job loyal man, so always on job even at time of being in bed with his wife. She was okay talking to me not so frank but she somewhere understood my intentions towards her

Coming to the story, one day my landlady asked me that our neighbors was unwell and Hanit is also out of station so she asked me to go and give them lunch. I went and knocked the door no one responded so I just pushed it and it opened and then I heard a voice shouting loudly "who is there I am changing please don't come in"

I knew what was in store for me. I went inside and caught Rami bhabhi in her nude state. She was surprised and left in mid air reacting surprisingly to take her dupatta to cover her nude body. She asked me to go away but instead I kept the lunch and moved towards her until I was really close and seeing directly in her eyes.

I slowly put my hand on her face and seducing moved it down on her body to her neck and suddenly put my lips on her she was pushing me away me but I capture her and finally opened her mouth with my tongue. I move downwards to kiss on her boobs. She was hesitant but offered no much reaction except that "I am married"

I continued touching her and feeling her large pigeons and then suddenly snatched the dupatta to leave her completely nude. Oh my! What a hairy cunt I think she never shaved since she started getting hair there. I immediately bent down and wandered my lips on her pussy to find her clit she was already wet and tasted salty.

Slowly and slowly, she was losing her composure and started to move her pussy in my face so that my tongue could penetrate more inside her. Then I took her and laid her on the bed and I fondled the breasts to my fullest pleasure. I squeezed them, I molested them, playing fondly with each nipple.

Her breasts bobbed with delight and they juggled as she protested with participation. I then undressed quickly and put my throbbing 7inch in her mouth to an intense feeling of her warm hot lips surrounding my meat. She almost choked on it.

She slowly began to suck my swollen dick like a huge lollipop and I was on the verge of collapsing on her with excitement. I held on to her breasts and pumped the spongy cakes merrily until I was ready to shoot my load uncontrollably into her mouth.

She was enjoying my work! I tongued her magnum cunt alternatively inserting my fingers and she now began to moan with pleasure:" oh please fuck me…fuck me a hundred times! I took my hard erect prick, bent her on nearby laying stool and rammed into her pussy lips from behind with all my might.

I battered her and she cried out: "oh…ahhhhhoooooooo…hhhh-hhh!!!!!!!!!! Meeting every thrust of mine she was a little loose but nevermind. I raised my intensity of ramming in her and after about 20 minutes I began to slow down a little licking her navel hole.

Then I began to cum, to my surprise she did not object and I came in her and I pulled out eventually. This has been by far my best sex experience since I always fancy fucking older ladies in my fantasies..........

Rami bhabhi was not talking to me after that day. I tried calling her many times on the way but she ignored always. I was very depressed... Some how many days passed, I went Chandigarh to my native place ... But suddenly one day I received call from a girl who asked me that she is house servant of Rami bhabhi named Pari.

She told me memsahib is vomiting & Hanit sahib and bade memsahib is gone to Delhi on some work, so I must rush her to hospital. I took a car & rushed to Patiala, went to her place. To my surprise Rami bhabhi was watching TV. I was shocked and shouted at her, "What the hell was this all a joke".

Why did she call me as I was in Chandigarh and rushed to Patiala just for her, I also fired Pari for this joke? She said memsahib asked to phone. The servant Pari also was a punjaban. Rami bhabhi said, "aap kyo naraaz hote ho abhi tumhari narazgi door karr deti hoo"(Why are you angry now. Here I will remove your anger). She came to me and just kissed me, I was amazed to her such a behavior.

She asked Pari to go to her room. She turned off the TV & passionately started hugging me, she put one hand on my manhood, which was now showing an erection. I was tensed she said don't worry no one gonna come today. I was waiting for this chance since long time. She unzipped my trouser and my tool came out.

She said, "aree tum kyu sharma rahe ho" (Why are you feeling shy) while asking me this she took my lund(cock) her hand and shook it up and down, it gets tight. She immediately took off my trouser & asks me to undress. I had no choice. Now I was naked and very happy in mind but equally shocked also as I have never seen such an attitude of Rami bhabhi.

She was looking at me and suddenly asked me to undress her but I was unable to reach to her and still feeling shocked. She herself removed each and every cloth of her. When she took her panty, I could not believe such a clean shaved pussy. I asked her how come this change?

She replied that last time I was shocked to see her hairy pussy. She now wants to give me equal shock and happiness as I gave her last time. She spread her legs and said she said don't worry come on. she hugged me. Now I was also getting little courage and started kissing her. I put my tongue inside her mouth. She asked me to suck her boobs, I obeyed it.

I felt a current going inside me as I was electrifying. Suddenly she lay down & asked me to come on her top, I did. My lund(cock) found a way in between her thighs & went inside her tunnel. I started digging the deep tunnel. My lund(cock) was going inside her choot(pussy) which was very much lubricated and it never stopped.

I found myself in 7th heaven. Oh my god she was crying oh please aur zoor se (More harder) ahhhhhhhhhhhh hhhh ohhhhh- hhhhhh hhhhhhhhhh ohmammmmmmmm ah mazaa aa gaya (I am having fun). Tumhare lund ka to zawab nahi (I don't have an answer for your cock). Kya iron steel ke jaise kadak hai (It hard like an iron steel). Meri choot ko yeah phaad hi dega (It will tear my pussy).

The way she was saying it made me more erotic. I started fuck- ing her hard. Back and forth. . . I was biting her nipple sucking the boobs. Pressing her every corner. Maine use mere badan se chipka liya jaise eik badan aur do aatma. Mera lund aab puri tarah se garam tha. Hathode ke jaise mai ghusha raha tha aur nikal raha tha. (I had stuck her to my body like one body and 2 souls. My cock was completely hot. Like a hammer I was shoving and removing it.)

Rami bhabhi ko bahoot hi maza aa raha tha. Thodi der ke liya mai bhool gaya tha ki uski naukrani Pari yeah sub dekh rahi thi. Maine kaha bhabhi tumhari naukrani dekh rahi hai.woh boli koi baat nahi.tum mujhe chodooo. Zoor se chodoo....... aab is lund ke liye to main Hanit se bhi zhagda kar sakti hoo. (Rupa my sister-in-law was having a lot of pleasure. For some time, I forgot that her maidservant Pari was watching all of this. I said sister-in-law your maidservant is watching. Dont worry you fuck me. fuck me harder. For this cock I can even fight with Hanit.)

Now even if he comes, I will not stop you. My god your lund(cock) is like a hammer. Zaldi karoo darling. Zoor zoor se dhake lagao. (Do it faster darling. Push harder and harder)

I pushed hard and hard and harder harder. My god it was really amazing. I don't know how I got such power. I was fucking harder/harder. She said, "aur zoor se chodo. Aur zoor se." (More harder fuck me. More harder)

Tumhara lund pura andar ghusa doo.aaz meri choot ko maza aa raha hai. shaadi ke baad pahli baar chudai ka maza sahi aaya hai. (Shove our cock completely inside. Today My pussy is having the pleasure. After marriage first time I have getting the pleasure of fucking) Aahhhhhhhhh hhhhhhhhhhh o hhhhhhhhh-hhhhhhhhhhhhh ghusa ke hi rakho. (Keep it shoved inside) After some time I said I am coming now. She said noooooooo this time come outside.

I pulled out and threw all my water on her belly. She sucked it. I was tired. Then I heard a knocking sound behind the door, immediately went to open the door, there I saw Pari standing and looking towards to me as I went naked to open the door, I saw hungry eyes of her servant Pari. She was a virgin girl.

I told Rami bhabhi tum to second hand hokar bhi mere virgin

lund ka maza le chooki aab mujhe virgin ladki ko chodne ki permission chahiye. (I told Rami my sister-in-law you are second hand and have taken the pleasure of my virgin cock. Now I want the permission of fucking a virgin girl.)

She said ask Pari… if she agrees okay.

Pari toh ready thi hi. mere puchne se pahile he (Pari was ready before I even asked her) she came all bare naked. She started kissing my lund(cock) and it became hard in next 5 minutes.

I started kissing Pari's choot(pussy).it was very tight.

Pari said, "babu yeah memsahib ki tarah nahi hai. bahoot tight hai. Tumhara hathoda shayad ise phaad nahi payee." (Mister this is not like Memsahib…It very tight…Your hammer may not be able to tear it)

Maine kaha challenge maat karo Pari. (I said don't challenge me Pari)

Uske kahne se pahle hi maine appne loday ko uski choot me ghusaane ki koshish kari. paar phisal gaya. Mere lund uski choot me nahi jaa paya. Pari ki choot bahoot hi narrow thi. Maine do/tin baar koshish kari. akhir haar gaya (Before she could say anything, I tried to put my cock inside her pussy but I slipped. My cock was not able to enter her pussy. Pari's pussy was very narrow. I tried two/ three times. In the end I gave up.) Then I asked Rami bhabhi for help. She said can help but I must fuck her one more time. I said okay but now she must help me in fucking this virgin cunt. She said okay and asked Pari to stand up.

She told me to lie down. Asked Pari to come on top of me and put her choot on my mouth. I started licking her hard. She asked me to lick her in this way I could make her choot hole wider. Idhar(here) Rami bhabhi (sister-in-law) came on me and started licking my lund(cock)

I told Rami Bhabhi pahile main Pari ki kunwari choot ko chod kaar achhe se khush hona chahta hoo. Phir tumhari choot ko bhi dubara choddunga. Rami bhabhi maan gayee aur mere lund ko muh me leker ek baar kis kaya aur hat gayee. Aab mein Pari ke uppar let gaya. Uska jism uska bahoot hi sexy kurmura tha. (I told Rupa my sister-in-law that I want to fuck Pari's virgin pussy nicely and want to be happy. After that I will fuck your pussy again. Rupa my sister-in-law agreed then took my cock in her mouth for once. kissed it and got away. Now I came on top of Pari lied down. Her body was very sexy lick a snack)

Usko dekhte hi achee acche ka lodaa khada ho sakta tha. Maine loday ko uski choot ke muh pe rakha aur Rami bhabhi ko kaha Pari ka mouth band karoo. kyoki shayad mere lund ke andar jaate hi woh chillayegi aur padosi aa sakte hai. (Looking at her many guys dicks would stand up.I kept my cock on her pussy lips and told Rami My sister in law to close Pari's mouth because maybe when my cock is inside her she will scream and neigh-bours may come) Rami bhabhi(sister in law) closed her mouth with her choot(pussy) I pushed immediately my lund(cock) in-side her choot(pussy).

I tried one/two attempt and finally I was able to penetrate my lund(cock) inside her virgin choot(pussy). oh my god my lun-d(cock) felt having a different feeling altogether. Rami bhabhi (sister in law) took away her choot(pussy) and Pari was crying babu baas aab chodooooooooo zoor zoorsesssssss (Mister now enough fuck me hard harderrr) sss ui maa(Mother) mmaaaa-aaaaa aaaaaaa aghj ahhhhhh hhhhhhhhhhhhhhhhh ohhhhhhhhh hhhhhhhhhhhhhhhhhhhh kya swarag ka anand aa rha hai babu aab yeah tumhara lund zindagi bhar meri choot me pada rahne doo.....(What a feeling of heaven Mister.Now your cock should be fallen inside my pussy for a lifetime)

Please believe me I pushed in her many times.kya jaam kar chudai kari thi. mujhe bhi bahoot hi maza aa aha tha..Pari ko bhi.......(What a fucking she wass giving me. I have having a lot of fun... so was Pari.) than I said, "now I am cumming Pari".

Pari boli koi baat nahi andar hi nikal do. maine kaha nahi Pari yeah bahut risky hai.tum pregnant ho sakto hoo. (Pari said no problem remove it inside. I said no this is very risky you may get pregnant)

woo boli koi chance nahi kyoki abhi end ke din chal rahe. Main dochar dhake zoor se lagaya aur woh chillayi zoorse babu zoor se chod. tera lund to wakai gazab ka hai. Aur mera pani Pari ke choot ke andar hi nikal gaya. (She said there is no chance as it is my end days. I pushed 2/4 times harder and she scream harder mister fuck me harder. Your cock is no wonder great.

And I cummed inside Pari. We slept for another 5 minutes in that fashion only.

Suddenly bhabhi (sister-in-law) came and ask me to get up. I said bhabhi (sister-in-law) no power left. She said I will give you more power. She asked Pari to go in kitchen and make almond milk cocktail for all of us. We drank. After 30 minutes now I was bit ready. She came on me. She started kissing my Lund(cock).

She took my lund(cock) inside her mouth and asked me to roam my tongue inside her choot(pussy). I did. My lund(cock) now was full erect and she did not want to lose this opportunity. She came down. I came on her and asked Pari to come near me. I inserted my lund(cock) inside Rami bhabhi's choot(pussy) and pressed Pari's boobs. She laughed.

Now Pari came back to me. She started pushing me. With Pari's pressure my lund(cock) was going more steeply in Rami bhabhi's choot (sister in law's pussy). Rami bhabhi (sister-in-law) was crying oh you are great. Tumhara lund to zoordar hai (Your cock is so hard). Ahhhhhhhhhhhhhhhhhhh, ohhhhhhhhhh-hhhhhhhhhh oi maa (Oh mother). Main zoor zoor se dhake laga raha tha aur woh chila rahi thi (I was pushing harder and harder and she was screaming).

Itne me achanak maine kaha bas Rami bhabhi nikalne wala hai bolo andar ya bahar(Suddenly I said enough Rami my sister in law it going to cum out do you want it inside or outside.)

Rami bhabhi boli iss baar andar hi loongi (Rami my sister-in-law said this time I am going to take it inside).

Aur maine Rami bhabhi ke choot ke andar hi chood diya aur 5 min tak Rami bhabhi ke uppar he leta raha (And I left it inside Rami my sister in law's pussy and for 5 mins I was lying on top of Rami my sister-in-law.)

Bhabhji ne mujhko kiss kiya aur kaha (Sister is law kissed me and said) thank you my husband Hanit used to fuck me once 15 days, and I used to cry for a lund(cock) and even when he used to fuck me, he just did it and slept. You have fulfilled my desire today. I am very happy today. You can come anytime you like.

Also, Pari said, "babu aaz tumne mujhe bhi aurat bana diya" (Mister today you have maid me a woman too). I said Pari your choot(pussy) was great. Pari sharmayee(embaressed). After this I came back to Chandigarh and slept but could not control myself thinking about the entire incident. Now Rami bhabhi (sister-in-law) is being fucked my me whenever I get chance.

But this year I completed my studies and come back to Chandigarh but still whenever I get chance, I visit Patiala to her house to fuck her.

11. Ranbir

I am Ranbir from Punjab, I am 32 years old. This story is about my encounter with my brother- in- law's wife, Mouni. Mouni is very fair and beautiful and has a figure of 38-26-38. I admired her figure always and used to fantasise about her and masturbate. She belongs to Lucknow. The incident took place in December 2005.

I had gone to Bombay to meet my sister-in-law and there my brother in laws wife Mouni had also come. I spent about a week in Bombay and as I was coming back to Lucknow my sister-in-law requested me to take Mouni also along with me as it is not safe for a lone lady to travel in train such a long distance. I agreed to it and told them that only one seat was booked in AC two tier on my name. We thought that we would be able to manage the second seat once we board the train, but the TT refused to give another seat. My seat was upper berth. Mouni and me waited till 10 in the night but couldn't manage another seat. Then Mouni said "Bhaiya ji challo hum dono ek hi seat par adjust ho kar soo jate hai(Brother let us adjust and sleep on one seat only)" I also agreed to it and we climbed on to the upper berth. As we lay side by side, I could feel the heat of her body and immediately my laura(cock) stood up. We talked for some time and then Mouni turned her face on the other side and went to sleep. I just couldn't sleep as my prick was aching to feel Mouni's hot cunt. After about half an hour I also turned towards Mouni and kept my hand on her waist. There was no response from Mouni. As she was wearing a saree my hand was on her naked waist. Slowly I moved my hand on her waist and pinched it. Mouni suddenly became stiff and whispered "Bhaiya ji yeh kya kar rahe ho (Brother what are you doing)" I didn't say anything and pushed my rod hard 7 inches prick in her arse and started rubbing it on her arse cheeks. I put my hand on her boobs and pressed them hard. Mouni started to push my hand away. I whispered in her ear "Mouni mujhe tumhari chut marni hai please marne do bahut din ho gaye hai, maine aapna lauda chut main nahi dala(Mouni I want to bang your pussy. Please let me bang as it has been many days, I have put my cock in a pussy)". I pulled her face towards me and before she could say anything, I kissed her full on the lips and pushed my tongue deep in her mouth. She tried to push me away but after about 15 seconds she just relaxed and started hugging me. I kissed her all over her face, neck and chest. She started breathing heavily. I pulled her saree pallu away and opened her blouse. She was wearing a black laced bra. I started sucking her nipples through her bra and my hand moved to her chut(pussy). I rubbed her chut(pussy)over the saree and immediately Mouni started moaning oooohhhhhhh aaaaahhhhh aacha lag raha hai, mere nipple jor se suck karo (It is feeling nice,suck my nipples harder). I immediately removed the hooks of her bra and started sucking her nipples hard. I pulled her saree up to her waist and put my hand on her chut(pussy). She was not wearing any panties. I left her nipples and moved down kissing her stomach and licking it with my tongue. Then I moved down and put my mouth on Mouni's chut(pussy)and kissed it she immediately started oozing juices from her chut(pussy). I put my tongue deep in her chut(pussy)and then pulled her clitoris and started sucking her. She started making soft moaning sounds aaaahahah bhaiyaji iiiii bah-huuuutttttt aacccchhhhhaaaa hhhhaaaaiiiii chuste raho meri chut (Brother it is very nice keep sucking my pussy) ohhhh. I then moved up and opened my pant and took my lund(cock) out. Mouni saw the 7-inch-long lund(cock) and got very excited and immediately pulled it and put it in her mouth. It was a great feeling. we moved into 69 position and after about 5 minutes when we both were on the brink of cumming. I changed position and sat in between her legs. I pushed my long hard laura(cock) in her hot chut(pussy)and gave a hard push. I was surprised that her cunt was very tight like a virgin. I said "Mouni tumhari chut to bahut tight hai(Mouni your pussy is very tight)". She said, "mere patti ka laura aap ka jitna mota aur lamba nahi hai, aur ab batein band karo aur meri chut ko aapna laura se phar do (My husband cock is not as big and long like yours and not stop talking and tear my pussy with your cock)". I started ramming hard into her chut(pussy) and after about 1 minute she became stiff and moaned and had an orgasm. I didn't stop and increased my ramming in her chut(pussy)and soon she came again and by this time I was also ready and I held her tightly and said "Mouni main aa raha hooo(Mouni I am going to cum)" and I opened my tap of cum in her chut(pussy) and filled it with my cum. She put her hand from behind on my balls and pressed them slowly and took out all the juice from them. I just lay on top of her for some time and then I kissed her on her lips and she said "bhaiyaji aaj tak mara patti ne kabhi bhi meri chut aisa nahi mari jaisa aap na mujhe maja diya hai(Brother till today my husband has never banged my pussy like you have given me pleasure)". Luckily there was no other passenger on the other three seats and the whole night Mouni and me fucked each other.

On reaching Lucknow we went home. Though I was to stay at Lucknow only for two days but after the night with Mouni in the train I spent 10 days at Lucknow as my brother-in-law, Mouni's husband was out of station and we enjoyed each and every position possible in those 10 days.

12. Ranbir 2

As I wrote in previous story once we reached Lucknow, we came to know that my brother-in-law has gone out of town for 10 days, we were really happy about it. I was to stay at Lucknow for only 2 days but when I saw that I had a good opportunity to be with Mouni and explore her body and each and every hole I decided to stay on till her husband returned. As we reached home the house was completely empty. I unloaded the luggage from auto rickshaw and took it in. as I put down the last bag I turned around and saw Mouni was closing the door. I didn't waste any time and went and held her from behind and cupped her large breast in my hands and started kissing her on her bare shoulders and her back. Immediately her body became very hot and she said 'oohhh bhaiya ji yeh kya kar rahe ho (Oh Brother what are you doing) aahhh press them hard its great oohhh it's so great'. I kept pressing her boobs hard and kissing her wildly on her neck and shoulders. She started moaning ooohhh aaaaahhhhhhhh aaaaaaaaaaaaa. I moved my hands slowly down on her stomach and massaged and pressed her stomach for some time. Then I moved my hands further down and put my left hand inside her suit and slowly started moving it upwards on her bare stomach. By now my 7-inch-long prick was on full mast(hard) and aching to come out of my pant. Mouni put her right hand behind and held my long hard prick and started massaging it over my pant. I pushed my right hand further down into her salwar (pant) and pushed my hand through her panties and touched her chut(pussy). It was very hot and oozing juices. I put one finger in her chut(pussy) and slowly started rubbing it in and out. By now I had moved my other hand up in her suit and was pressing her boobs from inside. Mouni was moaning loudly standing there in front of the door. "ooooohhhhhhhh aaaaaaahhhhhhhh aur joor se masalo mere chut ko (Squeeze my pussy more harder), it's so great." I kept this on for few minutes and then pulled my hands out and lifted her suit up and removed it slowly. Then I opened the hooks of her bra & pulled it off again held her nipples and pressed them hard in between my fingers. A loud aaaaaaaaa-aaahhhhhhhhhhhhhhhhhh escaped from her lips. I started kissing and licking her back. I kissed her neck and slowly moved down with my tongue licking her back. Mouni was getting very hot and moving her solid bums back and forth. I moved down to her waist and then opened the string of her salwar and let it fall down. In front of me were 2 beautiful round white buttocks covered with a small pink coloured panty. The buttocks were looking very tempting. I kissed on her buttocks over the panties and Mouni was now continuously moaning and shouting "aaaahhhhh ooooohhhh chumo mere gand ko aur jor se daba do is bari gand ko aur joor se (Kiss my ass. press my ass harder, more harder.) kiss me on my gand(ass) kiss and lick it hard". I removed it and was zapped to see the most ravishing gand(ass) I had ever seen. I couldn't hold myself back and shoved my face in between her buttocks and started kissing the hole of her gand(ass) it had a peculiar kind of smell and taste. I was turned on by this taste and smell. I started removing my dress also and was soon naked still lapping at her gand(ass) and her rear hole. After some seconds I turned Mouni around and her hot wet dripping chut was in front of my eyes. I saw her beautiful chut in broad daylight for the first time and it was beautiful with two pink coloured chut(pussy) lips protruding out towards me and hot juices flowing out. I put my mouth on the chut(pussy) lips and started sucking on it as if there was no tomorrow. The taste of her juices was driving me mad.

"Aaahhhhhhh ooooohhhhhh aaaaoooooooo hhhhhhhhheeeeeeeeee aaaaaaooooooooohhhhh suck it hard don't stop please suck it don't stop".

I pushed my tongue in her cunt and suddenly Mouni became stiff and screamed 'I am cuming aaaaahhh aaahhh ooohhhhhhhh suck my chut(pussy). mere chut ko chat lo (Lick my pussy) don't stop aaaaaaahhahahahahahh oooohhohohoooo aaaaaaaaaeeeeeeee.' I kept sucking with my tongue deep in her hot chut. After some time, I stood up and kissed Mouni on her lips and she licked all her chut(pussy) juices from my face. I held her tight and kissed her deep in her mouth and sucked her thick sexy lips.

Then Mouni pulled back and said "bhaiya aap to bahut hi aacha chusta ho chut ko. Mujhe aaisa maja kabhi nahi aaya. mera pati to sirf upper char ka aapna lund mera andar dalta hai aur jhatka maar kar niche uttar jata hain. Aaj ke baad mein aap se hi chudwaongi(Brother you are a very good pussy sucker. I did not get pleasure like this before. My husband just climbs on top, take his cock, puts it inside me and bangs and gets off me". Saying this she started kissing my chest and sucking my nipples. Slowly she moved down kissing my stomach and then she reached my long hard pole and held it in her hand and kissed the tip of my laura(cock) and licked the pre cum from the tip. A shiver went up my spine and it was a great feeling. She put the tip of my laura(cock) in her mouth and sucked it real hard. I felt the life going out of me. It was a feeling I hand never felt before. Then slowly she started pushing my laura (cock) in her mouth till it touched her throat and started doing in out motion with her mouth. It was a blowjob I had never got before. In between she started sucking my tatas(balls) and again sucking the laura(cock). I was in seventh heaven. After sometime I pulled her up and made her stand and kissed her full on the lips. I pushed her against the wall and opened her legs. She held my laura(cock) in her hand and directed the tip towards her hot wet choot(pussy). I pushed forward and the head of my laura(cock) entered her choot(pussy) which was literally on fire. As my laura(cock) went in she screamed "ooooooooohhhhhhhh aasta karo darad ho raha hai bahut bara laura hai aap ka please aasta(Do it slowly, it is paining, your cock is very big, please slowly) ". I didn't hear her please and gave hard push and almost half my laura(cock) went in her wet cunt. "aaaahahahahah aaaoooo meri choot faado ge kya. hai bhagwan! Maa! mar gai! aasta meri choot ko aapke laura ka size ko adjust hona do fir joor laga kar karna.(Are you going to tear my pussy. Oh my God! Mother! I am dying! Slowly ley my pussy get used to the size of your cock than you can surely bang me hard)" But I was on full heat and again pushed hard and my full laura(cock) went in and I could feel mu laura(cock) touch the innermost walls of her cunt. Aaaahhhhhh oooooohhhh-haaahhhhhheeeeeeeee, mar gai chutiya aasta chod muje. tera laura hai ya hathi ki soond hai(I am dying asshole, fuck me slowly, is this your cock or elephants trunk) aaaaaaahhhhhhh oooohhhhhh'. Hearing her say this I got more horny and started ramming harder. She kept screaming aaaaaaahhhhhhhh aooooooooooohhhhhhhhh chutiya chod mujhe aabhi aacha lag raha hai chood aaur joor se choooooooooooooood(asshole fuck me now I have feeling good, fuck me harder) . I kept ramming my hard laura(cock) in her choot (pussy) and was saying, "dekh Mouni mein teri choot kaisa chod raha hoon. Aaj main teri choot ko faar kar hi dum longa. Kal raat train mein itni aachi taran se nahi chod paa raha tha. aab dekh tere choot bhi mujhi se ukar rahi hai(Look Mouni how I am fucking your pussy. Today I am going to tear your pussy only then breathe. Yesterday night in the train I was not able to fuck nicely. Now see your pussy is attracted to me only"

"haaaaa joor se mar.... maa aa rahoi hoo.... joor se chod.. jhatka mmaaaar joor see (Yes bang me harder...Mother I am cuming.... Fuck me harder.... Push harder) maaaaaaaa main gir rahi hoo(I am cuming) aaaaaaahhhhhhhh oooohhhhhhhaaaaaaaaaaaa." She shivered and became very stiff as she came and kept coming as I kept ramming into her hot cunt holding her tightly against the wall. Suddenly I felt my tatta(balls) becoming hard and I screamed,"Mouni main aa raha hoon... teri choot mein aapna pani girana laga hoo(Mouni I am going to cum.... in your pussy I am leaving my water)"

She said, "aaja aaahh bhar de aapna pani se meri choot... bhar de is garam choot ko (Come aaahh fill me with your water fill my pussy... fill my hot pussy)". And I started cuming in her choot(pussy) and my cum wouldn't stop. After sometime we both relaxed and kissed each other standing against the wall with my laura(cock) still hard in her choot(pussy). We stood like this for some time and then I pushed back and Mouni bent down and licked my laura(cock) dry off our mixed juices. I pushed her back on the floor and took out my laura(cock) from her mouth and put my mouth on her cunt. We started sucking and licking each other as if we have not fucked for ages. We kept sucking for almost 15 minutes and then suddenly Mouni stopped sucking me and she started moving her hips with great force. I knew she was about to cum and I started putting more force on her clitoris. Soon her body became stiff and she cum. I kept sucking her choot(pussy) like a dog she relaxed and again put my laura(cock) in her mouth and started sucking. By now I was also on the brink of cuming and I started pushing my laura(cock) deeper in her mouth. Soon I screamed, "ooohhhh randi mei aa raha hhooo-oooo mooh mein hi lena pura juice mera(Oh my whore I am cuming...take it in your mouth the complete juice". She sucked my laura(cock) hard and I shot my load of cum in her mouth. She tightly closed her lips on my laura(cock) and kept sucking. I dumped my load in her mouth and she drank the complete juice. I slumped on her body with my face on her wet smelly choot(pussy) and my laura(cock) in her mouth. We remained in this position for some time and then I got off and kissed on her lips. Mouni said, "aapka juice to bahut hi aacha hai.... aab rooj drink karongi is ka (Your juice is very nice.... Now I will have a drink of this daily)". We held each other in our arms for some more time and then got up to have a wash.

13. Ranbir 3

Next day Mouni got up early in the morning to do the house hold chores. I got up after some time and went to the toilet and had a good bath and freshened up. By this time Mouni had prepared the breakfast and I sat down to have my breakfast. Mouni also came and stood near me, I pulled her closer and lifted her night shirt up and kissed on her belly button and started licking and kissing her stomach. Mouni started moaning aaaahhhhha ooooohhhhhh "yehi breakfast kahao ge yah plate mein se bhi kuch lo ge(Will you eat only this breakfast or will you eat something from the plate also)". I pulled Mouni on my lap with her back towards me. I pulled her night pants and shirt off and spread her legs with my legs in between. I picked up the toast of bread and put it on her choot(pussy) and rubbed it. She was already dripping her juices from her choot(pussy) and soon the bread was soaked in her juices. I applied some jam on the toast and had a bite. The taste was something I had never tasted before, the cunt juices mixed with jam. We shared the toast and soon we had completed our breakfast. My 7 inches long prick was hard by now and it was fighting to come out of the shorts I was wearing. Mouni got up from my lap, turned around and put her massive boobs in my mouth. I just went crazy and started sucking hard on her nipples. Mouni started moaning aaahahahah oooohhhhhhhhhh aaaaaaaahhhhhh-hhhhh. "bhaiyaji mat rookna chooste raho mere mamo ko(Brother don't stop keep sucking my boobs) aaaahhhhhh". I kept sucking her boobs and then put my hand on her choot(pussy)

and massaged it. I put my two fingers inside her choot(pussy) and pushed them hard inside. Mouni screamed aaaaaaaaaahhhhhhhhhhhh with desire and started moving her hips back and forth. Suddenly she pulled herself back got down on her knees and pulled my shorts in one jerk. My long hard laura(cock) sprang out. Mouni immediately put it in her mouth and started sucking my laura(cock) her head moving up and down at very high speed. I put my fingers in her hair and started pushing her head further on my laura (cock). I felt very excited as she took my 7-inch long laura(cock) almost completely in her mouth and I could feel the head of my laura (cock) touch deep in her throat. She choked on it once or twice but still continued sucking hard. After sucking my laura(cock) for about five minutes she stood up and I joined my legs and she moved forward and sat down holding my laura (cock) and directing it to her wet hot choot(pussy). I entered easily because of the juices flowing. Mouni gave one hard push and almost half my laura (cock) went in the cunt we both moaned together aaaaahhhhhhha ooooohhhhhhh eeeehhhhhhhhh aaaaaahhhhhhhhhhhhhh. She gave one more push and my laura(cock) was imbedded in her sizzling hot cunt. She started moving up and down and couldn't stop shouting "aaaaahhhhhhhh maja aa raha hai. mein is laura ko pura andar laga ke chodu gi (I am having fun. I will take this cock completely inside and fuck it.) aaaahhhhhhhhhhh aaahhhhhh ooooooohhhhhhhhh".
I hugged Mouni tightly and put her hard nipples in my mouth & sucked hard and bit them with my teeth. She could not hold her excitement back and screamed aaaaaaahahahhhhhhh and her body became stiff aaaaaahhhhhhhh

"main jhar rahi hooooo aaaaaahhhhhhhhh(I am cumming)"

And she came aaaaaaaaahhhhhhhhhh ooooooohhhhhhhh . we hugged each other tightly and she slowly stopped her up down moments. We remained like this for some time with my laura (cock) in her still pulsing choot(pussy). After about a minute when she eased, I picked her up with her legs wrapped around my waist, my laura (cock) in her choot (pussy) and I stood up and carried her to the drawing room sofa.

As Mouni was working in the morning she had forgotten to close the main door of the house which was connected with the drawing room. As I walked into the drawing room carrying Mouni completely naked with her legs still wrapped around my waist and hugging each other tightly, I froze in the mid-way as I saw a tall beautiful young girl in red top and black jeans standing at the main door of the house. She was staring at us with a look of shock on her face. I stood staring at her. Mouni felt something was wrong and she also turned her head and saw the girl standing. in a state of shock, we all 3 stood frozen for long. Suddenly Mouni pulled her legs and my laura(cock) popped out of her choot(pussy) with a splashing sound of the juices, and she ran to the bedroom. My laura (cock) lost its erection because of the sudden shock and embarrassment. I also turned around slowly walked to the bedroom with that girl still staring at my back. I entered the bedroom and saw Mouni looking scared and getting dressed. She told me immediately that the girl was Komal her cousin sister. Mouni got dressed and went out. I slowly took my time to get dressed and after about half an hour Mouni called me. I went to the drawing room and saw Mouni sitting with her cousin with a relaxed look on their faces. Mouni introduced me to her cousin. I moved forward and extended my hand and she also offered her hand for a hand shake. The moment I touched her hand a hot wave went through my body and my laura(cock) which was loose till now suddenly became hard in my shorts and immediately it was visible to both the ladies. I felt embarrassed so I quickly sat on the sofa opposite to them and folded my legs. After some talking Komal got up to go to have a wash as she had travelled in the bus and was feeling tired. As soon as she entered the guest room, Mouni told me that she had told her cousin that Mouni was not getting full satisfaction from her husband and so we were enjoying till her husband was out of station and after great persuasion her sister agreed not to mention about the incident to anyone.

After about half an hour Komal came out of guest room, her wet hair flowing down her shoulders and she was wearing a deep cut nighty which was up to her knees. She was looking really ravishing and that very moment I decided that I have to fuck this beauty. Komal came and sat opposite me on the sofa and we started talking. Mouni had gone to the kitchen to prepare breakfast for Komal and we both were alone in drawing room. My eyes were on her massive boobs, the shape of which were clearly visible because of the nighty having got wet in front and it was sticking to her body. My eyes went to her shapely legs and before I could stop myself, I blurted out "You have got really sexy legs". She met my stare and said "bhaiya(brother) even you have got a sexy body". I just smiled and said thanks. By then Mouni also came and we started talking other things. While we were talking Komal kept staring at me and looking at my nicker where I was finding it hard to hide my erection as I had not put on my underwear. Komal gave a mischievous smile and said to Mouni.

"Mouni, bhaiya to bahut sexy hai tumha bahut maja date honge(Mouni brother is so sexy giving you a lot of pleasure)". Mouni blushed and looked at me. I again couldn't stop myself and said, "you can also join us and have fun". Komal replied, "bhaiya(Brother), I am still a virgin and no one will touch my body till I get married". I took this as a challenge and decided that by tonight I will fuck this young beauty and break her virginity. After some talking Komal said that she was going to rest as she was feeling tired of bus journey and went to the guest room and closed her room. My laura(cock) was rock hard as I had not completed my fuck with Mouni in morning and also had become more horny after seeing Komal's sexy body.

Mouni started picking up the plated and cups from the centre table with her back towards me. I couldn't resist the sight of her sexy gand(ass) and immediately got up and held her from behind and started pushing my hard laura (cock)in her arse. She straightened and said, "bhaiya please mat karo Komal fir aa jaya gi (Brother don't do it kamal will come again)". I just held her boobs tightly and pushed her against me and started kissing her neck. She turned her face and I immediately kissed her on her lips and pushed my tongue in her mouth she started moaning ooooooooooooo hhhhhhhhhhhhhhh. I kept pressing her boobs hard and pushing my laura(cock) in her gand(ass) from behind. Mouni also started moving her gand (ass) and grinding my laura (cock) in the cut of her gand (ass). I moved my hand down and opened the buttons of her pant and put my hand inside and touched her hot choot (pussy) which was dripping with her juices. She moved her mouth away and loudly started aaaa-aaahhhhhhhhh ooooooooooooohhhhhhhhhhhhh aaaaaeeeee-eeehhhhhhhhhhhh. I put my finger in her choot(pussy) and started rubbing it and she kept on aaaaaaaaahhhhhhhhhhhh eee-eeeeehhhhhhhhhh ooooooooooooohhhhhhhh haai bhaiya bahut aacha hai. ek aur ungli andar dalo aur jor se karo (Brother it is very nice. Put one more finger and do it harder)'. I pushed my two fingers inside and gave a hard push she screamed loudly, "aaaaahhhhhh bhaiya thoda aasta darad hota hai(Brother little slowly it is paining)". I didn't hear anything and pulled my fingers out and again rammed it in again she screamed. In our excitement we had forgotten about Komal in the next room. Suddenly the guest room door opened and Komal walked out. This time she was not shocked but instead she had a smile on her face. Mouni and self-seeing her smile got motivated and we continued our finger fucking and my kissing her neck and back. Komal came and sat on the sofa in front of us and watched our moments. Mouni's pants were already down. With my free hand I pulled her t-shirt up and Mouni immediately removed it. Mouni was completely naked now and Komal was staring at Mouni's massive boobs which I was pressing hard with my left hand and my right hand was working hard in her choot (pussy). Komal's breathing was becoming hard watching this scene in front of her and she was pressing her legs tightly. soon Komal moved her one hand in between her legs and pressed her choot(pussy) with it and a moan escaped from her lips oooooohhhhhh. I knew that this was the right time for me to act if I have to fuck this beauty because she was already feeling horny seeing me finger fuck and kiss Mouni. I immediately left Mouni and moved towards Komal. She was staring at my erection in my nicker as I approached her with her hand tightly pressed in her choot (pussy) between her legs. I walked up to her and touched her cheeks with my hands. She closed her eyes and put her head back on the sofa back rest. I leaned forward and put my lips on her lips. Initially she kept her kips tightly shut but I pressed my tongue hard and soon she opened her lips. I pushed my tongue into her mouth and she started moaning ooooooohhhhhh aaaaaaaahhhhhh with my mouth on her mouth. I moved my hands down to her boobs and pressed them hard immediately Komal put her hands behind my back and hugged me tightly. We remained in this position for some time and then I pulled my mouth off her mouth and started kissing her neck and shoulders. And pressing her boobs harder. She kept her sounds on aaaaaaaahhhhhhhhhhhh ooooooohhhhhhhhhhhhhh aaaaaaaaahhhhhhhhhhhhhh ooooouuuuuuccccchhhhhhh. I moved my hands down and pulled her nighty up she adjusted her body a little and I pulled her nighty off. She was completely naked underneath. I was just amazed to see such a sexy body with perfect curves, 36 D hard breast and flat stomach. I fell on my knees and put the hard boobs in my mouth and started sucking on them wildly.

"aaaaaaaahhhhhhhhhh its great please suck them hard no one has ever touched me earlier I am enjoying it please suck don't stop aaaaaaaaahhhhhhhhhhhhhhhhhhhh ooooooohhhhhhhhhhhh".

I kept pulling and sucking her nipples and she was going mad. After some time, I left her boobs and moved my mouth down kissing her flat stomach and then her belly button. I put my tongue in her belly button and bit her with my teeth. Komal screamed with desire and some pain aaaaaaaaahhhhhhhhh oooooooouuuuuuuuccccccchhhhhhhhhhhhhh. I moved down and opened her legs which were till now tightly pressed together. The sight that met my eyes was amazing. Komals choot (pussy) was freshly shaved and her juices were flowing out and the sofa was already wet from her juices. I encircled her choot (pussy) without actually touching it with my fingers. Komal moaned loudly ooooooooooohhhhhhhhhhh aaahhhhhhhhhhhhh and said, "please meri choot touch karo please us mein ungli dalo please mujha mat tarpao please. (Please touch my pussy, please put a finger in it, please don't make me suffer please)". I still didn't touch her choot(pussy) and kept moving my hand around it and on her thighs. She was getting desperate for me to touch her choot(pussy). finally, she held my hand and pulled it towards her choot(pussy) but I pulled my hand back and held her thighs and pressed they hard and pushed her legs further apart. Komal couldn't hold any more and shouted, "bhaanchod meri choot mein kuch to dal. mein mari ja rahi hoo… andar dalwane ka liye (Sister fucker put something in my pussy. I am dying here…to put it in)". "Mouni issa bol yeh meri choot ke andar kuch dale please bol isko(Mouni tell him to put something in my pussy…. Please tell him)".

Mouni was busy finger fucking herself and she said, "bhaiya ise aur mat tarpao.. dal do aapna mauta laura iske choot mein aur faar dalo is virgin ki choot(Brother don't make her suffer more. Put your fat cock in her pussys and tear up this virgin's pussy)". I looked at Komal's choot(pussy) and then pushed my mouth on her choot(pussy) and kissed it hard. Komal screamed aaaaaaaaahhhhhhhhhhh oooooooohhhhohohohohohohohoooooohhh please karte raho please (keep going it please) aaaaaaahhhhhhhhhhhhhhhhhhhhhh. I put my tongue deep in her choot(pussy) and started licking it. then I put Komal's clitoris in my mouth and started sucking it. Komal went mad with desire and started jumping on the sofa. I held her gand (ass) tightly with her clitoris in my mouth and kept sucking it. She kept screaming ooooooooooooohhhhhhhhhh aaaaahhhhhh

I kept sucking and licking her choot(pussy). Now my laura(

cock) was almost on the verge of exploding so I pulled back my mouth and stood up. Komal got the hint and immediately and she pulled down my nicker and my laura(cock) sprang out. Komal who had never seen a laura(cock) before was amazed to see the size and thickness of my laura(cock). I put my hands on her head and pulled her face towards my laura(cock) and pushed my laura (cock) in her mouth. She was not aware what to do so I pushed her head back and forth to give me a blow job. She was a good learner and soon she was able to do it effectively. She left my laura(cock) and put my tattas(balls) in her mouth and started sucking them like a chocolate. The sensation was really great and I started moaning aaahhhhhhhhhh ooooooooooooohhhhhhhhhhh. By now Mouni who was still standing there, finger fucking herself came behind me and gave me a tight hug and held my laura(cock) in her hand and started masturbating me. I was in seventh heaven with Komal sucking my tattas and Mouni holding and masturbating my laura(cock). I didn't want to cum like this so I stopped both the beauties and told Komal to come and lie down on the carpet as this was her first fuck and I wanted her to be in a comfortable position to take my long hard laura(cock) in her. She moved down and lay on the carpet. Mouni got a cushion and lifted up Komal's gand(ass) and kept the cushion under it saying, "Komal yeh tere pehli chudhai hai is liya yeh cushion niche rekh le taki Ranbir ka pura laura tara andar achi tarah chala jai taki tujhe acha maja aayega. (Komal this is your first fuck that's why keep this cushion underneath so that Ranbir's full cock goes inside you and you get proper pleasure)" Komal then suddenly realized that how she is going to take such a big laura(cock) in her small virgin choot(pussy) and she became afraid and said, "Ranbir yeh itna bara laura(Ranbir this is a very big cock). how am I going to take it please I don't want to do it please" Saying this she started getting up. Mouni who was sitting near her immediately held her and pushed her back on the floor and pressed her down and said, "bhaiya jaldi dalo aapna laura is ki choot mein... fir aapne aap thik ho jayagi yeh (Brother quicky put your cock in her pussy... then on her own she will be alright)". I immediately knelt down and pushed her legs apart and in a kneeling position. I kept the head of my long hard laura(cock) at the entrance of Komal's virgin choot(pussy) and pushed slowly. As the head of my laura(cock) went in her choot(pussy) she became absolutely still with her eyes staring at me. I gave a hard push and she screamed at top of her voice ooooooooooooooooooohhhhhhhhhhhhhhh aaaaaaaaaaaahhhhhhhhhhhhhhhhhhh please mat karo mein mar gai bahut darad ho raha hai please (aaaaaaaaaaaahhhhhhhhhhhhhhhhhhh. I didn't hear anything what she was saying because the heat in her choot had driven me to such hights that I didn't want to stop and pulled back my laura a little and again pushed it with full force in her choot. She screamed aaaaaaaaaaaaaaaahhhhhhhhhhhhhhhh hhhh uuuuuuuuuuuuuuuuuuuuuu "bhanchod mar gai… mat kar… bhanchod phar dalega kya meri choot ko… please mat kar(Sisterfucker am dying…don't do it…sister fucker will you be tearing my pussy.. please don't do it)".

I again pulled my laura (cock) out and gave a hard push and my laura (cock) went fully in her choot (pussy). This time she literally jumped up with pain and started crying and screaming.

"naaaaahiiiiiii main mar jaungi… please nikal de aapna laura(No I will die…please remove your cock) please please aaaaaaaaaahhhhhhhhhhhh uuuuuuuuuu mmmaaaaaaaaaa mein mar gai I will die)".

Mouni said,"bus ho gaya aab aaur pain nahi ho ga aab sirf maaza hi maaaza hai(Enough now there will be no pain. Only fun and more fun)" I slowly pulled my laura(cock) out a bit and saw blood flowing out on Komal's choot(pussy) . I was satisfied that I have been able to fuck another virgin today. The heat from her choot(pussy) increased because of the blood and I was getting mad and I started humping hard on her and she was screaming aaaaaaaahhhhhhhhhhhh oooooooooohhhhhhhhhh aaaaaaaaaahhhhhhhhhhhhhhhhh

"Please mat karo please(Please don't do it please)".

Her tears were flowing out because of pain but I was so mad fucking a virgin that I didn't stop and kept humping her. After about a minute or so her pain reduced and slowly her cries of pain turned into cries of ecstasy. Now she started moaning with desire.

"aaaaaahhhhhhhhh ooooooohhhhhhhh do it jaan(honey) its great I am feeling nice now, fuck me hard, fuck my choot(pussy) with your big laura(cock) hard, don't stop please." I kept my humping and soon she said, "aaaaahhhhhhhhh kuch ho raha hai(Something is happening) aaaaaahaaaahhhhhhhh and suddenly her body became stiff and she had first orgasm of her life aaaaaaaaaahhhhhhhh ooooooooooooooooooohhhhhhh-hhhhhhhhhhhh . She kept coming and I kept fucking her with increased energy as her choot(pussy) convulsed with orgasm. Seeing her cum I couldn't hold back and I also started cumming in her choot (pussy) downloading loads and loads of semen into her choot (pussy). I fell on top of her and we hugged each other tightly and lay in this position panting. After some time, I got up and gave a long hot smooch on Komal's lips. She said "Ranbir it was great I never knew sex was so nice I really enjoyed and this was my first orgasm ever in this life. Mouni, aapne bhaiya sa chudwana ka liya bahut bahut thank you (Mouni thank you very, very much for letting me get fucked by your brother)".

Mouni also looked at our satisfied faces and said, "tum dono ne to chood chood ke aapna maja le liya hai. par meri choot to abhi bhi garam hai, isse kaun thanda kare ga(You two have fucked and fucked and had your fun but my pussy is still hot. Who will cool this down)"?

I said, "main hi karunga bus dus minute aaram karne do fir tumhe bhi chood kar thand kar deta hu(I will only do it Just let me rest for 10 mins then I will fuck you too and cool you down)".

14. Ranbir 4

As I lay on top of Komal after having fucked and de-flowered her, Mouni who was looking at us with her finger in her choot (pussy) said, "aap dono ne to chood chood kar aapna maaza le liya hai… ab mujhe kaun chodega aur thanda karaga(You two have fucked and fucked and had your fun…Now who will fuck me and cool me down)".

I replied, "bus dus minute aaram karne do fir tumhe bhi chod dunga" (Just let me relax for 10 mins and then I will fuck you too). Hearing this Mouni also came and lay next to us putting her arm and leg on top of me and hugging me tightly. Her body was hot from want of a fuck. I turned my face towards her and put my mouth on her hot sexy lips and started sucking her wet lips. She was moaning aaaahhhhh…..ooooooo. I slowly pulled my laura(cock) out of Komal's choot(pussy) which was still semi hard. I kept kissing Mouni while lying on top of Komal and feeling the heat of her body. I moved my left hand and put it on Mouni's right boob and pressed it hard. She moaned hard aaaahhhhhh ooooohhhhhhhhhh. Komal was holding me tightly as she was also enjoying my body on top of her. Mouni in the meanwhile put her hand between my and Komal's body and held my laura(cock) and started pressing it. I immediately started getting hard and I knew that it is not long when I would have to put my laura(cock) in Komal's choot(pussy) to satisfy her hot choot(pussy). I moved my lips off her mouth and started kissing Komal on her hot lips. Seeing this Mouni pulled at my hair and said "bhaiya ji abhi to us ki choot ko thanda kiya hai aura bhi fir us ko kiss kar rahe ho meri choot aap ka laura andar lane ke liya taras rahi hai, please mujha ek baar chood do please (Brother you have just cooled down her pussy and now you are kissing her only. My pussy is is yearning to take take your cock, please fuck me once please)".

Komal smiled and said "Ranbir pehla Mouni ko chood do... uski choot garam ho rahi hai fir hum dono chudai karanga.(Ranbir first fuck Mouni...her pussy is getting hot then we both will fuck)".

Hearing this I moved off Komal's body and lay next to Mouni between two hot sexy bodies. I again started kissing Mouni on her hot lips and sucked her lips and tongue holding her tightly against my body. I broke off the kiss and turned Mouni around and started kissing her on her shoulders and back. She enjoyed the sensation of my tongue on her back and said "aahhhhh bahut maaja aa raha hai aaah please meri gand par bhi kiss karo (I am having a lot of fun aaah please kiss my ass too)". I moved down on her back and started kissing her low back and then moved further down on to her ass and started kissing the round globes of her gaand(ass). She was writhing under me and moaning "aaaaaaaaahhhhhhhhhhhhhh bahut aacha lag raha hai(I am feeling very nice)" I kissed her gaand(ass) and then spread the two globes of her gand (ass) and slowly kissed her gand (ass) hole. She screamed in joy and jumped up and said "aapni tongue meri gand mein dalke chooso... bahut aacha lag raha hai, mare pati na kabhi bhi aaisa nahi kiya.(Put your tongue in my ass and suck...I am feeling very nice. My husband has never done this)" I pushed my tongue in her gand (ass) and tasted it. It tasted a little odd but it was good. I bit her lightly on her gand (ass) lips and she started pushing her gand (ass) more into my face. Then I turned her around and started kissing her on her belly button and pushed my tongue in her belly button and started licking it. She was getting wild and said " please aapna laura meri choot mein daalo aur choodo mujhe please mein aab aur nahi rukh sakti please choodo mujha please(Please put your cock in my pussy and fuck me please. I cannot wait anymore please fuck me please)". I moved down kissing her stomach and then moved down kissing her thighs and then moved closer to her hot wet burning and dripping choot(pussy). I put my tongue on her choot(pussy) and licked her dripping juices. By now Komal who was lying next to us came closer and caught hold of Mouni's boobs and started pressing them. Mouni was enjoying this. Komal then put Mouni's right nipple in her mouth and started sucking her hard. I pushed my tongue deep in her choot(pussy) and licked her juices. Then I put Mouni's clitoris in my mouth and sucked it. This was too much for Mouni and suddenly her body became stiff and she started coming in my mouth. I licked hard on her cunt and sucked all the juices. I then moved up on her body and kissed her on her lips and she tasted her own juices in my mouth. As I was lying on top of her. Komal held my laura (cock)and directed it on Mouni's hot choot(pussy). Due to her recent orgasm, she was very wet and the moment Komal put my laura(cock) on her choot(pussy) it just slid inside. Mouni again moaned "aaaaaaaahhhhhhhhhhhhhh ooooooooooooooooouuuuuuuuuhhhhhhhhhhh" I rammed it hard and pushed my full 7-inch laura(cock) in her hot choot(pussy). I started ramming her hard and pushed my laura (cock) deep in her choot (pussy). Mouni was screaming by now "chood mujha phar day meri choot please aapna seemen meri choot mein bhar da aaaaahhhhhhh joor se phar daal meri choot (fuck me tear my pussy please. Put your semen in my pussy and full it aaaaahhhhhhh harder...tear my my pussy)". hearing all this I became more excited and increased the speed of my fucking her choot(pussy). Soon Mouni was again ready and she screamed "mein aa rahi hoooooooooo joor se karo (I am cuming do it harder) aaaaaaaaaahhhhhhh" and she started cuming and her choot (pussy) muscles started sucking my laura(cock) hard as it convulsed in an orgasm. This was too much for me and I started coming in Mouni's choot(pussy) and loads and loads of semen was dumped in her choot(pussy). I fell on top of Mouni exhausted and my laura(cock) in her hot burning choot(pussy). As I lay on her Komal also cum and lay on top of me sandwiching me between two hot sexy bodies and we rested in this position only.

Now I am feeling horny narrating this incident and my laura(cock) has again become hard. I now need to go masturbate again.

15. *Raveena*

My name is Sandip, my sister's name is Raveena and we live in Mumbai. My sister & I have been really close for as far back as I remember. Growing up we did every thing together, we eat, played, went to school and even slept together until, I think, about when I was 14. I am now 38 and my sister is 2 years older than me.

She still has beautiful black shinny hair, deep smoldering brown eyes and curvy body which would not look out of place on a catwalk and the most beautiful breast that seem to contradict all the laws of gravity. When we reached the age of going out to socialize, we always went together and had the same group of friends that we hung around with.

We always looked out for each other like a team. If she ever had too much to drink, I would look after her and she would look also after me. One night after she had too much to drink, we decided to head for home. We called a taxi and she slept on my lap the whole way home.

I always had feelings of sister love for her but this night my feelings turned to something more. As she slept her head was resting right on my crotch and my dick was reacting to this. I began to stroke her head so that she would not wake but we reached home after about 15 minutes so I had to wake her.

I carried her to her room taking care not to wake anyone. Our house was very big. You could have had a party at one end of the house and not heard a sound at the other end. When we got to her room, I put her down on her bed but since she was totally out of it I took off her top and her jeans.

As I pulled her jeans off her white panties slipped down around her hips to reveal the most beautiful pussy. I quickly took off her jeans and pulled the panties back up to cover her. There was no reaction from her so I had this urge to look again.

I locked the bedroom door even though everyone was asleep and slipped her panties off. My cock was throbbing at this stage but I just wanted to put my mouth on her pussy lips to see what it tasted like. As I lowered my mouth to her pussy and to my surprise, she instinctively opened her legs to me.

I didn't need a second invitation I continued to lick and kiss and suck on her pussy and gently massaged her clitoris with my tongue, licking it like an ice cream. She started to moan. My heart almost stopped with excitement but she did not wake so I continued to suck her.

After about 20 minutes my jaw started to ache but the pleasure, I was giving to sis was driving me on. As she climaxed, she let out a kind of whimper, her whole body went into spasm for about 30-40 seconds and a flood of juice flowed from her pussy which tasted like a sweet dry wine.

I continued to lick and suck her slower and slower until the spasms slowed down. She looked so beautiful lying there on the bed with a very faint smile of satisfaction on her face. I put her panties back on and kissed her goodnight on the lips.

I went to my room and stroked my penis for about 10 minutes but the thrill of what just happened was too much. I came with such intensity that I almost passed out. Thick white sperm gushed from the tip of my penis. I still could not get over what had just happened.

When my sister woke up in the morning, she came into my bedroom to find out what happened the previous night and from the glowing look that she had I could see that she enjoyed herself. She knew that she had a good time because she felt so good but she said that she did not remember what happened.

Weeks went on and needless to say the frequency of nights that I offered to take care of my sister increased. I quickly became an expert at oral sex. Each night I took her home put her to bed and climaxed her into a deep sleep.

One night her orgasm lasted for over a minute. I thought she was ill when her body started shaking uncontrollably. She was moaning so deeply I was worried that she was not Ok but when she whispered in her sleep "mere pyaare Anil... Meri choot chaa"...(My sweet Anil...My pussy needs a lic....) I knew that everything was fine.

Again, I continued to kiss her slower and slower to bring her down from her climax and then went on my way to relieve the pressure building up in my penis. One night on returning home and putting her to bed I had an urge to go just a little bit further. I made her climax as usual but then I thought what if...?

I turned her on her side and lay down behind her. I had no difficulty in entering her at she was as wet as I was. I slowly made love to her for about 20 minutes kissing her erogenous zones, her neck, underneath her breasts and the side of her body but as I started to explode inside her pussy.

I became aware that she was stroking my hair and as I looked at her to my surprise, she was awake!! She smiled at me and kissed me deeply on the mouth as I came, in a wave of pure pleasure, inside her. As soon as I recovered, she put me on my back and kneeled down on top of me, he breasts hanging like ripe melons waiting to be picked, and slid my semi erect penis in to her wet pussy.

She fucked me like a crazy woman; lowering her pussy all the way down my shaft and rising up to the tip of my cock and down again, like a steam train. It wasn't long before I was hard again. We continued to make love all night. To finish she lowered her mouth to my cock and started to give me the most amazing blowjob I think I will ever get in my life.

She licked, sucked, kissed and stroked me to an intense orgasm and when I climaxed, she sucked and swallowed every drop of cum from my penis. Then with a naughty smile on her face she said.

"That's for all the nights that you made me come so hard!! "

She had been awake every night that I brought her home and she said that she had looked forward to each and every night!! We still look out for each other but she has since married and we both agree that our love making had to stop.

I will never forget the experience that we had together but I am sure that I will experience an orgasm just as intense as I did with sis and I am sure that I will make someone come just as hard.

16. Lets us not count

I first had sex with my mother when my wife had gone to her parent's house for her delivery. That was in an afternoon on a Sunday. When we finished, I had thought that was to be the last sexual encounter between me and my mother. But that was not to be.

After I shot my juice deep into my mother's cunt, we lay side by side for about half an hour. Then mother touched me again. I was still limp. With my mother's touch, I got hard again. Without much talk, I mounted her again and entered her. This time I slid inside her cunt easily.

Also, since I had shot my juice twice, I was in no hurry. So, we fucked slowly and I took more than 15 minutes to shoot my juice inside her. After that, my mother said, "I think you must have cooled off by now. Take rest and sleep. We will see in the evening". With this she left.

I went to sleep and slept like a log till seven in the evening. When I woke up, I was fresh. I took a bath and went out. I came back at about 9 and had my two pegs of whiskey as usual and went to the dining room for dinner.

Mother was ready with dinner as usual. She was bathed and in a fresh saree. We both remembered the afternoon of passionate fucking, but said nothing. I had dinner, mother also had dinner after me, and I went to my bedroom and slept. I masturbated as usual before sleep. I went to sleep.

I don't know why, but I woke up at 4 in the morning. I tried to go back to sleep but could not. I was disturbed. I was also hard. I got up, went to the kitchen for a drink of water and returned back to my bedroom. I tried to go back to sleep but I could not. I slowly got up and went to my mother's bedroom.

The lights were off and she was deep asleep. I went in and put on the light. She was still asleep and was in a saree which was now up to her knees. I thought of last afternoon and I got real hard. I slowly lifted up her saree till her hips. She was wearing a black panty which I peeled down.

There was that cunt again. It was now closed and not yet ready for sex. But I was so aroused; I bent down and kissed it. I was in shorts and T Shirt. I got up, took them off and became nude. I again sat near her and kissed her cunt. She moaned a little and opened her eyes. Seeing me sitting naked near her she said, "What's the time?"

I said, "Its 4:30"

"Go to sleep then. What are you doing here?"

"Mother, I am back to do what we did last afternoon"

"Son, once in a while it is OK, but a son having regular sex with his own mother is not proper."

"Mom, I am not thinking about what is proper or not. I am aroused, I need sex. I have no one but you, so why don't we do it?"

"When I started between us, I was prepared for occasional sex but not twice daily" mom said

"Mom lets us not count. When you or I are aroused, let us do it."

"Son, I was thinking of your dad this evening. I somehow felt odd"

"You yourself told me mom, that dad hasn't got half the cock that I have. You are a woman. I am a man, apart from that, we need not think about any relationship. Come on mom, forget about dad and let us enjoy each others body once more. You know I have not lost my erection since evening. Let me mom. Forget everything else and let me enter you."

I kissed her on her lips. They were soft and moist. I thrust my tongue inside her mouth and my tongue played with hers. I started rubbing her breasts. Slowly she was getting aroused too. I started licking her all over and when I reached her cunt, she was fully wet. I kissed her cunt deeply.

"Mother, has my father satisfied you ever? Sexually I mean?"

"No son. Not like you have"

I got on top of her slowly. She said, "Let me become fully nude. I want to feel your skin on mine." She got up and took off her saree. She soon became fully nude and got on bed beside me.

"How often do you have sex with you wife?" she asked.

"2-3 times a week mom"

"What all do you do?"

"Just fuck"

"Haven't you tried oral?"

"She doesn't suck me mom. I lick her sometimes"

"On bed, a man is his woman's slave. But a woman has also got to orally please a hard man"

"You used to suck dad's cock mom?"

"Yes"

"And did he lick your sweet cunt?"

"Not much"

"Then the old bastard didn't get as much pleasure as he should have"

"Will you lick me?"

"Of course,"

I dove between my mother's thighs and started sniffing at her cunt. I slowly started licking her and drove my tongue up her sweet hole. I licked and savored her for some time.

"Don't you want your wife to suck you son?"

"I do mom but she doesn't like it"

"Come on sit up"

I sat on the bed and she knelt below me on the floor. My mother peeled my foreskin back and started licking my cockhead. I was slowly oozing precum, which she licked. Slowly she took my cockhead inside her mouth and started sucking. She rolled her tongue around and soon got wild.

I caught hold of her hair and thrust my cock in her mouth. Mu cock was in my own mother's mouth. I held her head and started mouth fucking her. Soon I was about to juice. I didn't warn her. I shot my juice in her mouth. She was surprised but swallowed nevertheless.

It was the first time I was ejaculating inside a woman's mouth, and that too my mother's. She loved it. I wanted to return the favor. Soon I was between her thighs and tongue fucking her. She came in five minutes and almost crushed my head when she came. We were both tired and soon we went to sleep hugging each other.

17. *Manisha*

My name is Joshva. I am 32, Bengali and a Central Govt. Employee from Kolkata. My marriage is an arranged one and the name of my spouse is Manisha. She is 28 and she is for me the most beautiful lady in the world. She had a nice pair of breasts (34), great ass (38), pussy and wonderful pair of buttocks and her face cuts are just beautiful and every man dream to have her

Though we married 8 months back we are still enjoying our sex for 4 to 5 times a day. I want to share with you the greatest first night encounter we both had. It is the first night of our marriage. Manisha and I never talked with each other up to now. I entered into the bedroom at 12:30 at night the bedroom was well decorated with flowers.

She was seated on the bed in the room with nice saree and after a bath. She was looking gorgeous in her green silk saree. The view of her heaving breasts through her saree and her nipples pointing sharply towards me is just fantastic. My cock was saluting straightly at her beauty.

I entered the room and closed the door and sat on the bed. She felt shy and I was too. Then I started to talk and I said as this was our first night and we will be together throughout our life. I moved closer to her. I said I want to share many things with you about life on this night but your beauty is killing and then the show started.

I took her hand into my hands. This was the first time I touched a lady in my life so I felt very much excited. I said we are not only just wife and husband; we will also be good friends and we have to share everything in our lives especially sex.

It is just a symbol of love between us and we cannot find more enjoyment anywhere as in sex and kissed her on her forehead softly and slowly started to press Manisha's soft buttocks and I pressed her stomach and moved hands all over her back and I again kissed on her forehead and I said I love you.

She felt shy more at first, as this was the first time, she was spending time with a man. She returned back the kiss and said I too love you too. Slowly the shyness in her was gone and her face started glowing as I talked very friendly with her.

I asked her to be cooperative in sex and she said that she will and I will be yours and you can use me in whatever way you want. We stood up and hugged each other and I started kissing all around head and I kissed the neck portion and bit on her shoulders smoothly.

A small moan of ooooooooo.... Aaaaaaa.... What are you doing...? She was feeling shy and closed her eyes. She then hugged me tightly and planted kisses on my lips. I put my hands on her shoulders and I moved my body close to her so that my chest will touch her boobs.

She understood what I wanted she started to rub her breasts against my chest and soon I locked her lips with my lips and started kissing her lips and she just hugged me taking my kisses. We continued to do slow french kisses for some time and after sometime I increased the pressure on her lips and she also started to kiss fast.

Now we were kissing in such a way that we are chewing bubble gum. While sucking each other lips Manisha moaned. Please press my milk ball. I removed the anchal of her saree from her breast and I started to press her huge boobs slowly through her blouse and bra.

I pressed and kissed on them. She started moaning heavily like such press harder press harder please don't stop and she was feeling the pressure to the extreme. The sight of her milk ball through her skin color transparent blouse and red bra is clearly visible.

By seeing that sight, the sexual desires in me started to raise high and I started to press her ball harder and harder and she was moaning pleaaaaaaasssse press harder ....continue don't stop please......she said please suckkkkk me fuckkkkkk meeeee please don't stop........

I am also happy and my sexcitement was also picked up to heard these words from her and I removed the saree from her body now she was only in blouse and saya and inner garments and pressed her stomach and she was rising high and moaned ahahahahahaaaaaa.... ooooooooooo... uhuhuhuhuuuuummmm-mmmmmmt...... ooooooo....

I started to unhook the buttons of my shirt and she said, "You opened my sari, I will open yours".

And she slowly unhooks the buttons and remove my shirt from my body. She then started to move her boobs over my chest and she moved like a snake rubbing her big milk melons over my chest. She even knelt down and knows her boobs are touching my cock.

She knowingly started to rub her boobs against my cock and by kneeling down she started to press my buttocks simultan-eously. I looked down at her and my cock is simply saluting her and I did not want to interrupt her because this is the kind of wife I just wanted and I always wanted a wife who will be full-filling my sexual desires to the extreme.

Then she stood up and we kissed each other on lips for 10 minutes nonstop. I become fully erect now and suddenly pushed her towards me and taken off her blouse and that was the first time I saw the beautiful boobs under red bra in my life. I pushed her on to the bed.

I am not able to control myself and I started to press her boobs very hardly. And I open her bra from back side and I have seen beautiful naked breast first time in my life and then I tasted all the breast part with my mouth and sucked and bit her nipples. Now she was moaning like anything.

She is moaning aaaaaaaaa....... uuuuuuuummmmmmmm... what happiness .... Suck me....... Suck me harder....... Please don't stop.... harder... uuummmmmmmmm.............aro. After that Manisha lay behind me and took off my pant. I was only in brief now.

My bulge stood straight and the head of my bulge is visible to her through my brief. I then remove off her saya and her skin color panty was visible, she touched my bulge from my brief and I asked her, "Manisha tell me what is it"?

She said, "I don't know".

Then I said, "Hold my big cock"

And she started to rub my lund(cock) from my brief by her hand.

I said to her, "Do you like it"?

She just presses her head and then I also kissed her and I touched her pussy over her panty and I feel her hairy pussy for first time and due to first time she was also shivering like anything, then I entered my hand under her panty and felt her wet hairy cunt and then I took off her panty from her body.

She removed my brief off we are both naked before each other for the first time in our lives. Then she closes her eyes in shyness and also trying to cover her chut(pussy) by her hand but I held her hand and put it on my lund(cock) and started to fingering her chut(pussy) by one finger.

She also rubbing the foreskin of my lund(cock) by to and fro motion. Then I started to suck her chut(pussy) and she is moaned like uuuummm suckkkkkk aaaaaaaaaa uuuuuuummmmmmm and pressed my head on her chut(pussy). I suck pussy lip and her pre cum for the first time and the test was so good this is the first time feeling like that.

Then I inserted two fingers into her pussy hard suddenly she screamed loudly, "its hurting slowly this is the first time I am getting something into my love hole".

I said to her, "It will hurt a little first time then you will see how much happy you will be".

She begged me for the first time be slow then you can do it in whatever way you want.

I hugged her tightly and she too did so and we locked each other lips and started kissing then she stops me Don't show me that. I can't cry.

I asked her Which one should I insert?

She touched my lund(cock) You are so big and you want to put it in my ass and fuck it and she felt very shy and hid her face under my chest.

Then I pulled her leg on my shoulder and I inserted 3 fingers into her pussy.

She moaned aaaaaaaa......it hurts and she said holding my 7.5-inch lund(cock) that I want it. You put it in my ass.

Then I sat on her legs while she is lying on the bed and slowly inserted the head of the cock into her.

The head of the cock went into her without paining her as she was very wet inside. I pushed the cock further inside and she moaned loudly. aaaaaaaa.....oooooooo please astteeeeeeeee(s-lowly) its my 1st time please be slow....... plllllleeaaaaassse oooo. Fuck me slowly on the hearing this word from her.

I am very much sexcited and press the lund(cock) more near about half of the cock entered into her. it is very painful for her and I asked, "Shall I take it out"? but when I asking her this at that time. I also entering my lund(cock) more and more and I felt the hymen and I press more so that the hymen would tear and she crying loudly like aaaaaaaaaaa uuuuuuuuuuuuuuu.

Its too much and simultaneously I was sucking and kissing her lips and pressing her boobs within a few second my lund(cock) totally entered to her cunt some tear also comes out from her eyes and she fell on the bed totally motion less then.

I started to and from motion after a few minutes she was co-operating with me by motioning her ass. She started to move my cock to and fro and she was shouting in pain oooooooo Don't stop now. It hurts a lot... Do it slowly...slowly fuck me... Fuck me but slowly.

I continued making to and fro moves. Suddenly her voice changed and she said, "It paining fuck me slowly"

After a few minutes her pain has been gone out and she also moves her body slowly.

I continued fucking by making to and fro movements and she now seems to be enjoying this and she was also moving her body up and down in order to take the whole cock into her. My cock completely entered into her and we both were moaning with pleasure like any thing.

She was very near to her orgasm and I too was going to cum very soon. We both started to make fast movements of our body. We hug and kiss at that time and I also press her boobs very hard and this time she wanted to be on top of me and she made faster movements lying on the top of me.

As we were very near to our climax the pace of our desires and love for each other keep on increasing. She responded to me by moving her body rhythmically. The pace increased and she was moving her body very fast and said harderrrrrrrr moreeeeee oooooooooooooo moreeeeeeeeeee harderrrrrrrrrrr fuck meee-eeee don't stop and moves her body more up.

I was also going to climax and moved faster after about 10 minutes we both hugged tight and I pushed my lund(cock) tight into her chut(pussy). I then cummed into her and as soon as I cum she had her orgasm and both our love juices are being exchanged for the 1st time and that moment is just wonderful.

We exchanged our juices for the first time with sweet kisses. We both were happy to lose our virginity by a wonderful pleasantable love making. We fucked for more two times and slept at 4:30 am and we saw the next morning that some blood spot and love juices on our bedsheet.

18. Radha

I am Anil from Chandigarh. I'm 18 yrs old doing my Engineering from a reputed institute in city. The story here involves my lovely encounters with my aunty (my father's sis). Her name is Radha. She is 36 yrs & a very hot woman. Her vital stats are 38-26-38. So, she posses a little plump but nevertheless has a sexy curves body.

She had been married some 8 yrs back but her hubby was in America & ever since he hasn't called her. So, she used to stay with our family. Mine is a large house in a village few kms from the city. The house resides my family & the families of two of my uncles. Radha aunty as I use to call her was a very caring woman when I was in my childhood.

I use to spend most of my time with her but as I grew, the separation became more prominent & till the time I left home for my education there was hardly any dialog between us. But I noticed a sudden changed in her behavior when I visited my house during vacations.

I observed that she was taking a very unusual interest in me. Like she often used to come to my room when I would be alone and will inquire about my girlfriends. During this time, I often noticed that her, pallu will always be down and her suits always exposed her boobs generously. I was 19 yrs old healthy guy and such scenes ignited the fire of lust in me.

Now I too started taking interest in her (or in her body). I would always look for a chance to view across her tight suits or see thru kameezs that generously revealed her hot body. It was one such occasion; we were coming back from the city after watching a movie. I was there with my aunty & we were driving back to village.

Others were coming in different vehicles. It was all dark and we were moving through the dark fields leading to our village. Just then near a hand pump, aunty told me to stop as she wanted to get fresh. I stood near the jeep as she went behind the pump wall but after some time, she called me.

As I went there, the scene I saw was biggest and most pleasurable shock of my life. I saw her naked boobs. Perfect round melons, huge much larger than I had thought. Pink nipples and dark brown areolas wow for a moment I froze. It was first time I had ever seen such beautiful boobs that too in full nudity.

They were just killing. More killing was her hot body with upper half completely naked. She said what are you looking Anil I know you want them badly. Even I want you Anil c'mon hurry up give your Aunt's boobs a nice suck. I moved forward and took them into my hands. Oh, they were so soft; I started kneading her boobs hard.

She started moaning, I pressed them hard trying to squeeze milk out of them and then mouthed her right nipple, pressed it sucked it bite it. I was hungry and there she had offered me chicken biryani I was not going to let it go easily. I went like maniacs kissing sucking squeezing licking biting each and every part of her wonderful breast.

All she could do was respond to my brutal assault, and then I threw some water on her breast and started sucking it from her nipples. I remained grossed in her boobs for a long period of time. There was not a single inch on her breast that didn't have marks of my teeth on it. He boobs had become red with my biting and rubbing.

Finally, she stopped me and reminded me for being late. It was difficult but then we left and through the whole way I kept pressing her boobs over her clothes. That night I couldn't sleep for a second even when I did, I fantasized of making a hot steamy love to my sexy aunty. I woke up to find my underwear wet with my cum.

I went straight looking for her but was disappointed to know that she has left to attend marriage in a neighboring village. I don't like going to parties so I stayed home. She came late at night and by the time I had already gone to sleep.

When I woke up, I went through the house and found that most of the members had stayed in the marriage only and those who had come back at night were fast asleep. This again was good opportunity for me, so I went straight to my aunt's room. She had just come out of bath and was looking fresh as a rose.

Her back was facing me, and she didn't notice me coming to her room. She was compiling some clothes and was in bending position. I saw her big ass which was in full prominence. It was jutting out of her thin gown. I was highly ignited by such display of her assets. I bolted the door, went behind her and grabbed her ass hard.

She was shocked initially and told me to control myself but I made my desires clear by kissing her ass hard. She moaned as I lifted her gown up to reveal her beautiful ass. Wow her butts were great. They were hard & tight. I started squeezing them, pinching them, licking them as my tongue rolled up & down on her big round buttocks.

She was now in a bending position with her hands & knees on ground. I kneaded her flesh as my hands parted her butts to reveal her hot & wet cunt. I poked in my nose to smell the intoxicating aroma that her delicious pussy was emitting. Ohhhhh!!!! .... Ahhhh!!! She screamed lightly as my fingers touched her clit.

It was first time I saw a woman's genitals. It was a small tight hole with reddish material from inside hanging and encircled by pink flesh. I probed her virgin pussy with my cunt as liquid from her cunt wet my tongue. I can't describe the feeling of exploring a woman's pussy for the first time. It was great, a heavenly experience.

I kept licking her cunt as my tongue went up & down along the length of her cunt. She was moaning with ecstasy but was keeping it low less some one heard it outside. I feasted on her pussy for a longtime & in the meantime she cummed thrice. I tasted her delicious juices for a first time and was not ready to go.

But she stopped me saying she couldn't take anymore and now it was her turn to seek pleasure from me. I told her to do as she wants. She turned me around and pulled my shorts down. My butt was now naked before her. She moved her fingers all over my butt, sometimes pressing them hard into my flesh and then started kissing my butts.

She licked them wet with her tongue as she took the flesh of both my bums into her hands and squeezed it hard. Now she tried to poke a finger into my ass but I stopped her. She said, "You filthy dog. You have taken your share of pleasure and now you are denying me mine.

I said that it will hurt me as I have never experienced that before.

She said Ok but I won't leave you like that & she took my face into her hands and planted a hot steamy kiss on my lips. I too responded & soon there was shower of kisses on my face. My forehead, eyes, cheeks, lips, nose & neck every part was drenched with her saliva. She was behaving like a sex starved goddess & I was her satisfier.

She kept on kissing my face for a long time sometimes smooching me so hard that I had to gasp for breath. Wow this bitch is really hot I said to myself. She would have continued her monsoon of love or lust but for a call from my grandmother made her depart. I cursed my luck & came back to my room.

In the afternoon my mother insisted on me going to attend the marriage function. I was reluctant but Radha was also going so I agreed. I spent the day going here & there just doing some simple chores for time pass. I pretended to be happy but my eyes were always on Radha.

She was wearing a sky-blue color suit and due to summer heat, it had become almost sees thru. Her white color lacy bra was distinctly visible along with her black panties. Her boobs were also jutting as if trying to break free from her bra. The sleeveless & low cut kameez was exposing her smooth white flesh to every single man's desire.

I could see many of them ogling at her & often trying to touch her hot body on one pretext or other. But I knew that I was the luckiest among them as sooner or later her body will be mine. There was a mehnadi function at night and we all were dressing my mom came to me.

She told me to take Radha back home as she had forgotten some jewelry and her dress for the occasion. I instantly agreed & soon we both were on the way back. I kept telling her all the way that today I will not spare her & she kept saying that we will see. By the time we reached our house it was 10 o clock.

As soon as we entered our house, I grabbed her breast hard and pushed her to the charpai that was lying in the backyard. I came over her & started squeezing her huge boobs over her clothes. Nibbled, licked, fondled, caressed & pressed hard. I could locate her nipples over her clothes & I pinched the hard, tuned them & licked them.

She started moaning as I placed my hands on her boobs over her bra inside her kameez. I slowly pulled her kameez up and then gave a huge bite at booth her boobs. She cried with pain. As I eagerly unfastened hooks of her bra & released those huge mounds.

I once again started my feast on her naked boobs. Again, her boobs went for a good long session of nibbling, squeezing, pressing, and biting. She grabbed my head and pushed it tightly on her boobs as I made different scars on her boobs with my teeth. I sucked her nipples so hard that they turned red.

I looked at her face it was amazing; she had closed her eyes in ecstasy. Her rosy red lips were moving over each-other in an attempt to absorb the immense pleasure that mauling of her boobs was giving her. I couldn't control and placed my lips on hers but she pushed me back hard.

I was surprised but then she smiled as she took my face in her hands & gave a strong kiss on my lips. She held me tightly as her bare boobs pressed into my chest & my cock rubbed against her crotch. My lips were being sucked by her and my hands were moving all over her naked back massaging her white smooth flesh.

I felt her tongue inside my mouth. It was a great experience. After few minutes of this beautiful tussle between our mouths, I proceeded to remove izarband of her salwar. Soon her salwar was pulled out of her legs and I saw most killing view of my life. Her smooth white legs with fleshy thighs were before me.

The sweat was sprinkling here and there while her pussy was being covered by a black scanty panty. I moved down & started kissing from her ankle, then her legs finally her thighs. She moaned hard as I pulled her panty down with teeth to reveal her completely shaven cunt. It was her most treasured possession that I had long wanted.

I parted her thighs and brought my mouth over her dripping cunt. She started screaming loud as my tongue explored her wet cunt all over. OHHH! Ahhhhhhhhhh!!!!!!!! Yes, suck me ya tear my pussy you bastard ohhhhh your tongue is such a nice sex toy you bastard fuck your aunt with your filthy tongue.

This increased already burning fire in me as I gave her very hard bites on her cunt. Taking her clit in my mouth I almost parted it she gave a huge groan and told me to go slow. I didn't stop and continued at same pace. Soon I was rewarded with her cunt juices that flowed like some waterfall from her pussy. Second time they tasted even better.

I looked at her face. It was having an expression of partially satisfied woman. She looked at my crotch. I understood her signal and pulled my pajama down (I was wearing a safari suit). She remained at charpai occasionally pressing her boobs. Now I lifted my kurta & pulled my underwear down. My monster emerged from the bushy jungle.

She smiled & I moved to hold her in my arms but she drifted away started running in opposite direction. This was frustrating as my erection was at peak and I was dying to eat that forbidden fruit which she was denying. I followed her. It was a wonderful sight to see this naked beauty run wild with her boobs and ass swaying up & down.

She ended up in a small tanker of water which was adjacent to the pump. As I reached there, I found her splashing water all over her body. My already hard cock became stiffer as I saw water flowing down her lips over to her jutting boobs, then to her navel & finally disappearing in her cunt.

Eager to join her I removed my remaining clothes and jumped into the tank. We splashed water on each-other as I held her tightly from behind rubbing my cock on her ass & pressing her boobs hard. We kissed for a while & then she made me sit on the edge of the tank with my legs hanging down. Now she grabbed my cock & put it into her mouth.

Soon she started sucking it hard; believe me guys first blowjob is a mind-blowing experience. Everything seemed so good, the cool breeze that was blowing, a hot wet naked lady of 36 sucking my cock & I felt I was in heaven. I thanked god for this ultimate ride.

She kept sucking my cock in all directions, sometimes squeezing it, sometimes rubbing her face all over it, and licking along its length kissing every single muscle on it. There seemed to be no end to the pleasure she was deriving out of my cock but then there was no end to the pleasure I was getting from her.

Finally, pressure started building inside my balls but since it was my first time, I wanted to shoot it into her mouth and see how it feels to cum inside a woman's mouth so I let her carry on. My cock busted in her mouth. The white sticky gel from my cock blew and fell all over her face.

Seeing me cum she opened her mouth & took her tongue out trying to gather every single drop of cum that my cock was oozing. She licked my cock clean. My heartbeat was coming to normal as well as my cock too. Seeing my limp cock, she came forward and took it and crushed it between her boobs.

Then she started moving her boobs along the length of my cock. The feel of smooth flesh of her boobs on my cock was really exciting due to which my horny bastard again rose to power. This time she came out of tank & told me to lie down on the floor. I obeyed her.

She came over me with her legs across my belly held my cock, positioned it for her cunt & slowly sat over my crotch taking my cock into her cunt. She moaned with great pleasure as my cock entered her pussy. It was not as tight as I had thought which made doubtful about her virginity but nevertheless it was not right time for such thoughts.

She started moving up and down as my cock touched her clit every time she came down. I too responded pushing my cock in rhythm with her motion. The wetness & warmness of her cunt was driving me mad. On top of it her big boobs were moving up & down with her wet body. All this busted my dam much early than I had thought.

This time even I couldn't control my timing and soon her cunt was splashed by my liquid. But she was still not done yet & kept on pushing herself on my cock. I relaxed after my orgasm as she continued pushing her pussy with increased pace. After few moments she too came as I felt her cunt gripping my cock hard. My cock was lashed by her juices.

She too collapsed on me & we remained like that for few moments. Then she reminded me that we were late & I realized that we were here on some pretext. I saw it was 11:35 we were there for 1 ½ hour though it shouldn't have taken more than 30 mins for us We cleaned ourselves, dressed up & left for the wedding.

We were lucky no one noticed when we arrived back. When we came back from wedding it was 2 am. I was tired and fell asleep as soon as I touched the bed. In my dreams it seemed that my aunt was playing with my hard cock, she was stroking it hard like the gear of a car.

I opened my eyes to sheer surprise that my aunt was actually stroking my cock. I was scared that we could be caught but she told me that everyone was fast asleep. She said that she wanted repeat of the night experience. I was only too willing. She lifted her gown up till her waist flashing her cunt to me.

She positioned herself on my cock and slowly took it inside her cunt. Now she started the joy ride pushing her cunt up down on my cock. I remained lied down letting her enjoy the pleasure. She kept on pushing herself on my cock in-between my cock slipped 2-3 times from her cunt but she repositioned it & carried on.

As she carried on, I opened buttons of her gown & let her big melons free. I started squeezing them hard. Pinching the nipples & tuning them. Soon my cock busted filling her pussy with my cum. She too came at almost same time.

Our combined juices flow through her thighs on to bed sheet. She came down, pulled my shirt apart & started kissing my bare chest. She kissed my chest, nipples, belly & licked my navel. Her tongue rolled on my body making different designs with her saliva.

Finally, it stopped at my nipples & I shredded with sensation as she mouthed my nipple & started sucking it. She encircled the nipple with her right tongue, and then gave a strong suck to it squeezing it in between. She continued her vengeance as she played with my nipples as I had done with hers.

Overcome by lust, I pushed her down came over her locked my lips with her. We started sucking each-others mouth very badly with saliva constantly moving from one mouth to another. I sucked her lips which were at their rosy best. Our tongues inter mingled as we explored each-others mouth.

My cock was now rock hard & was urging to enter her cunt. I pulled my shorts down, came at her legs and pushed her gown till her waist. She spread her legs wide to accommodate my monster into her hole. I slowly pushed it inside her hole, placed my hands on her thighs for support & then started moving in out of her wet lubricated cunt.

Soon she started abusing OHHHHH. Ahhhhh yes fuck my pussy with your big filthy cock yes ram it ram it hard push it hard into my hole. Your cock has made me mad. It is so big so thick ahhh I love its roundness. I retaliated saying aunt even your hole is quite good. your breast are mind blowing.

Anyone guy would love to play with these ripe mangos of yours. Your ass is too good; it always makes my cock hard. You are my fantasy queen aunt & sexiest woman I had ever seen. She was really touched by my appreciation & moved forward to hug me. I kept fucking her.

Due to our motions her gown had slipped down from her boobs and was now only hanging through her nipples. I could see her black aureoles, this further excited me & I cummed soon after filling her pussy with my seeds. She too came and I felt my cock drenched with shower from her pussy. Now we again started smooching.

This time we carried our kissing like maniacs. Meanwhile we removed our clothes & started feeling each-others body. We rolled over from one side of bed to another, sometimes she came on top & sometime me & we carried on our smooching journey. In rolling over we tripped from the bed but didn't stop kissing as our mouths remained lock.

I suppose we sure had made some world record. Then she came over me & started moving her hands all along my bare body. Massaging my chest, pinching my nipples, then my abdomen, and then to my cock. It was sensuous feeling to have her gently massage my cock along its length.

The pleasure was inexpressible. Then she turned me to turn around & lye with my face facing the floor. She then took my bums & started massaging them. I could feel her soft hands moving all around my butt & gently pressing it. It gave me great relaxation.

She continued her massaging service till I stopped her told her that I wanted to taste her ripe melons. Now she lied down, I came over her & started massaging her breast in same manner. I moved my hands along the roundness of her boobs. Tuned her nipples, mouthed them, sucked them hard, & licked every single corner of her twin beauties.

She had her eyes closed; simply relishing the pleasure I was giving her. She moved her hands all over my body, feeling each part, & then again squeezed & sucked my nipples. We continued like that lost in our own heaven till we heard certain sounds coming from the ground floor. It was indication that others were wakened up.

We half heartedly agreed to part as she quickly adjusted her gown gave me a good bye kiss & left. I remained in bed till late afternoon just relishing my conversion from a boy to a man. So this was a story that happened with me.

It was just the start, after that we enjoyed many times but those were other encounters.

19. Shilpa

My wife Shilpa and I are broad minded persons form a Rich family. Shilpa aged 29 and had sexy figure 38-26-38. I am 31. We are married for last 6 years and we had a love marriage. My friend Salman always visits at my house and we are free with him. He is not married and staying alone.

He is working at a studio and is a Professional Videographer. Last year in summer, at night we were watching xxx movie. I said "Salman sala english blue film mai wo maja nahi atta hai jo indian blue film me atta hai" (Salman Sala there is not fun in an English blue film what fun is there in an Indian Blue film) but in market you don't get quality indian blue film. Normally either model is not good or quality of video is not good.

Salman said why you don't make your own video. Your wife Shilpa is good looking and sexy and your personality is handsome. Shilpa was there in room with us but did not react. Salman said he will shoot for us. I asked Shilpa if she was ready. She said no. I still got up took out my handicam and started making fun by shooting.

I was acting in funny manners to make atmosphere light. I know it is matter of time before Shilpa agrees for shooting. After some time, I gave the handy cam to Salman and asked him to shoot. He took the camera and looked at me. I said don't worry. He started with me and did not focus on Shilpa.

I moved near Shilpa and held her hand, she did not resist. I kissed her and she did not respond but I knew she will be hot soon and nothing can stop her then. We have discussed this situation many times watching blue films. I put my hand over her shoulder and touch her full 38″ boobs. She smiled and I know she was ready for action.

I took my other hand inside her skirt and touched her underwear she was wet and hot. I put my fingers from side of her underwear to touch her pussy. Her pussy was hairless. I was shocked and asked her "bal kab kate tune" (when did you cut your hair) but she said nothing. She must have just shaved at the time of her evening bath.

Salman and I used to go for sex together since our college days and many times fucked together. I know how he likes to see shaved pussy. More over my wife had big round type pussy and not flat one, and it looks great without hair. I know Salman is always hot towards Shilpa.

In free time we always talk about girls we fucked together and, on many times, he compares them with my wife. He was never indecent but always his remarks end with you are lucky to have good looking wife like Shilpa. Shilpa always insisted he marry but he replies were if I find some girl like you then only, he will marry.

My wife knows all about our activities and we talk lot about it in bed. I started kissing Shilpa and now she responded positively. My both hands were busy, one on her boobs and other on her pussy. Slowly her hand moved on zip of my pant and she was trying to open it. My cock was rock hard and fully erect.

Salman was busy with the camera. She manages to take it out. She started stroking up and down. My cock of 7″ is now fully erect. She said "aaj tumhara aur bada lag raha hai." (Today yours is feeling bigger). I smiled and said "yeh to phir bhi Salman ke samne kuch bhe nahi hai, aur Salman ka lund to mere se kafi bada hai." (This is nothing front of Salman. Salman cock is much bigger than mine) she could not believe it.

I took opportunity to fulfill my long-time dream to have sex with Salman and Shilpa and me. I moved away from my wife and asked Salman to fix camera on bed. He was quick to do it and started the camera. He now knew what was in my mind. He was mentally preparing himself to fuck my wife.

Shilpa was not sure what will happen next as I push her on the bed. She was fully clothed till now only with her skirt up showing her new black underwear. I was excited to see that sexy underwear and knew that she must have deliberately put them on.

Shilpa is fair and had big butts and long sexy legs her height is also 5'10" well above average Indian girls. Salman was enjoying show. I asked him to sit on the bed which he promptly did. In my wife's ears I whisper "darling, ab tak jaise sab ladkio ko ham chod te they. aaj tumhare sath waise he karge." (Darling till now how we used to fuck girls, we will do the same with you) chill went through her body and she held me tight.

I could feel her nails on my back but she said nothing. I knew it, she was ready for action. To break the ice, I told Salman to look at her new underwear it is nice and beautiful. He smiled and said yes. I said and her clothes are also very soft and have a good feeling. I then asked him to touch it.

He gently put his hand on her butts as if he was checking cloth of underwear. He was not sure about the reaction of Shilpa. Slowly he started rubbing her butts. Shilpa started her moaning with his touch. She was breathing heavy. She started kissing me like mad.

I pulled Salman near us as Shilpa's back was towards Salman. She was unaware that Salman was sleeping next to her. I signaled Salman to remove his clothes. Also, I started removing the top and skirt of my wife. She responded with removing my pant. In no time we were nude. Shilpa still managed to hide her treasures from Salman.

Salman could only see her back and butts. I took Salman's hand to place it on her big boobs. Her nipples ware hard as rock. He could not cover her boobs in his hand as he tried to measure her boobs before pressing them. With his eyes closed he was in heaven. I knew his life time dream was coming true.

Shilpa was pulling my cock like mad and I was fingering her wet pussy. I took her hand from my cock moved it towards Salman's cock. She realized what I am trying to do. She tried to resist so I had to use some force. Salman was still few inches away from her body. I stretched her hand towards her back to reach for his cock.

She grabs his cock and realized his thickness she opened her mouth in disbelief. I enjoyed the expression on her face. I asked her to open her eyes and look what she was holding. See his size, his thickness and see his color. Since her back was towards Salman. He also could not see her pussy nor did he try to touch her there.

He was all the time busy pressing her hard big boobs. She opened her eyes to look at me. I asked to turn towards Salman. Now she was holding two cocks and playing with them. I helped her turn around. Now her face was towards my friend Salman. She looks down at what she was holding. Her eyes widened to see his cock.

She could not believe about size. Salman's cock is 9" long, double and thicker then mine. I have seen such reaction from many girls we fucked together. She was mad when she looked at his naked cock. Salman was also mad to see her shaved pussy and her round shape. He put his hand on her pussy and started rubbing it.

He put his one finger in her and tried to insert second finger. Shilpa cried and requested to stop him. I know he always insert two or three fingers in all girls we fuck. But he could not insert more then one. Shilpa's pussy is much tighter than girls he used to fuck.

I then climbed up on my wife's face and put my cock in her mouth. My friend also moves to her shaven pussy. His tongue started playing with her pussy. Shilpa could not keep control on her self and started making loud noises. I know now it's was time to finish the game.

I asked Salman if he liked to fuck first, he did not wait to tell me yes and immediately removed his face and placed his cock on her pussy. I climbed down her and removed my cock from her mouth. I know it will be difficult for her to adjust Salman's cock inside her.

I place my mouth on her lips and held her face tight in both hands as Salman prepared himself. He was now between her legs and his cock touching her pussy. Shilpa put her arms around my neck when he starts rubbing his cock on her pussy.

I could not see what is going on below but my wife's hand moments indicate she was preparing herself for Salman's big and thick cock. It seems from her movements she was worried now as he was preparing to enter her. I know my wife's pussy will be too tight for thick cock like his.

I was also worried about her reaction when he will enter his cock in her pussy. Salman preferred to tap me gently on my back to indicate that he is going to start fucking her. I locked my lips more tightly on her lips and ingress grip on her face. Salman in one strong and great stroke rammed his entire cock in her pussy.

She tried to scream in pain but I was ready and in full control on her lips. She tried to push my head but failed. Tears started rolling. She was crying in pain and I knew it will hart her. He took some time to adjust his cock in her pussy before removing his cock. He then removed his cock slowly and waited to see her reaction.

She was somewhat relieved and tried to breathe normally but that was time for second stroke. Soon Salman started pushing his cock in and out with great speed. In few seconds I removed my lips from her face to see what Salman was doing. I could see his cock going inside her.

I have seen it many times but those girls were not my wife. He is a great fucker and normally takes more than 15 minutes to finish. But this time it was Shilpa and he could not fuck her more than three minutes. He cum inside her and did not move for some time. I asked him to move so I can take her.

He rolled to one side and I could see what mess he made with her pussy. His come was dripping from her pussy. Shilpa's pussy hole was still open and I could imagine it will be loose for me now. I was eager to try how loose it will feel to me. I climbed on her to fuck. I was burning in fire and my cock was ready to shoot full load immediately.

Shilpa requested me not fuck her for some time as her pussy was in pain. I asked if she enjoyed, she said yes. I have to respect her feelings as she was in pain. I know I may not be able to fuck for few days. I took her hand on my cock and ask her to finish with it. Salman was smiling at my condition. In few strokes I cummed in her hand.

We got up and put on our clothes. Salman checked if the camera was recording the movie properly. It was fine. For few days we keep watching the great blue film we made. Now Shilpa can take both of us and we have done it many times.

20. Seema

I am Sharukh from Kolkata. After tasting pussy, I was just like a hungry Tiger and I was searching for a woman to enjoy eagerly.

Many times, I got chances to press boobs, ass and cunt in our favorite Kolkata's private bus service especially mini buses in office times. This incident also happened in a mini bus which was bound to Behala from B.B.D bag. After finishing my office as usual I was waiting for my bus in a queue. In that queue a lovely looking lady also there.

I thought to take chance with her. She was of age about 30 years and statistics are 36-30-36 and she was wearing a black saree with golden border and a sleeveless blouse if you can imagine how sexy she was looking at that time. When our bus arrived, we entered in that and I purposely sat beside her.

Then bus started and it is running towards Esplanade. She was free in nature I asked her name and she told me her name as Seema. I asked her where she works, she told me in a Multi-national Bank. Then while talking to her I started to touch her thighs at the same time I was looking her reaction also, she was normal at that time.

I enquired about her life she told me that she is married to a businessman and when asked about her hubby she told me that he's out for approx 20 days a month for tour, listening this I thought there might be a chance here, then with sympathy I put my hand on her thigh, she looked at me.

I gathered some courage I asked her about her married life, she remained silent and bend her head downwards. I asked her again she just looked at me and said I am lonely, that's the chance I was waiting for, I asked her can I help you to remove your loneliness. She glanced at me and nodded her head in agreement.

It was about 6:30 pm and we are near Victoria Memorial hall in Kolkata I asked her to get down the bus and we moved in to Victoria hall's garden we discovered a vacant and isolated bench there and we sat down without wasting a min I hugged her passionately and planted a French kiss on her lips.

She too responded like a horny babe and started to lick my tongue and I was licking her too. I asked her "How long ago was your groom engaged to you?" She replied "one and half month's before". Then she replied "Today I am very happy. Please caress me more. I want to get lost in your lap". I was on seventh heaven after hearing this I started to press her boobs vigorously she was moaning very slowly aaah hhh aaaaaaaaaaaahhhhhh more harder plsssssssssss After eating the fruit, Tear my nipples today.

Listening to this I lifted her blouse and black bra and I gave a bite on her nipples this time she shouted "AAAAAAHHH What are you doing everyone who comes near will hear everything passing by". I realized that she was right. Then I started to bite slowly and started chewing her nipples she was enjoying every moment and moaning lightly.

"aahhhh uuuu uuuhuuuhuhhhh, I am getting happiness after many days aaaaahhhhhhhh, Why haven't I met you before? When your cock grows up, no girl will get out of bed; her hands will always be here and there. aahhhhh harder more harder".

I was listening every word of her which was making me more and more horny in the mean time I entered my hand in her panty and it was amazing to observe the softness of her skin inside her saree she was simply superb. I observed that her cunt juices are started oozing from her cunt and drenching her panty.

I liked to lick cunt but the situation is not favorable so I just entered my finger in her cunt and tasted her juice and in the mean time my prick was also in her hand she was vigorously stroking it. After few minutes I cummed on her hand and she wiped my cum with her saree.

And some time she unloaded a huge orgasm on my hand and in her panty. I wiped my hand with her saree. She was looking quite happy and she asked me about my life. I told her that I was unmarried and looking for one. She told me that "aaaah if I had met you a year ago, I would not have had to rejoice in secret today. We could take off all these clothes in our bed and make love like Adam and Eve"

I told her "We can still do it like Adam and Eve if you want". She asked how? I told her "I can make love to you in the absence of your bora, tell me when I come to your house". She got little bit afraid and told me that it is not possible.

I asked her why she replied, "My father-in-law's mother-in-law is at home." .... I said ok. Then we went out of Victoria Memorial and caught the Behala bus and I left the bus in Alipore and she proceeded to Sakher Bazar.

Then few days we used to return in the same bus and start repeating our play for half an hour and then again back to our home. After a month or so she called me and said to me that she is now all alone for one week as her father-in-law and mother-in-law have gone to their daughter's house.

It was great news for me and we had enjoyed for a week, but that's another story I'll tell u in next part.

21. Seema 2

After our incident in Victoria Memorial, we started to meet very frequently. She used to wait for me in BBD Bag Bus Stop stand and then we both used to go to Victoria Memorial or Rabindra Sadan or Dhakuria Lake in evening hrs, these are the best place to make love especially in Kolkata. I always used to do oral sex with her as there is no other option left for us in public places.

These went on for approx a month or so. One day I got a call from her side. She told me that her hubby is going out for business tour for one week and that she is now all alone for one week as her father-in-law and mother-in-law have gone to their daughter's house. Listening to this I was in seventh heaven, now my dream is turning out in reality. She told me that she'll call me at perfect time.

Next day at about 3:00 pm I got a message from her. She told me that she'll be waiting for me in our usual place at 5:00 pm. At about 5:00 pm I went to that place and we moved to her house I called my mother and told that I'll be in my friend's house for the night and will come on next day evening after office. She took me to her home; it was not a home it was a palace in Behala. She opened the lock and we entered in her house. I lost my control and I grabbed her from behind and put my hands round her below her arm pits and squeezed her boobs from her saaree top. She moaned and said, "Aaaaaaahhhhhh Stranger we have a whole week of jumping around. You can fuck me in this one week, from where you want as much as you want, whatever you want, just wait a minute and get a little fresh".

I kissed her on her lips and let her free and she went to the bathroom and I was waiting for her in her living room. After 15 min she came out, I was shocked to see her in her night gown she was wearing sleeveless satin night lingerie which is in three pieces. She asked me to fresh up I went to her bathroom took a bath. I saw her bra and panty was lying there in bathroom. I picked her panty and smelled that. The smell of her vaginal sweat was mind blowing and making me crazy. I started masturbating there and unloaded my excitement there in her bath room. When I got out, she was ready with dinner we ate and finished up quickly I can't concentrate on food coz she was sitting right in front of me, her cleavage and smooth fair skin was inviting me all the time. After we finished our dinner, we washed our hands and I just can't control my temptation and grabbed her and took her to her bed room and with in a sec I undressed her lingerie's upper piece which was like a gown. She was now in her satin transparent bra and panty and I was in my underwear. I put my lips on her lips. She starts breathing heavily and I tasted her juicy lips. And with my both hands I was pressing her melons.

Her breathing was becoming hot and hot with every seconds of time. Then we parted and I removed her bra and started to suck her boobs, she was moaning heavily and shouting "aaaaahhhhhhhhaaa aaaaaaaaaa Very good, today you fuck me so much that there is no hope left. After many days, someone is sucking my tits, aaaaahhh harder harder aaaaaaaaroooo aaaaahhhhhuuuuuuufffffff Very good plsssssssssssss more harder aaaaahhhhh... I was becoming furious by these words, in the mean time I removed her panty also, and started to kiss her belly button she was still moaning loudly. And when I kissed her cunt she moaning said 'aah for so many days you licked me in hiding, today lick me with with all your might. For many days I have controlled my lust. Lick me and empty my juices... plssssssss" I inserted my tongue in her vagina which was wet previously. As soon as I inserted my tongue... she gave a jerk and moaned loudly aaaaaaaahhhhh kiiii arrrrrrrraaaaaa-aaammmmmmm More more lick me plsssss Eat it today, give it to me today, take this pussy today, my husband has never been here to give me such happiness till today. aaaaahhhhhh uuuuufuuuuuuffffffffffffff, where have you been all this time? I haven't seen you for so mnay days. My fire would have been quenched long ago. You can bite me first. My pussy feels so good oooooooooooohhhhhhhhhuuuuuuuffffffff. And within five mins she unloaded huge amount of orgasm in my mouth. I drank every drop coming out of her pussy. I asked her, "How did it feel sweetheart". She replied, "I have been married for so long and have not received such pleasure. Come on and fuck me. My husband does it for only two or three minutes and falls asleep".

I asked her to suck my cock. She said, "After I said all this, I am sure your 7-inch rod much have become hard. I used to suck your cock in darkness. Today in broad daylight I will suck your cock. She took out my penis and put the whole prick in her mouth and started sucking it and with in few min I was also cummed in her mouth she dranked few drops and split out rest. Then we kissed each other and grabbed each other and again kissed on each others lips and now I asked her to lay down she laid on her back and I put a pillow behind her ass and slowly inserted my cock in her vagina, she screamed and said aaaaahhhh fuck me slowly slowly if you fuck me hard I will scream due to pain..... Your is so big and twice the size of my husband... looking at you no one will say that you have such a big cock, aaaaaaaaaaaahhhhhhhhhhhhhhh. I slowly increased the speed and by this time she was jumping with joy, then I laid my self on my back and asked her to sit on me, it was my first experience in this position. She sat on my prick and slowly started to move up and down. Now by this time I was shouting aaahhhhhahhh-hhhhhh ooooh ohooo it was really painful for me. But slowly slowly everything was normal and we enjoyed in that position also. After about 20 minutes we both cum together which we never had done before. It was about 1:00 am in the night we lay in each other arms naked and after half an hour we had our second round, thus in that night we fucked three times. I left for my office in the morning and applied for four days leave and then we enjoyed the whole week fucking, sucking and outing. We went to Darjeeling and enjoyed there. She told me that it was just like her second honey moon. Still, we enjoy when ever we get time mostly oral in famous parks of Kolkata and all this in absence of her husband. Now she's expecting my baby in her tummy. You can say I'll be a "kunwara baap" (Bachelor Father) and her hubby would be official baap(father).

22. Swathi

This is about my experience with an aunty who lives in my Apartment Complex in Chennai. Her name is Swathi, she is around 42 years of age, and blessed with great assets. She has 2 daughters who are 13 & 11 years.
Her husband used to be an Association Member in our Apartment Complex and I used to work with him for some routine work in the Apartment. Recently I went to his house to meet with him and settle some account balances and that's when I had a close look at Swathi, she was wearing a cotton saree and was looking very sexy...

She offered me a cup of coffee and was asking me about my job. While she was talking to me, I scanned through her body and couldn't resist watching her boobs....and when she walked back, my godddd..... Her ass really made me go crazy. I was feeling jealous about her husband and was dreaming of having sex with Swathi.

From that day, I started visiting their house frequently and over the next few months we became good friends. Both Swathi and her husband started talking to me about their financial problems and some issues with their parents. Swathi's husband Pranav was working for a Chemical company as an accountant.

He was worried that the company was not doing well and he might lose his job. After a couple of weeks, I ran in to Swathi at the entrance of the apartment complex, and she asked me for the first time if I will be able to find a job for Pranav uncle.

She told me that he was really worried and because of this they have been having frequent problems between them and even the kids are finding it difficult. She was not interested to talk to her parents about this as she wants to keep her issues within them. I consoled her and told her that I will certainly do my best to find a job for Pranav.

The next day I met with Pranav and worked with him to get his resume updated and later forwarded it to some of my contacts in Chennai. Over the next few days Pranav uncle started getting interview calls from these companies and in the mean time my company asked me to go to Singapore for a project implementation.

Before I left to Singapore, I went to Swathi's house and informed her about my trip and promised her that I will follow up with my friends regarding uncle's job and call her & give her an update from Singapore. After 2 weeks, while I am at Singapore, one of my friends called me and told me that his company is ready to hire Pranav uncle as an Accounts Manager and he can start his job 2 weeks later.

Hearing this good news, I called Swathi at 11 am on a Tuesday, just to make sure she is alone at home and conveyed the good news to her. She was so excited to hear the news and started praising me and thanking me for the help. Suddenly an idea popped up in my mind.

I asked her what will be my treat for getting this nice job for Pranav uncle. She immediately told me that they will take me out for dinner when I get back to India. I responded back to her saying that I was expecting something special than an ordinary dinner. Then she asked me what that special thing I was referring to was.

I kept pushing it back to her saying that it was up to her to guess and started giving her some clues...... After a good 5 minutes of guessing, she eventually guessed what I meant as a special treat, and told me that she did not expect such a thing from me and also told me that she is not a person of that nature and quickly changed the topic.

Since this discussion was not planned to happen, I was not sure how to handle and told her that I was really looking forward for a positive reply from her and told her that she can think about it and let me know later. Then I completed the call with wishes to them and told her that I will call her later.

After 2 months, I finished my project and returned to India. During the week I was busy with work and was not able to meet Swathi. Later that weekend, I saw Swathi and her family at the Apartment entrance and they were excited to see me and enquired with me about my Singapore trip.

Pranav uncle thanked me for the job and he told me that his new job is very interesting and his salary was twice that what he was making with his old job. I immediately made an eye contact with Swathi and she gave me a smile and invited me to their place for dinner. I turned it down and told her that it was OK and silently walked away.

After a few days, Swathi called me to her house to talk to her. I immediately went there and she was alone in the house and was wearing this pink cotton saree. She was looking like an angel and I could not take my eyes off her boobs. She asked me why I turned down their invite and told me that Pranav uncle felt really bad about that.

I told her that I have made it clear about what I wanted from her, and keeping my face dull, I told her that I am not a lucky person and it was my fate that I don't get anything I wish in my life. She started crying and told me that she thinks it will be risky to do something like that.

She tried her best to convince me but I was strong, and after a good 30 minutes of discussion, she finally told me that even if she is ready to give me that gift, it would be a big risk to do it at home. As soon as I heard that sentence, I turned around and went close to Swathi.

She immediately went back and told me that she needs some time to think about it. She promised me that she will call me in my cell phone and let me know about the next steps. Two days later I got a call from Swathi and she started the discussion asking if I really wanted to do this, for which I said "YES".

I asked her if she can come out of the house during the day. I told her that I will book a room in a nice hotel and we can meet their and have fun. She thought for a moment and told me that she will have to come up with a reason to leave home for such a long time and will have to make arrangements for the kids until she returns home.

She told me that she will call me the next day and confirm the date. I was so happy to hear that and was in cloud nine.... I couldn't sleep that night and was dreaming about the day and all the fun I am going to have with the sexy woman....... The next day Swathi called me and told me that Wednesday will be a good day for her.

She has taken care of all the arrangements at home. I immediately made a booking for the same day at a 3-star hotel in Chennai. It was Wednesday, the luckiest day in my life.... I called up work and told them that I was sick and took a day off. I left the house at 9.30 am and went to the hotel and checked in.

I called Swathi from there and gave her the hotel name & the room number. She told me that she will be there by 11am. It was 10.45am, and my heart was beating fast and I was getting sooooooo excited.... After 2 minutes, the door bell rang and there you go......

It was Swathi dresses like a princess in a black silk saree with a matching blouse and she had a nice handbag matching her saree color. She was looking tensed, and came in and closed the door. She asked me for a glass of water and I gave her. She drank the water and told me that she was worried if anyone will know about this and was tensed.

I told her to relax and asked her to forget about everything. The next 10 minutes we both were silent and she was still looking tensed. I took the lead, walked up to her and kept my hand on her shoulder. She immediately looked at me and gave me a weird smile. I went close to her and hugged her for some time and slowly moved my hands behind.

She was quiet and did not move...... Then I kissed her in her cheeks and her forehead and finally planted a soft kiss on her lips. Her eyes were closed and she did not give any reaction. Then I started kissing her lips again and this time she opened her mouth and took my lips inside. That's it!!!

The next few minutes I kissed her passionately and in the mean time my hands started exploring her neck and gradually dragged it down on her boobs. As soon as I kept my hand on her boobs, she opened her eyes and told me that she never thought I will be so bold and she told me not to mention about this to anyone.

I cajoled her and this time went behind her and kissed her ears and my hands were on her navel area starting to move up....... She started enjoying and turned around and kissed my lips.... I then slowly moved her back and took her to the wall and she rested on the wall and we kissed again.

I slowly took the pallu of the saree and dropped it down.... There I saw a beautiful cleavage in front of me.... I kissed in that area and licked her lower neck and pressed her boobs. She was feeling shy and closed her eyes and was waiting for my next move.......

I then removed the saree completely and started pressing her boobs and slowly started unhooking the blouse... One button at a time....... After unhooking the second button, I saw her black bra holding that massive breasts....... I just couldn't control and kissed her boobs and the cleavage area.

She just did not open her mouth and was thoroughly enjoying the show. I finally unhooked all the buttons in her blouse, and saw those melons hanging stiff in that black bra.... I pressed it hard, squeezed them and kissed them a million times and finally removed the blouse completely.........

Once I took off her blouse she felt shy and hugged me tightly..... In the mean time, I moved my hands behind and lowered it slowly and felt her ass.... It was soft like cotton and I pressed it hard and she moaned.......... I then turned her around and kissed her ears and aroused her....

At the same time my hands were squeezing her boobs and she loved it........ She moved her hands around my shoulder and started moaning....... I just didn't want to stop, but then wanted to try different things. I then sat on the bed, and she was standing right next to the bed, and we started kissing again.

I slowly untied her skirt (pavadai) and in a moment it dropped down on the floor. She then stepped out of the skirt and was standing in front with her black bra and panty...... I just could not believe my eyes..... She was looking so sexy and was inviting.......

I just couldn't believe the shape she has maintained all these years..... At 42 no one can be in this shape...... No kidding...... She was just perfect and I was feeling so lucky......... I moved my hands behind her and massaged her ass and spanked them a few times..... She was enjoying it and asked me to remove my shirt.

I then removed my shirt and she ran her hands in my bear body and hugged me tightly. After exploring her back with my hands and then slowly unhooked her bra...... O' boy!!!! I just couldn't believe..... She had a beautiful pair of breast, which was so stiff even without the bra and I just couldn't control myself......

And kissed her nipple gently.... She moaned again and hugged me...... I kissed the other nipple this time and squeezed her boobs and licked her nipples and made it hard......... I lifted her slowly and placed her on the bed..... She was lying with her panty and I removed my pant and joined her in the bed.

The next 15 minutes, I kissed her entire body from her forehead till her feet...... And again came back to her boobs and kissed and pressed them hardly...... I slowly slide my hand inside her panty and it was smooth..... There was no hair in that region...... And not to mention, it was wet.......

I started fingering her and at the same time, kissed her boobs and lips and she started moaning again........ While this continued for the next 5 minutes, I kissed her belly button and gradually moved down and removed her panty......... There you go..... I saw my Swathi without any clothes and she was looking like an angel.......

She was biting her lips and was moaning........ I went down and parted her legs and saw her pussy for the first time....... It was wet and was oozing....... I just parted her pussy lips and licked her pussy lips and the outer portion of her clitoris......... She was enjoying it sooo much.... And she was raising her hip to get the attention of my lips.

I licked her for some time and all of a sudden, her lower body was moving a lot and she gave a loud moan and she came....... I saw the liquid oozing out and she told me to stop licking....... I looked at her and she was lying there with eyes closed and was breathing heavily........

I kissed her lips this time and she opened her eyes and gave me a smile...... She then hugged me and her hands went down and she removed my underwear........ She then placed her hands on my dick and started playing with my dick and my balls. .....The nails in her hand were making me more aroused......... And she started stroking my dick......

I just stopped her and went on top of her...... She took her hands down, got hold of my dick and slowly took it to her pussy...... She rubbed her pussy with my dick and then slides it inside and took my dick inside........ As it was wet inside, my dick just went in smooth and I started stroking her pussy and gradually increased my speed.........

She started moaning again, and asked me to do it slowly........ I just reduced my pace when ever she told me to, but then was stroking continuously.......... After a few moments, I was feeling that I am going to cum..... I opened my eyes and looked at her...... She gave me a sexy smile and she told me to cum inside her........

After hearing that I increased my strokes, and started ramming her pussy........ She moaned loudly and within a moment, I came inside her......... It felt as if I was cuming for ever....... When I opened my eyes, she looked at me and gave me a kiss on my lips.......... She asked me if I got my treat........

I gave her a kiss and she hugged me and we kissed again......... We both were still lying in the bed, and I looked at the watch and it was 1.30pm...... Swathi told me that she got to leave by 3.30 so that she can get there on time and take care of the kids......

She was telling me that Pranav uncle is very happy with his new job and because of this, they do not fight with each other these days and the kids are also happy....... She thanked me again for the help and told me that she will never forget this help.......

I just kissed her again, and told her not to worry about anything and she can always call me for any kind of help........ Saying this I kept hands on her boobs and started squeezing them........ She then moved her hands down and took my dick......... Then she went down and kissed my dick...... And she asked me if she can give me a blowjob.......

I smiled and said yes......... She took it inside her mouth and did it slowly....... Although I was in little pain, I enjoyed it and in a moment my dick became hard and I got all the energy for another round of pleasure........ I made her stop the blowjob and asked her if she can lie on top of me and take my dick inside.........

She said that she was feeling tired already, but then I convinced her and there she is....... On top of me this time........... She took my dick inside and she started moving slowly....... Every time she moved her boobs bounced and that was a great sight to watch........ It turned me on so much.....

I started pressing her boobs again and she increased her movements and started doing it faster.......... I was feeling little uncomfortable and paused her for a second..... She gave me an additional pillow for my neck so that I could feel comfortable...... Yes, that really helped...... And she started stroking again.......

As my head was up, I could see her ass on the mirror that was right in front of me........ Every time she stroke, her ass was bouncing which I could see in the mirror and her boobs were going nuts........ This turned me on big time, and I cum inside her again........ I just hugged her tight and could hardly open my eyes........ It was pleasure at its best........

After a few minutes, Swathi got out of the bed and started dressing....... Within a few minutes, she got dressed up and she came and sat next to me in the bed........ She then told me that this cannot happen again, as it was not fair for her to cheat on her husband and requested me to understand her situation.....

I promised her that I will not tell anyone about this wonderful day and all the great things I did..... And at the same time, I will not ask her to do this again....... It was 3.30pm, Swathi gave me a kiss again, and she left the hotel room.

I was there for another hour and then went home after settling the hotel bill. It was a great experience and I am not sure if I will be lucky another time.

23. Nandini

I am Nandini 43 years old, living in small village nearby big city. I am a widow with two daughters. My husband passed away five years ago. I have to take care of my home with what ever property my husband left me with the help of my elder sister.

Sometime in June 2003, one of the relative of my aunt all of a sudden came to my house. He is very good by nature and he wants to help us as my father helped his Aunt long time back. I am proud of myself and I told him I do not wish to take any help from him. He used to come my house twice in a month to check on us. I felt his intention were clear as he is a really good person. He is also around 50 by age.

He also kept a distance from me. We had a lot of talk with him in different subjects. He was very kind giving me a lot of advice and helping children in their studies.

After year had passed, I saw no sign vulgarity from him. He helped me giving money to my children for education. Sometimes I thought, what a man he is, no selfishness and tries to lift me by giving moral support by the time we became closer. Now I started liking him very much.

Sach kahu mai maan hi maan mai use pyar karne lagi thi (Truth be told I started loving him heart to heart) but he never thought of. I am feeling love without sex. He now changed my name and called me as sakhi(friend)

Ohh abhi tak mere bare mai kuchh suna hi nahi hai aapne (Ohh till now you haven't heard anything about me) I have a white skin, attractive body 38-28-38, broad lips. Men wish to kiss me. Round face, grey eyes soft cheeks. The most important part are my big boobs. They very soft but tight. Men would like to play kiss and press it. The other best is my pussy like double roti (Flat bread) and one slit with no hairs on it

But he never looked at the beauty of my body. I never wear bra. I am only in gown and petticoat so he can see my body. Every day passes by I love him. Wish he would do something to me but I know still… I am in vain

Once he came home, I asked, "kya apni sakhi ko kabhi bahar nahi le jaoge".(Will you never take your friend out sometime.)

Why not we went to garden with children. We sat side by side first time in rickshaw and on every jump, we touch one other naturally.

He tried a lot but could flirt. I was pleased and planned for a tour.

When he came next time, I proposed to have a one-day tour on Sunday. At first, he said no but both children requested him for the tour.

He agreed on one condition… we shall be back by night

All said ok. I was pleased.

Next Sunday we had a tour about 150 km away at a holy place where hotel and dharmshala are available.

We reached at 12-00pm enjoyed bus traveling with children between us. After the preliminary tour surrounding and lunch, we went to hotel one suit was available on third floor after observing he said we may go to another place.

I asked why

Because only one suit was on the floor he said.

But the children and I insisted for the same. We entered the room with two separated beds. He said I am coming soon and went outside. After one hour he came back. Both children were just sleeping in one bed. I closed the door and sat on bed and told him to come sit near me.

Thinking whether or no to sit he sat.

I wore a bra, blouse and sari with panty and petticoat. After some moments oh some thing was under my blouse and I tried to remove it but I could not. help me. The were two beans stitched in it as the blouse was so tight, I had to remove it

mai chillai kya kar rahe aap meri choli ke niche kuchh hai. usne pith par haath lagake dekha to kuchh hone ka ehssas hua. kya sakhi ko madad nahi karoge. (I scream...what are you doing something is there inside my blouse. He put his hand on my back and saw then I felt something was there.Will you not help your friend)

Mai uske karib gayi. usne dhirese blouse ke batan kholne sharu kiye. do batan ko kholke nikalne ka prayas karne lage tab mai chahuki ye kya kar rahe ho choli phat jayegi. aakhir ek ek karke sabhi batan khulte hi bean girgaye par maine use do chuchiyo par pkad kar dabahi diya. usne lakh koshish ki par.... (I went near him. He slowly started opening the buttons of my blouse. Efforts on starting to open remove 2 buttons I was shocked. What are you doin my blouse will tear? Finally, once all buttons opened up one by one the beans fell down but I caught them between my 2 boobs and pressed them. He tried lacs of times but...)

Yeh kya kar rahi ho mai tumhe pana chahta hu (What are you doing I want to get you)

kya yahi tarika hai ha mere sakha. ab mujse raha nahi jata muje chumo daboao aur 5 saal ke baad pahli chudai kar ke meri maag bhardo. maine chehera upar kiya, mere hoth kapne lage, mai kapate huye hothose boli tumahari sakhi varna paagal ho... (Is this the only way my friend. Now I cannot control it. Kiss me squeeze and now after 5 years fuck me for the first time and fill me up. I lifted my face, my lips were shivering, with my shivering lips I said your friend will go mad or....)

usne dhire se dono hotho ko bada diya phir pyarse mere rsile hothoka raspan karne lage us doran apne hatho ko meri chuchiya par rakh kar halke halke dabane lage. ras pan aur mardan pan paa kar mai dhanay dhanay ho gayi. thodi der ke baad meri bra ko alag kar ke kaidi kapoto dekhne lage. (He slowly brought both lips near then with love sucked on my juicy lips. During that time put his hands on my boobs slowly slowly squeezed them. Juiced and squeezed by him I had become blessed, blessed. After some time, my bra was separated and the blind prisoners started looking.)

oh, sakhi kitne khubsurat hai tumare ye phal. aao unka ras pan kar ke tumhe asli pyar ka maja doo. Dono chuchiyo masalne lage dhire bed par lita kar chuhiyo ka ras baari baari pine lage Mai mast ho chuki thi ki chumte chuste dabate usne aapne sabhi kapade nikal diye. (Oh friend how beautiful are these fruits. Come let me squeeze the juice out and give you the real pleasure of love.)

meri najar uske lund par padte hi dil me ek dhakka laga. kitana bada choda lund tha puri 8-inch ki lambai ka. mere pati ka lund uske aage kuchh bhi nahi tha. chuchiyo ke saath khelte khelte usne meri saari peticoat ko nikal kar farsh par dal diya sirf panty hi thi. (I sight fell on his cock and my heart skipped a beat. How much big fat cock it was full 8-inch long. My husband's cock was nothing is front of this. Playing playing with my boobs he removed my Saari, petticoat and kept them on the floor, only panty was left.)

Usne bath chath kar meri chuchiyake saath dhoodh pite bach-heke tarah chusane chbalane lage ki meri chut mai se pahli baar paani nikal gaya mai puri aveshit ho gayi. usko lipt kar pyar se usko chmane lagi. usne dono tango ke bich uglidaal kar meri javani to panty khich kar nanga kar diya. (After licking my boobs like a child drinking milk, sucking biting that made my pussy release its water and I was completedly horny. I clinged to him and with love and started eating him. He put his finger in between my legs and made my youth naked by pulling my panty.)

Mai jor se liptkar pure badan ko chumane lagi. usne bhi garami hui. javani ko khub masana dabana chut kigali mai bhi ugli daal kar mere sapne ko sajane mai jut gaye puri tarah taiyar hogayi thi. muje apne sine lagake jor se kas kar kaha sakhi tumhe vo sukh dunga jiske liye tum tadap rahi ho bas phir kya tha. (I clinged to him harder and kissed his full body. He too became hot. Youth was a lot squeezed, pressed, hole in the pussy had his finger in it made me decorate my dreams in which I was completely ready.He roughly pulled me on his chest and said friend I will give you that happiness for which you have the thirst for. Thats is now what will come next.)

Mai aahhhhhhhhhhhh mar jaugi mujse ab nahi raha jata... hay re... bolo meri sakha...muje sirf tumhara kasa hua land chahiye. apnalo muje...ha ha tab usne dono tange falai chut dekh kar loda puri tarah tan kar khada ho gaya. usne jhuk kar dhire dhire chut ko chumne lage. (I aahhhhhhhhhhhhh will die I cannot control it anymore... Oh my...tell me my friend... I just want your hard cock. Accept me...Yes yes then he spread both my legs, saw my pussy and his cock had become completely erect. He bends down and slowly slowly started kissing my pussy)

Mai chilla uthi bas karo mere pyar ahhhhhhhhhhhhhh oy maaa oyammmmmaaayah kya kar rahe ho... meri kucch na suni aur uski jubaan ko meri chut mai daal de ki vo hayyyyyyyyyyyy reeeeeeee yah kya ho raha hai. Ab bahut mat tarsao apni sakhi ko. Meri tange khud kholdi usne puri 5-minute tak chusa. (I scream out aloud...it is enough my love ahhhhhhhhhhhhh oy maaa oyammmmmmaaayah what are you doing... My words were not heard and his tongue he put it in my pussy hayyyyyyyyyyyy reeeeeeee what is this happening. Now don't make your friend yearn. My legs he himself opened and sucked me for 5 minutes.)

Chut garama chuki thi. ab intjar karana thik nahi maine dono pavo ko upar karke use… ab mat ruko meri chut masatani hogayi hai tab maine lund ko pakad kar chut par rakh diya vo aahe bharne lagi chhod do muje… tab main dhire chutmai lund dabaya ohhh oooohhhhhhayreee. (Pussy had become hot. Now it was not alrright to wait. I held both my legs up in the air…now don't wait my pussy has become wit. Then I caught the cock and kept it on my pussy. It sighs a heave of moan Fuck me…thas when I slowly press the cock in my pussy ohhh oooohhhhhhay-reee.)

Meri chut chudai me uske lund ne dusara dhakka mara to vo khul gayi hayyyy ahh ahh ahhh mar jaugi. tab mera tisara aur ek do ek do karta hua lund apni manzil ki aur aage badhgaya par mai ahhh ohhhh ohh karti rah gayi. sach usko chut kuvari si lagi par ab vo kab manane vala tha. (In fucking my pussy his cock gave a second push and it opened up hayyyy ahh ahh ahhh I will die. Then my third and one two one two started the cock to reach its destination but I ahhh ohhhh ohh started doing. Truth he fely my pussy was a virgin but where is he now going to per-suade it.)

Dhakke par dkka dhaka dka dka faka faka fka f faka chodne laga manzil ko cchu liya pura lund ne. dono chuchiyo kas kas kar dabatedabate ji bhar ke mast se chudai ka maja lene lage mai bhi masta chuki thi vo bhi puri tarah chodne lage ab vo bhi dil kholkar chuchiyo ka aur chudai karne laga. (Push after push push push push faka faka fka f faka fucked me till the destination was completely touched by his cock. Both boobs were roughly roughly squeezed and squeezed till hearts content. Now he too with all his heart squeezed my boobs and kept fucking me.)

Mai ahhahahh bahut maja aa raha hai jor jor se ab chodo mai tumahari hochuki hu chhodo chhod mere bas vo kas kas kar chodne lage tab dhire dhire donobahome bharkar maine apni upar khicha aur tej aur tej muje puri trarh chudai ka maja milne laga. speed badhate gaye aur tej faka faka faka aur tej fach fach fach ahhh fach facha fach fach fach. (I ahhahahh a lot of fun I am getting. Fuck me harder harder, I am become yours fuck me fuck. He fucks me hard harder then slowly slowly in both arms I was pulled on top more faster more faster I got the complete pleasure of the fucking. He increased the speed and faka faka faka aur tej fach fach fach ahhh fach facha fach fach fach.)

Vo tejise chodne lage pura bed garamagaram ho chuka tha. usne koi sharm nahi rakhi aur apni sakhi ko pura maja dene lage. mai eka baar aur paani nikal chuki thi par vo aasman ki uchai ki aur muje savargiy sukh dete ja rahe the. vo dhana dhan chodate rahe aur apne pyase land ki puri tarah chod chod kar pyas bujane lage. (He fucked me with speed the full bed had become hot hot. He did not keep any shame in giveng his friend the complete pleasure. I once more released my water but that was in the heights of the skies and I was received the pleasures of heavens. He bang bang kept fucking me and quenched the thirst fucking fucking me of his thirsty cock)

Mai ahhhhhhhhhhh ohhhhhhhhhhhhh ahhhha haaay re kk-kkkkkarrrrtttttttttttiiiiiiiiiiii phir jar gayee ahhhhhhhh aur puri tarah mere par chha gaye aur pahli baar apna viryadaan karne liye betab ho gaye muje kas kas kar dhakke marne lage ek do teen char panch chh saat ek aur lagaye phir mara das bas ho gay mai jarne laga. (I ahhhhhhhhhhhh ohhhhhhhhhhhhhh ahhhha haaay re made noises then cummed ahhhhhhhh and completely he was over me and for the first time he was desperate to give me his spermdonation. He pusher hard and harder one two there four five six seven and one more push my man that was enough I as cumming again.)

Ab vo muje jorse liptgaye kas kar. chuchiyoko upar aate daboch liya. mai kahar uthi… hamara dono ka milan hua. hamari sanse tej chalane lagi aur maine dono tange kas kar mere sine se aur kas diya –sakhi-sakha ek ho gaye. mai jit gayi aakhir dono bachche abhi bhi so rahe the jab vaps ghar ke liye bus mai baithe. (Now he roughly clinged to me tightly. My boobs came up and he grabbed them. I got arosed. Both of us had our meet. Both our heartbeats were running fast and I held both my legs to my chest tightly and made them more tighter. Female and Male Friend have become one. Both the children were still sleeping when we sat in the bus to return home.)

To kabhi andhera ho chuka tha picchevali sit par koi nahi tha. humdono saath baithe aur mauka pate hi maja lutne lage pure safar ke doran. koi pichhe nahi aya mai khushi khushi se pagal hogayi Is tarah safar ke saath meri manokamana bhi puri hui. (So, it had become dark. Behind seat no one was there. We both sat together and once we had the chance, we started having fun the whole journey. No one came behind. I was so happy I was going mad. So, this way along with the travel my desires were also completed.)

24. Lata and Seema

I am Rohit, just 19 of age from garden city Bangalore, well-built body,5′ 6″ height and 65 kg weight. I met a lady aged around 32, very sexy and hot, named Lata who is really filled with shy top to bottom. Seduction of this woman would be a dream of every Indian guy. Figure 38D-26-36 especially attractive by huge boobs. She is 5′ 4″ tall and a bit heavy looking lady coz of those 2 round boobs.

Whenever she walks, hai rabba mai mar jawa (Oh my God I will suerly die) can't just explain by words, that cat walk. Her eyes are just like two stars twinkling with urge for sex and a single look at those stars would make a man go crazy about her. Her ass was not that huge but very sexy to look at and to play with in is a different enjoyment which has to be experienced.

I had worn jeans and I wore a simple designed full arm t-shirt and had left for my admission in C.A institute where I found a mind blowing lady(Lata) she got impressed by my looks that day and spoke to me nicely. She is a North Indian with whom I had to speak for my admission as there was a confirmation.

At my first sight I became crazy about this lady, which would had happened to everyone who ever spoke to her. Think if this was my condition just for being 5 min in front of this lady, what would be the condition of the office staffs? Fortunately, my English was fluent when I spoke to her even thought I was a bit nervous after seeing her.

That day I got myself admitted. But at the same time, I decide to join for the couching classes in the institute itself so that it would help me in seeing Lata every now and then. After some days the classes began for P.E-1 and I started going for classes.

Whenever got chance I was not missing it out to see her naked naval which was visible as she wore saree below that naval. Just like that, 3 months passed away and in those three months somehow, I had managed to get close to her by going to her for asking one or the other thing about the details of the course.

In the mean while I used to sit close to her by which I could smell her perfume. Many times, even I could view her private places through the opening of her blouse when her pallu was little misplaced. After those three months I got a chance to go out with Lata as she asked me to just drop her to her place as she was very late for some function.

I left the institute with Lata on my bike. My devil mind started working and whenever I got humps or any dug places, I would put sudden breaks so that her melons would press my shoulders. Like this only I reached her house and dropped her home. But for my surprise her husband asked me to get in and have a cup of tea.

I readily agreed thinking I could spend time in her house. When I was in her house I came to know one thing that her hubby was not such a good person and she was not happy with his behaviors thought that was not the right time for me to sit for some more time and I left.

The next day she came with a dull face and I was thinking she might have fought with hubby so she is like that. But she had a very good friend named Seema who was an accountant in the same institute with whom she would share all her feelings.

That day in the afternoon I went to her chamber to speak to her but I found Seema also and stayed out to wait till Seema comes out of the chamber. But fortunately I heard Lata saying yesterday night her hubby fucked her very badly and she had a swollen pussy which was paining a lot. She told she was not even satisfied when he finished fucking.

I felt my luck kicking me badly and I decide to seduce this lady. After that day I tried to mingle with Lata in a matured way. I sometimes asked her about her married life and some time I also asked her why she is not having children. Whenever I asked such questions, I could see some sadness on her cute face. Slowly I started asking her about sex.

Initially I asked her whether I can send her some non-veg messages, she agreed without any hesitation. From this I got a little bit courage and I started sending her extreme non-veg messages which had intercourse jokes, jokes on pussy, facts of sex and all. She was getting naughty day by day and she also started sending such messages to me in return.

I was enjoying this very much. But one day I gained some courage and asked her whether she liked having sex and was she satisfied by her husband. I was shocked by her reaction; she left the place without saying a word and did not speak to me for 3 days. I felt very bad by her reaction.

Later I was regretting for what I had asked. But to my utter surprise after some days, I got an msg from her which read- "hi Rohit, this is Lata. I felt very bad when you asked me that question but when I went home, thought about it, my mind told it's not a wrong question to be asked.

From next day I could observe urge of sex in her eyes. Being so shy she was so hot; I don't have words to explain. From that day I became very close and one surprising thing is me, Lata and Seema three of us started to speak vulgar things whenever we sat for chatting. Like this only 5 months passed away.

One day when we were speaking about sex life Lata openly told that she is not at all satisfied by her hubby. He always comes and just fucks her for 5 min gets satisfied and goes. He never thought what his wife wanted. He was a business man who would go on long tours for 1 month like that.

So he would come someday, finish his sex with her and would leave again for tour. Lata was really fed up on this; she needed a new sex partner which she had not expressed. Like this only one Sunday I visited her house just to spend some time with her. Her hubby was on tour for that whole week.

I thought this is the right time to fulfill my dreams if not I will loose a great chance. When I got into her house, I found her in a light blue saree and the blouse was sleeveless coz of which she was looking damn beautiful. We both called up Seema to accompany us in Lata's house.

We started our usual chat on sex and all. I got some courage to ask Lata, was she expecting a sex partner as she had not got satisfied by her hubby. Hesitantly she said yes I need one right now. Seema suddenly got excited by our speech and she caught hold of my 6" cock. We both were shocked by this move of Seema.

I did not know what to do and how to react for this move, so was sitting idle on the chair enjoying Seema's strokes on my half-grown cock. Really the atmosphere was getting too hot so we all entered the bedroom, put on the A.C. Lata come on to the bed where me and Seema were busy in our kissing session.

After 5 min of kissing, I shifted on to Lata with her lips on mine and we both were sucking each other's lips like hungry beasts. After finishing the French kiss I asked both the ladies to kiss each other and also asked them to strip each other with all sexy acts.

When they started removing each other's dress I had my cock out from the zipper and was stroking to make it grow up completely. Both the ladies were naked in front of me sucking each other's nipples one by one. I was aroused fully by that scene and this continued till 10 min.

It was too much for me to cum but I controlled my emotions for a while as I had to satisfy both the angels who were completely nude in front of me. I started rolling my hands on Lata's ass now, she was sucking Seema's boobs when I started rubbing her ass with more pressure, she understood what was happening to me sitting there seeing them sucking each other.

She came to me bent her head and took my manhood into her mouth. She started sucking it like a lolly pop. At the same time Seema was sucking Lata's pussy with her tongue in it. Both the ladies had an exceptionally good structure and spare parts (vagina, boobs and ass). Those pussy lips of both were so beautiful I felt like sucking it till I die.

I was going crazy about them and we were talking and doing this entire thing. Lata told me that if she had a chance, she would have married me and would have had sex with me every now and then. But it was too late to do that as she was already married.

Then I took my turn on both the pussies, I licked them on their pussy which had hair first for which they started hopping and moaning. I inserted my tongue into Lata's vagina and started tasting her pre-cum. I started fucking her with my tongue her pussy walls were very wet.

She had a loose pussy as her hubby would treat her like an animal all the time. But she tasted great with her pussy. After 5 min she gave a loud moan and ejaculated in my mouth and that was the first time I had sucked a pussy as well as drank cum of vagina.

What a great experience it was, really mind blowing. They both sucked my cock to make it completely erect. I could not control any more myself from fucking both the dream ladies. I placed my cock on Lata's vaginal lips. Just coz of touching her pussy with my manhood I was in heavens and started pushing it inside the vagina.

She was very slippery and I felt very easy to slide in as she had a loose hole. I started jerking in and out very easily and vigorously but suddenly I felt like ejaculating. I did not want to finish the climax so easily, so I took my cock out and rested for some time. The heat came down a bit but I was keeping on finger fucking Seema at the same time Seema to Lata.

I kept them hot but I cooled a bit and again I came in to act. This time I took Seema and placed my cock on her vagina and pushed it little and found difficult into her as she was very tight to enter. Somehow, I made myself in her completely but this time I used one idea I started stroking her slowly and fucked her for 10 min like that.

This idea started working I keep on fucking her at the same pace as I had started it. By this the climax got delayed and I got ample time to fuck Seema. It was so great to prolong the climax by reducing the speed. We both were in heavens that slow fuck continued for 45 min, what a satisfying intercourse it was.

Oh god, I can never forget that in my life time. I ejaculated after such a long time and collapsed on her. After 15 min I again took action on Lata. She was really waiting for her turn and was totally arouse by our intercourse. I started entering Lata with a great force as I had again become impatient coz more than Seema, I was eager about Lata.

But she asked me to fuck her in the same way as I did with Seema. This time I kept jerking slowly into Lata, her vaginal walls were very slippery by this time so felt easy access into her. I felt her enjoying the slow-motion jerk. I was getting the feeling of the warmth inside her vagina. Heat was increasing time by time.

She was pushing her ass rhythmically with my strokes to meet the dept of the stroke. We both were enjoying this very much. I spent very long time in Lata's pussy than in Seema's. Whenever I felt Lata's vaginal walls contrasting, I would slow down and again I would start so that her orgasm would get prolonged.

This made her to get satisfied very much. She was so satisfied that she just hugged me with her arms when I was jerking her and she had her legs wrapped around my waste. After one hour I came in her and for my luck she also ejaculated at the same time.

This was very satisfactory for us. From that day whenever we got chance, we would not miss it not even in institute bathroom. Lata and Seema told me that they felt lucky to have me as their sex partner and wanted their hubbies to be away from them.

25. Yash

Pallavi was my mother's kid sister. She was a twenty-four-year-old blue-eyed blonde with a figure straight out of a porno flick. She was a tall, leggy chick about five foot nine in bare feet. Her tits were about a 36C and her ass was as perfect a specimen as ever filled out a bikini brief.

Her long blonde hair and stunning looks were everything a horny eighteen-year-old like me desired. I had fantasized about sinking my cock into my luscious aunt so many times I was in danger of pulling my dick out by the root!

I was staying at her house for the summer before returning to my studies after the summer break. Pallavi had taken to using her swimming pool just after her husband Chand had left for his work in the city. Chand had a high paying job that meant that my aunt didn't need to do a tap herself.

She was very much the lady of leisure, able to lounge around poolside all day. I was happy with this...Boy was I happy with this.

You see I had worked out that if I got up early, I could look out of my bedroom window and enjoy the view. The view consisted of Pallavi in a tiny bikini. Today was a little different, today Pallavi and Chand were arguing. I surreptitiously pulled the blind back to see what was going on.

She was wearing a small yellow bikini that accentuated her curves. I loved that bikini. Chand was only feet away in a sharp business suit. Christ! If he was any more straight–laced he'd be a fucking waxwork!

"You're ALWAYS too tired Chand!! ...I have needs you know!! A woman needs to feel wanted...I need sex Chand!! If you don't give it to me, I'll look elsewhere!

Chand was never one for confrontation. He spun on his heels and disappeared through the gate in the twelve-foot wall that surrounded the property. I heard his car spin on the gravel and he was gone.

I turned my attention to Pallavi. She dove into the pool and swam furiously, obviously trying to burn off the frustration of not getting fucked. Dammit I thought to myself, a perfectly good piece of prime pussy going to fucking waste.

I had planned to try and get to see more of Pallavi's curves. This little episode finally pushed my libido over the edge. I knew Pallavi always did twenty laps then went back to her bedroom to change. Luckily for me the house was a large, meandering affair that would enable me to reach there without being seen by my aunt.

It took me no time at all and I had no problem in finding a hiding place. The large drapes covering one window were still drawn and afforded me a good view of the whole room. I quickly ensconced myself and waited.

It wasn't long before Pallavi arrived. She let out a huge sigh. Boy was she on a downer! She went to a draw and took out a towel and headed to the shower in suite of course. I waited until I heard the water splashing and padded quietly to the door. I took a quick look into the bathroom.

Pallavi had her back to me and was already well scudded. The soap ran down her little body as the water jets hit her blonde hair. Was it my imagination or was my young aunt spending an inordinate amount of time soaping and rubbing her pussy? I was tempted to join her but the time was not yet right.

Pallavi reached to turn the flow of water off and I beat a hasty retreat to my hiding place. Pallavi returned to the bedroom. She was totally naked. My aunt perched her perfect ass on the edge of the four poster bed. My hand went to my cock as I saw her begin to towel herself dry.

I was hard as iron at the sight of the hot blonde slowly rubbing her blonde bush. It was neatly trimmed to allow her to wear those small bikinis. I had only ever dreamed of being close enough to tell that my aunt was a natural blonde.

She returned to the towel draw and took out a small vibrator. It just couldn't get any better!! I was about to see Pallavi use a sex toy to get herself off!! But no…she just sighed once more and replaced it in the draw.

Then much to my dismay she walked to my hiding place and pulled the drapes back. Busted!! I stood there looking eye to eye with my aunt. She looked stunned as her jaw dropped earthward. Quickly taking the initiative I moved forward and took her in my arms. My mouth mashed against hers.

I had hoped her pent-up hormones would take over and Pallavi would demand my sexual services. Boy was I wrong. She pushed me away and grabbed the towel to cover her ample charms. She was wide-eyed and looked like a rabbit caught in car headlights.

"Yash…what do you think you are playing at!!"

She edged towards the bedroom door, the only route of escape from her horny nephew. I wasn't prepared to lose my prize now though.

"You try for the door I'll rip the towel from you."

Pallavi stopped in her tracks. Realization was dawning. Her eighteen-year-old nephew was making a major play for her body.

I moved slowly towards her. The blonde retreated until the backs of her knees bumped against the bed. Pallavi gripped the towel tightly in front of her for protection.

I smiled at her and kissed her once again.

Pallavi looked uncertain as to how to react.

"What do you want?" She asked. Her voice barely a whisper

"I heard your argument with Chand. I want to give you what he won't. Sex"

I gripped the towel firmly and pulled downwards. Pallavi's grip gave way and she was naked before me once more. Her one hand instinctively covered her tits and the other her pussy.

"You forget I just saw you naked…saw you go to use a vibrator you are feeling that horny. Put your hands behind your back and show Yash what's on offer."

"Please Yash…nothing's on offer. I'm your aunt."

In response I pulled my Tee shirt off and shed my Speedos. All I was wearing. My nine-inch cock sprang forward. It was fully erect and begging for attention.

"I heard you telling your husband you wanted cock…well here you are. Now I want some pussy and you want cock. Fair exchange?"

Pallavi's eyes were nearly popping out of her head. She still looked unsure. Time to make her mind up for her I thought.

"Hands behind your back NOW Pallavi. I want to see what I'm about to fuck."

Pallavi decided to do as bid. I reached out and gently touched her now exposed breast. She made no move to resist as I teased her nipple to fullness.

Finding her voice, she expressed her fears.

"Yash please, I'm your aunt. What if your mother finds out I let you fuck me…what if Chand finds out!"

I moved my hand slowly to her perfect ass and pulled her as

close to me as I could get. My cock was digging in to her and her reaction was what I anticipated. She moved her lips to mine and we kissed deeply. Her hand found my tool and gently ran its full length.

"I'm not going to tell! …Are you? I mean if we keep quiet and I can satisfy your sexual needs and Chand can keep you financially satisfied. Everyone is happy"

I led back on the bed and beckoned towards Pallavi.

"If you want this as bad as me get your ass on this bed NOW!"

Pallavi climbed on and I led right back. She led alongside me and gently massaged my balls with her delicate hands.

"Sit on my face"

"What…"

"I said sit on my face Pallavi. I want to taste that pussy."

Pallavi slid herself up and lowered herself to my mouth. Her pussy lips were full and moist. I ran my tongue slowly over the entrance to her cunt. My fingers spread her sex open to my wet, probing licks and its darting motions were too much for the blonde.

She pushed herself onto my face and her pussy mashed into me. She was losing herself totally. Her juices were flowing freely over my face. The poor, sex-starved bitch had given it up to me. She was pushing against me until I almost smothered.

I managed to flip her over on to her back. I didn't have to say a word as she willingly spread those long legs of hers. I decided to tease her. Quite a feat as every sinew of my body was screaming inside me to just spear the pussy in front of me.

"You want to be fucked now Pallavi don't you."

I pushed her legs even further apart and ran my fingers slowly around her pussy lips.

"Answer me Pallavi…do you want to be fucked?"

Pallavi remained silent but nodded.

I inserted a finger into her cunt and quickly located the button of her clit. I playfully teased it, pushing into her pussy. I removed the finger and slowly ran my tongue over it, tasting her juices. I took my dick and inserted an inch into her moist opening.

Pallavi tensed slightly but my full length slipped easily into her slippery cunt. My body covered hers and those long legs of hers wrapped around my back, drawing me into her, extracting every pleasure she could from my long, thick rod.

"God you're huge!!" She moaned as I slowly picked up pace and made her body mine. I took a tit in my hand and squeezed none too gently. My mouth locked on to her large, tanned globe and I feasted on its gloriously engorged nipple.

I kissed her deeply and our tongues entwined. We broke free as Pallavi's back arched when a glorious orgasm wracked her body. She was panting like a dog, or should that be a bitch as I piston my cock into her soaking pussy. Her nails raked my back, scouring deep gouges from shoulder to flank.

This was the final spur to my cumming. I was in seventh heaven as waves of ecstasy combined with Pallavi's thrusts pushed me over the edge. I came in a long, shuddering climax, pouring my cum into my young aunts all too welcoming cunt.

I looked deep into her deep blue eyes.

"I'm glad you decided to give it up to me bitch. Now the fun really starts."

26. Yash 2

Ever since Shilpa my cousin caught a glimpse of my naked body when I stepped out of the shower, she hasn't stopped bugging me for another look. I guess seeing a stiff 9-inch cock on her 20-year-old brother is quite a curiosity to a 19-year-old girl who hasn't so much as kissed a boy, let alone had a throbbing cock up her tiny cunt hole.

Now every time I go for a shower, she stands at the door almost begging me to show her my body again. She has quite a dynamite body for a 19-year-old. I must admit that I have had a hard-on before looking at her firm, perky tits and her silky-smooth thighs that lead up to a rather tight little arse.

But the thing I can't get out of my mind is that she is still my sister. No matter how much her begging and promises of doing anything I wanted, made me hot I just couldn't bring myself to doing the deed with my own sister. I thought that boys were the only one to go through that entire hormone thing but my sister had it bad.

I used to go passed her room at night and hear her squealing and panting. One night my curiosity got the better of me and I just had to take a peek inside. Opening the door just enough to see in, there was my sister lying on her back with a cucumber up her twat moaning my name over and over.

Her constant whimpering was starting to get to me. She was a crafty little bitch I'll give her that. The more I refused to show her my cock the more she would do things to try and get my attention. She would parade around the house naked when our parents were not home and would always leave the bathroom door open so that I could see her taking a shower.

I even started to dream about her last week. Now that really got me worried. Here was this gorgeous teenager who wanted me so bad, and yet I refused to go near her. I didn't have this problem with other girls, I would fuck them to their hearts content but the fact that this one came from the same family as I did made all the difference.

It wasn't long before I started to ask myself what difference it made that she was my sister. I mean, the Egyptians used to do it all the time didn't they? I started to wonder about the meaning of the word "love". I could love my sister the same way I loved another girl and yet I wanted to get in the other girl's panties but felt funny about getting into my sister's.

I probably loved my sister even more than the other girls and I knew everything about her and yet there seemed to be this invisible barrier that stopped me from going any further. After one rather intense session of trying to explain to my sister that I would under no circumstances do anything with her she suddenly had a devious look in her eyes and told me "I will find a way big bro, don't you worry" and left, a little giggle escaping her lips as she did.

I had no idea what she meant by that then but I didn't realize how desperate she was to get into my pants either. I was in a kind of relationship with this girl from school named Natasha. Now Natasha had a gorgeous body, her soft Auburn hair came down in ringlets around her soft features and her tits were large and firm with big nipples that enjoyed sucking.

Her pussy was completely bare and I had to take my shoes off to count the number of times I had lapped at that bald cunt with abandon. Shilpa was friends with Natasha's younger sister who was how I met her in the first place and so Natasha got on really well with Shilpa. The three of us went out on occasion, having picnics or going for long walks.

When Natasha and I got amorous we used to send Shilpa off to do something and got stuck into a heavy fuck session while she was gone. Looking back on it now it was last Saturday that Shilpa's plan to get into my pants started. She told Natasha and I that she had scored three tickets to a movie on Saturday and asked if we would like to go with her.

We enjoyed basketball and so we all agreed. Then behind my back the sneaky bitch called my dad that I had a lot of undone homework to do for Monday and so my parents said I couldn't go. Shilpa didn't seem all that upset and said that Natasha's sister could go instead and that was that.

It wasn't until later that I found out what really happened that evening so what I tell you now are in retrospect. After the game the three girls went back to Natasha's house. Her parents were going out for dinner and asked if Shilpa would like to join them. She politely declined and asked if Natasha could give her a lift home.

Natasha said that she was just going to have a rabbit dinner (at least that's what I call her diet) and would take Shilpa home later. Shilpa said that she wouldn't mind a small dinner like that and so Natasha and Shilpa stayed at home alone to have a quick dinner before she went home.

It wasn't long before Shilpa started asking questions about me to Natasha and they had a real chinwag about yours truly. After about half an hour of general chitchat Shilpa started to move the conversation to a more personal level and asked Natasha if she had ever slept with me.

Natasha was a little embarrassed about this but as they knew each other fairly well she told Shilpa all about our sex life. Shilpa knew exactly what she was doing and before long Natasha was getting horny thinking about all the things we had done together. She could feel the moistness in her panties as she continued to relate story after story to Shilpa.

Natasha was getting a little uncomfortable now as it sounded like she was a real slut for doing all the things we had done and especially since she was talking to my sister about it at the time. Shilpa saw this and gently rested her hand on Natasha's knee saying that she really liked her and that she enjoyed listening to the stories as well.

Something strange happened next. Natasha was feeling so horny and here was a young girl with her hand resting on Natasha's knee and she felt warm inside. It was a gesture that Natasha felt deeply about and was confused about all the signals she was getting from Shilpa. Suddenly Shilpa leaned forward and gently kissed Natasha on the lips.

Natasha pulled back in amazement and looked intently at Shilpa wondering why she had done that. Telling her that everything was all right and that she just felt an urge to kiss her. Natasha had always had feelings for other women but never had the nerve to explore that side of her sexuality before.

Before long Shilpa had broken Natasha's barriers down and was passionately kissing her and fondling her ample bust. Natasha was fighting to resist the urges she was feeling but felt safe and let herself go. The slid to the floor and began to undress each other.

Shilpa's tongue was eagerly probing Natasha's mouth and the sensations that racked her body were incredible. Just then Shilpa pulled Natasha's panties off and lowered her head to my girlfriend's shaven snatch. Dipping her tongue into Natasha's glistening cunt lips she started to search for that little excitement bud she loved to play with when she masturbated herself.

Natasha's mind was racing; here she was with the 19-year-old sister of her boyfriend licking her pussy the same way that I had always done it. She thought about how much alike Shilpa and I was and found herself deeply attracted to her as she was to me.

Shilpa could see that Natasha was becoming eager to try her young cunny so she quickly turned around and thrust her tight little blond-haired pussy into Natasha's face. The smell was so overwhelming. She had smelt her own cunt when I kissed her after licking her pussy but now, she had her face buried in the young snatch of another girl and the sensations she was feeling were incredible.

Natasha began to feel her way inside Shilpa's hot snatch with her tongue and she located those areas she knew would bring excitement. Shilpa now had her finger inside my girlfriend's hot cunt and was making slow circles getting deeper and deeper as she went.

This went on for about half an hour before the two horny girls couldn't hold out any longer. First Natasha started to quiver and buck under the snaking tongue and delving fingers of my sister. She started to arch her back as her first lesbian orgasm flooded through her body.

The intensity of Natasha's orgasm brought on my sister's and she too arched her back, thrusting Natasha's tongue deeper into Shilpa's juicy snatch even further. Both girls just lay there as the last tingling of their orgasms faded away.

Natasha looked into the eyes of my nympho sister and was at a loss to say something to her. Shilpa simply looked into Natasha's eyes and said one simple phrase that shocked the living daylights out of her.

"I want you to help me fuck my brother!!!!"

For nearly a minute the room was silent as Natasha tried to absorb what my sister had just said. It was becoming so hard to tell the difference between her encounters with me and that which she had just had with my sister. The thought of taking part in a threesome with the two people who made her body quiver with such passion was too much for her to resist and she simply nodded to Shilpa.

It seems that Shilpa had thought of everything. Sunday came and Mom and Dad were going to see friends that night. Shilpa and I were alone in the house and I sighed to myself that I would probably spend the entire night fighting my little sister of instead of being with someone I could really fuck, like Natasha.

To my surprise Shilpa didn't seem interested anymore and didn't ask me once to fuck her. We had a quick take-away dinner and sat in front of the TV watching some stupid show. About 7 o'clock the doorbell rang and standing at the door was the person I most wanted to see, Natasha.

She came in and I couldn't wait to have my cock buried deep inside her tight snatch. I told Shilpa that I was taking Natasha up to do a bit of study but she didn't even look away from the TV. I couldn't believe my luck. The house was empty, my sister wasn't bothering us and I was about to fuck my girlfriend like a wild man.

We hadn't even made it to my room before both of us started taking our clothes off. It seemed that Natasha was just as anxious to screw as I was and we started to grope and fondle each other as we made our way to the bed. Natasha pushed me onto my back on the bed and whispered that she wanted to be on top this time.

I wasn't about to say no and watched with glee as she started kissing her way down my chest towards my eager stiff prick. Once there she gently guided my swollen cock into her mouth and started to take me deeply with slow but steady strokes. There seemed to be something extra in the way Natasha devoured my shaft.

I couldn't work it out at the time but there seemed to be a newfound lust in the way she moved and the things she did. Without even asking she quickly released my cock from her hot throat and straddled my body. She reached behind with her hand and gently shoved my cock into her steamy cunt.

She was extremely wet and my cock slid right up to the balls almost immediately. Natasha was always a good fuck but every now and then I wished that she were a little tighter. Not that the way she can take a hard cock up her snatch isn't the most exquisite sensation on earth, just that I would like to feel the walls of her vagina tightly wrapped around my cock just once in a while.

Our rhythm was becoming wilder by the minute and I was madly thrusting away inside Natasha's engorged cunny lips. She was impaling herself on my swollen rod on every down stroke and moaning softly in my ear. Just then I felt Natasha move her body kind of jerkily and she raised her hips up just enough to let my cock slip out of her creamy cunt.

I was just about to ask her why she let him escape like that when the most tingling sensation started to make my rock-hard cock quiver. I looked at Natasha curiously and there was a devious smile on her face. I couldn't for the life of me work out what it was that was making my prick feel so good.

I gently moved Natasha to one side so I could get a good look at my cock and there was Shilpa!!!! Sucking my cock like a mad woman. The sudden sight of my little sister with my 9-inch cock buried up to the balls in her throat was too much for me. I screamed for her to hold on as I started to squirt my hot cum down her throat.

It didn't faze her at all, she clung to my gushing cock taking every stream down her throat. My cock was on fire, it was going berserk with my climax and more semen shot itself out the deeply devoured end. It was too much for her now and sperm started to dribble down the side of her mouth.

With one final suck she drew the last drops of cum from my bewildered cock and slid it from her mouth. Wiping the sperm from her lips she made a snide remark about "I told you I would get you" and started to jerk my half hard cock.

I looked at Natasha to see what her reaction was to my sister's head job and she was dumbfounded to see her gazing lustily at my sister!!! She looked at me and gave me a brief rundown on what happened Saturday evening. I was totally amazed.

My sister had seduced my girlfriend, finger-fucked her to orgasm and made her an accomplice in seducing me too. That's when I lost all inhibitions about fucking my sweet little sister. She had worked my cock up to another erection by this time and I jumped off the bed and made my sister lie on her back with her legs gaping wide, desperately waiting for my huge cock to fill her.

"If you wanna fuck little sis, I'll give you one ... And them I'm gonna fill that tight little cunt with your brother's sperm", I whispered to her as I started to work a finger into her young snatch. Natasha moved around to Shilpa's head and placed herself over my sister's waiting mouth.

Shilpa eagerly lapped at Natasha's juicy cunt and I made way for the tightest fuck I had ever had in my life. Teasingly I moved my fat cock around the entrance of my sister's juicy cunt. I worked the head from the little pink bud of her clitoris right down the glistening golden curls of my sister's slit.

She started to moan from under my girlfriend's dripping snatch and Natasha looked at me in a way I had never seen before. Her eyes were wide open and she was obviously experiencing something that I alone could not give her. The sight of my sister's prone body lying beneath my hungry cock with my girlfriend's pussy being licked and sucked into frenzy was enough for me.

I pressed the head of my cock against my sister's tight opening and started to push it towards heaven. At first, I thought that it would never go in. It just seemed to resist any attempt at entry. Then with a sudden squeal from Shilpa the head of my monster cock slipped into her vice-like cunt.

I couldn't believe how tight her quivering pussy was holding me. I started to push further and the pressure on my cock made every ridge along the shaft feel like an earthquake. Shilpa pulled her face away from Natasha's burning clit just long enough to tell me to thrust harder.

Hearing my sister say that made me go for broke. I thrust my cock as deep as I could into her ever so tight cunt and started to pull out with a long, hard stroke. Back in again I began a slow rhythm where my sweet little Shilpa could feel the full length of her brother's cock slide in and out of her juicy snatch.

My mind was spinning and the sensation of such a tight little cunt was making my balls ache with a gallon of sperm. Natasha could see that I was nearing the edge of my ejaculation so she pulled away from Shilpa's lapping tongue so that I could see the look on my sister's face when I shot my load into her incestuous snatch.

Shilpa looked at me with sisterly love as her orgasm gripped the head of my cock. Feeling such a tight pussy get even tighter pushed me over the edge and my cock started to shoot glob after glob of brotherly jism into her hot snatch. Her eyes opened wider and her mouth opened only to allow a high-pitched whimper escape.

Her cunt was twitching like crazy as another glob filled her womb. She pulled my hips tight to hers with her encircled legs as the last squirt of cum filled my sister's fuckhole. Then she went limp.

We must have lain there for about an hour before any of us come too. I looked at my satisfied sister and asked her if it was worth all her begging and scheming. She looked at me with that devious smile again and said:

"It was fantastic … Just wait until I tell Natasha's sister all about it. She is going to want you to fuck her too!!!!"

27. Yash 3

It was all good for the first few days with my Aunt and my Cousin, that is until my mom decided to visit me. I really dreaded this because she would be constantly on my case and most importantly, I wouldn't be able to have fun with my aunt or cousin.

My mom wasn't really very strict, but very conservative. She was the type of mom who would freak at the word sex. She was of course my Mama (Uncle)'s(uncle) sister, so my aunt and her weren't related. She and my aunt for some odd reason got along really well and would always talk for hours.

My mom got to my Mama (Uncle)'shouse on a Friday afternoon. As usual she was wearing her long conservative skirt and a loose top. She wore very little make up and as I met her, she gave me a big hug and told me how I was.

"Oh, Yash how have you been, oh thanks a lot Pallavi for taking care of him, has he been any trouble," she said as she hugged my Mama (Uncle), aunt, Shilpa, and me.

"No, he's been great," my aunt said as she winked at Shilpa.

"Yeah, Aunt Pallavi, having Yash has been a lot of fun," Shilpa said as she smiled shyly.

"Don't worry about him Pallavi, he's been a real help, especially when I go away, it's great to have a man with these two gals," my Mama (Uncle) said proudly.

My Mama (Uncle) and I helped out my mom with her stuff and we headed home. When we got home my Mama (Uncle) asked me if my mom could stay in my room, and I could sleep in the living room, and I of course agreed. That first night was crappy, as I slept in a little couch, and worst of all didn't get any from my Aunt or cousin.

My Aunt and my mom stayed up real late in the kitchen, which also sucked because the light from the kitchen could clearly be seen in the living room.

"Having fun Yash," Shilpa whispered as she walked in.

"No, this bites," I whispered back to her.

"I bet my mom and your mom will go out some time so that we can have fun," Shilpa whispered back as she left for the kitchen. She stayed with my mom and my Aunt till about two in the morning when they all finally went to sleep.

As it turned out we would go out everywhere as a big family, and as much as I tried, I couldn't have time for myself. It was like this for the whole weekend until my Mama (Uncle) left for another business trip that Tuesday. That day my aunt and my mom went to the airport to drop of my Mama (Uncle) while Shilpa and I stayed at the house alone, finally.

"Hey Shilpa we're finally alone," I said as I gently caressed her thighs.

"I think I noticed Yash, but I don't think we should do this right now, I mean what if they get back early and see us," she said trying to wave of my arm.

"They won't be back early, I mean I bet we have at least an hour or two," I said as I tried to convince her that we should do it.

I finally got to her and convinced her that we should go at it. We started of slowly by kissing and touching each other. She would touch my dick, and then I would go and touch her tits or her ass. Then suddenly we heard the door open and there my aunt and my mom stared at us on the sofa on top of each other.

"Oh my, what do you think you are doing Yash, do you know how wrong this is, get of her this instant, I'm so sorry Pallavi I didn't know this was happening, oh my, where did I go wrong," my mom said as she pulled me off Shilpa and tried to explain everything to my aunt.

"Calm down Pallavi, I think we need to talk," my Aunt said as she sat my mom down on the sofa.

"Rupa this isn't wrong, okay, it's completely normal to have sex, and I don't think you should condemn a young man for sex, even if it is with his own cousin," my Aunt said as she tried to explain to my mom what was happening.

"But Pallavi this is so wrong, I don't think it's right especially with your own cousin," my mom said, as she tried to clear out everything that was happening.

"It's not wrong Rupa, I mean, haven't you ever fantasized about one of your own relatives," my Aunt said, trying to make a point.

"Yeah but it's just a fantasy."

"No Rupa, it's not just a fantasy, it's something that you should do, I mean wouldn't you have loved to fulfill that fantasy, and anyway I don't think that having sex with anyone is wrong, in fact it's beautiful."

This statement of course left my mom kind of shocked and then kind of relieved at the same time.

"Now that we got this out of us, I got to kind of confess something, my fantasy was with umm, with you and Shilpa," my mom said as she lowered her head and talked to my Aunt.

"Well why don't we fulfill that fantasy, and I bet you won't mind if Yash joins in, I mean it was him who started this whole thing," my Aunt said as she leaned over towards my mom.

"Uhhh, well okay, but don't tell anyone one, but, ohh, okay, what the heck," my Mom said as she started to undress.

To my surprise my Mom wasn't half bad, I mean I had always seen her as the type of person who would be unsexy, but she was the total opposite. As she started to undress, she revealed a tremendous set of legs and also a nice firm tight ass, and most beautiful of all, a nice shaved pussy which really gave me a hard on.

As she took her top off, she also unveiled a tight stomach and nice firm tits. As she let her hair down, she looked like a model, I mean my mom was actually fine. She then went over to my aunt and then started to take off her clothes. She kissed her as she started to undress her and then my aunt would finger my mom's already wet pussy.

My mom started by taking my aunt's shirt of then her jeans, she then unstrapped her bra, and then slipped my aunt's panties off, all while the made out. This had to be the most incredible sight. This two people, both in their thirties, were all over each other.

"That's one hell of a sight to see," Shilpa said as she started to undress and joined the excitement

"What the heck," I said to myself as I undressed and hoped to join the whole thing.

This was truly one of those things that you truly will probably ever see, especially be involved in. It was incredible, my Mom and my Aunt made out while my cousin, Shilpa ate my mother up. All the while Shilpa fingered herself and my mom fingered my Aunt Pallavi.

This was unbelievable, I was watching three beautiful women have sex, and best yet I could join in. As I moved towards the action, I noticed Shilpa and she pointed towards my mom's ass. My dick was really hard, so I started by leaning over towards my mom's ass and licking it so that my dick might go in.

My mom kind of shook a little but kept on making out with my aunt. I then stood up and opened her cheeks and pushed my dick in her tight little ass hole. She kind of shuddered a little but just went with it. I pumped my dick in and out of her ass as fast as I could. I didn't take long for her to come to an intense orgasm.

As she started to orgasm, her tight asshole gripped my dick real tight, which made my load come out in her asshole. As some of it leaked out Shilpa licked it and then moved to my mom's asshole and licked the cum out of her asshole. My mom was kind of dumbfounded by the whole thing and exhausted, but my aunt had other ideas.

"Hey Pallavi, I think that Yash didn't get enough, how about we take turn sucking his young hard dick, wouldn't that be fun.

"I think that I should start since I discovered him first" my aunt said as she kneeled down and started to suck on my dick.

"Wait mom, I think that we should do it together, I bet Aunt Pallavi wouldn't mind," Shilpa said as she kneeled down and started to suck on my balls.

"No, I think I have other plans for Yash," my mom said as she laid down and tried to recover from the intense fuck she had gotten.

The dick sucking was incredible, my aunt would suck on my dick, and all the while Shilpa would move around my balls and put them in her mouth. This was so intense that I had to sit down. My aunt was unbelievable, as my aunt and cousin both joined in sucking on my dick, sometimes both of them sucking on my dick while others they met lips while sucking.

It only took a few minutes for me to produce a whole new load of cum. This was incredible because both women licked the cum of my dick and as some of the cum got on Shilpa's tits, my aunt started to suck on her tits.

After a while my mom signaled me to go over to the sofa where she was. She then laid down and told me to get on her stomach. I did as she told and sat on her stomach. She then noticed that my dick wasn't hard and started to play with it, massaging it, this then got my dick hard again. As my dick finally got hard, she got it and stuck it between her tits.

"I always wanted to do this, but your father always said no, now I want you to relax and cum all over your mother's titties," my mom said as she started to massage my dick with her nice tits. As she did this my aunt and Shilpa fingered each other and made out. I then leaned over and started to fondle and suck on my mom's tits.

"Oh yeah Yash suck on them good."

"Oh cum on mom, faster, don't you want my cum all over you."

My mom then started to squeeze my tits and rub them faster. My aunt and my cousin all the while fingered each other and made out.

As my mom squeezed harder, I let out a huge load of cum, some of it reaching her face, the rest streaming down my mom's tits. She was very satisfied with what she had done, and as the last of my cum came out of my aching dick, she called Shilpa and my aunt.

"Why don't you two help us get cleaned up," my mom said to Shilpa and my aunt, which automatically got up and started to lick on my mom's tits. Shilpa went to my mom's tits and licked all over them, clearing all of my cum and then slurping on my mom's tits.

At the same time, my aunt went over to my soft aching dick and sucked on it. This wasn't like any other blowjob, but painful yet very pleasurable. She didn't just lick it, but she literally sucked it, making my dick get a little hard and a making a little cum come out. This was incredible because this gave me an intense orgasm and also dried me off all my cum.

When we had finished, we all laid the living room exhausted, sticky, naked, but most importantly of all satisfied.

"So, what do you think of having sex with relatives," my aunt said.

"I don't know, I'm too tired to think, all I know is that I feel really tired, but yet very Satisfied, thanks Pallavi," my Mom said.

28. *Lisa*

I am Luv working as Teacher for a Higher Secondary School. My first time was with my colleague Lisa. She was a virgin. We are living in the same colony in Mysore (Karnataka). I am fair, well-built person. Lisa gorgeous girl white fair in color, she has big boobs and a very nice structure about 38-85-30.
Coming to story, I have to say thanks to my colleague Dilip, since he loved her. He asked me to be a mediator. I always lusted after her, so I agreed to act as a mediator. I got many chances to speak with her regarding the gifts and cards given by my friend. She rejected my friends' love and this is how our friendship began.

She was from a conservative family, so I made a plan and acted accordingly. First, I found out that she is fond of luxuries gifts. So, I had foreign chocolates sent daily as I have a cousin in the States. She became very close to me. We sat together and spoke a lot in our leisure time.

I intentionally placed my hand on her thigh. She didn't care. The public place we hung out won't allow me to go beyond that. Every night I used to masturbate thinking of her.

My chance finally arrived. Her birthday is on Sep 10 and it is Wednesday. I gave her a big dairy milk chocolate and a rose. She became very happy. She asked me what I wanted. Waiting for this chance I said "I want a kiss ". She was stunned for a second, looked around and said that don't speak like that again. I apologized for that and said I was just having fun.

I thought that I have to take her alone to some other area then only I enjoy her. So, I asked her to come for an outing outside Mysore. She said ok immediately. Our outing is about 1/2 hour from our place. The next morning, we told our parents we are going to school as if we were going to inform them about our outing

On that day she looked very beautiful... She wore blue sari with free hair. When we left for the place we headed separately as she has a fear if someone saw us together it may create a problem. Before meeting at the place, we met up at a different place as planned as she owned a scooty bike.

Once we met, I was driving her vehicle her breast used to touch my back on every speed bump this made me horny. She did not know I used to apply the brakes intentionally. I took this chance and told her that we are near the island of Krishna Raja Sagara. Once we reached, we went inside the island and found no one was around.... As I expected only ten to fifteen people were on that island (all lovers). On seeing them she relaxed. We went to an isolated place.

I placed my hand on her hand. She didn't respond. After 15 minutes I said "Normally my friends will put their hand on their girlfriend when they are with a girl". She smiled and said "O.K.". I said o.k. And then I placed my hands on her shoulder covering her back. She was getting horny.

Then I slowly moved my hand from her shoulder to her hand. I freely moved my hand on her back but slowly. Then I moved on her hair, ear, cheek, neck and she stopped my hand when I about to touch her nipple. I got angry and removed my hand from her.

Then after 2 mins she placed her hand on my thighs and smiled cunningly. I did not respond. She caressed and placed her hands on my crotch. The pleasure was unbelievable. She rubbed it gently. She is moving her breast up and down with excitement.

I don't know how my cock also started getting stiff. She started giving me a very good hand job. I shot my load into her mouth. She swallowed it without spilling and she cleaned my tool with her tongue. Then I kissed all parts of her body.

We came out. I wanted to take full advantage of that day. I already got a key of that island's guest house in Krishna Raja Sagara. I told Lisa today it is very hot, we can take rest for some time and then go. She nodded. We took lunch and then went to the room; it was a lonely guest house.

My intensions were very clear by hook or crook today I must screw Lisa. Once inside the room she went to freshen up. I showed her the bathroom and to my surprise after 1 minute she came out looking hotter that before. I placed my hand on her shoulder. I began to open the buttons of the blouse on her back side.

My mouth was watering to see her naked back. Gently I opened her buttons. More I moved down more flesh I saw on her naked back with bra strap. I lick her naked back and kiss it too. She stood up from the chair. I hugged her from back. She was getting a sexy sensation so she pushes her buttocks out. Her buttocks than hit my hard cock.

I felt an electric current running through my body. I was going mad. I turned her and started kissing her face her lips and then I came down to the neck. I again kissed on her lips and then started licking them. Then I shove my tongue into her mouth and licked inside her mouth. While we kissed, I felt her hand move to my crotch.

Then I removed her sari and then moved down to her the light blue petticoat. Now she was only standing in her bra and panty. She was looking so sexy. I never seen a woman's body like this. Her buttocks were so full round and tight inside the panty. I was feeling and massaging her soft smooth skin on her back. She had worn a white bra in which she looked very sexy.

I remove the straps from her shoulder and skipped the bra

down. She had big pair of boobs and pink nipples that made her look like a sex goddess. Her nipples became rock hard. I caught her tender boobs in my hand and press them hard. She was constantly moaning aaaaoohhhh. She than removed my shirt.

My cock was tearing my pant and coming out like a hot rod. She removed my pant and underwear. I continued to pull her light blue panty down. When I was doing that, I was also kissing her ass. Now Lisa was fully naked in front of me. She had a very nice hairy pussy.

I put my hand on her pussy and started rubbing it. Then I put my hand inside her pussy hole. She cried uuuuuueeeeeeeeeeeeeeee. She was one tight virgin pussy. I laid her on the bed and opened her legs. I was licking her hard. She asked me to lick her faster. After sometime I put my 7-inch cock near her virgin pussy.

I took her quickly in my arms and put her pussy on my cock and showed her how to do it. She was afraid at first but she was a quick learner. I slowly put my cock at the entrance of her pussy and made a hard stroke. Just one inch of my cock was entered in her pussy. She screamed uuuuuueeeeeeeeeeeeeeee.

I again made a gentle stroke and her cries were increasing with every stroke. After two or three strokes my cock was stopped by some obstruction. I understood that it was her virgin seal. I made a harder stroke with all my might. A cry broke from her aaaaaayyyyyyyyyyyyyiiiiiiiiiii Luv please stoppppp.

I continued making smaller strokes and after my cock had entered her pussy completely. I again start making harder movements to and fro. She again started crying but I continued to fuck her. I made several harder strokes and loved to hear her moan. Then I rolled onto my back and she got on top and offered me with her breasts while she rode my lund (cock).

I loved the feeling of having my lund(cock) in her choot (pussy). We cummed at the same time and she collapsed on top of me and pressed her body on mine. We are banging each other continuously until it was evening. Then I told her it is enough for today. We then returned back to our place.

After a week of our first experience, I wanted to have another session with Lisa. She too was very eager to meet me. We applied for a leave and went to same place. I took some porn books that would provoke more...As I asked her, she wore lace purple thongs this is the first time I fucked her ass... First, she rejected then responded well.

After that day I have spent many days and nights with her.

29. Paalika

I'm Lohit from Delhi. I like to share my first sex experience as it is the only and most exciting experience of my life, which I never disclosed to any one before.
I am 27 years old, belong to Punjab and a graduate from I.D.E.A.S. college Nagpur and now working for Multinational company in Delhi. I stay in company provided flat in Gurgaon. It's not that I belong to economically weak family, but in my college days I used to have a mobile which used to be expensive both the phone and the bills so I thought this is my luxurious passion so I must earn on my own and should not let my parents pay for it.

So, during my education in Nagpur, I use to get my earnings from home tuitions. The story, which I am going to tell you, is 4 years old. I posted some add in paper for home tutor. Then I received a call from some Uncleji. He asked me about my qualification. I told him everything honestly.

He was impressed by my college name and told me that his daughter is student of 12th and preparing for engineering entrance. So, I was the right person for them. As I passed this exam only 2 yr. ago. He invited me to his home, which was not very far away from my college. I rang the bell.

A girl of around 18yrs opened the door, I instantly understood that I'm going to teach this girl. Paalikae, as she was called by her parents with love. I taught her for one year. She was so cute and charming that I have never seen any girl so lively and beautiful.

I later knew this that how horny she was at that age. But in the beginning, she looked very innocent and gentle. I was very fair with her but one day I was amazed, rather shocked by a strange event. This was a hot Sunday of summer when I was working on my pc in my hostel. I got a call on my mobile phone.

It was from Paalikae's home phone. She was having an exam on Monday. When I picked up, she told me that she is nervous for exam, so requested me to come early to her home. I told her I be there in 20 mins. She thanked me.

When I arrived, she opened the door, I was amazed to see her. She was wearing tight top of white colour and tight jeans of blue colour. Her top was so tight that I could see her black bra and even the nipples were protruding out. She requested me to sit on sofa and got water for me. She then sat next to me.

I asked about her parents, she told me that they are out at her uncle's house so that there is no noise in the house so that she can study. I asked her what happened. She said that she is getting nervous and placed her head over my shoulder. I pressed her head closer to my shoulder and held her hand and told her not to worry, I'm there to help you.

I pressed her hand and kissed on her forehead. I asked her why she was so nervous. She didn't answer. I was more encouraged with her 'no reply' response. Then I pressed her closer to me and my hand encompassed her at her breast area and my left hand touched her breast over the t shirt. She never opposed this to me.

This was a tacit consent of her to carry on. I understood what she was wanting at that time. Though, reluctant at that time but more stimulated with her condition. This was more prompting for me when she put her head on my thighs and lied on the sofa. I broke all the barriers and put my lips onto her cheeks.

She was like a fresh rose. She never opposed so I got encouraged and I kissed her lips for five minutes and soaked all the juice from her succulent lips.

This was really the first time of Paalikae because she was trembling and quivering with enjoyment and fervour of first interaction with any male. I was also out of control. I requested her to stand up for a while and pulled out her t-shirt and opened the bra also. Then I put my lips on the apple-sized boobs.

She was moaning and shivering with the excitement. I was also on the seventh heaven when I found an 18-year hot virgin, which was flaring-up. She was looking like a nymph. I later came to know that Paalikae had seen a XXX movie which she was hidden in her brother's computer. Her brother went to Mumbai for his job so she got that computer.

Because of that movie she was like 'near to erupt' volcano as she watched that movie for 3 hours late night yesterday alone in her room. She was in my hands like a gift from paradise. I took off her jeans now, as I was taking her cloth and she with a little resistance allowed her 'Sir' for appeasing her seemingly unquenchable fire, which she had blown in her body after watching that pornography.

Now she was in panty only. I requested her to remove but she opposed and requested me to wait for few moments and told me to suck her nipples for some more time. I was delighted and I started to suck her nipples and then kiss her body from head to toe. Her nipples were the most delicious part of her gorgeous body.

I sucked the nipples one by one, as these were the two fountains sprouting the nectar, which I was drinking. Then she herself inserted hand in her panty and I understood her signal and remover it and saw her naked for the first time. Then I moved to her delicate and fragile pussy. This was the really magnificent.

When my lips touched the lips of her pussy, she produced a moaning noise and stretched her legs in the manner as her pussy became like a sealed gorge. I was wild by that time; I held her both white thighs in my hand and put my mouth in the area between her legs. She was like a fish out of water she was nearly screaming.

Her clit was wet and was leaking with the fluids of joy. She held her small breasts in her hands and starting pressing her in a haphazard way. I had inserted my tongue in her clit and my tongue was tasting the world's tastiest juice. She held my hair in her hand with the lust. But I was absorbed in the little world of hers.

All of a sudden, I felt she was near orgasm. She pressed her clit firmly and her legs bent with a sprout of fluids from her clit. After this she cooled down and when relaxed she kissed me deeply and started looking for her dress.

But I managed to get her dress before she could reach there, now I was moving all around in her house and she followed me and requested me for her clothes, but I refused. Then I reached her bedroom and saw a mirror behind her. I caught her and twisted her to see the mirror. I saw both naked bodies standing side by side and my dick was hard rock.

She held my cock in her hand and started touching it to her ass. I was fingering her by now. Then I again twisted her and touched my penis to her vagina. There she stopped for a moment and requested me to leave. I asked her why? She said that she 'd get condom from her dads' room. I left her.

She went to her dad's room, I followed her, as soon she picked condom out of drawer, and I gripped her from back. We programmed to watch the movie in her bedroom. We both were on the bed when the movie started. It was provocative. I at once went on. Paalikae looked at me and smiled. She wanted to enjoy it full.

I took initiative. Her splendid body was warming me. I sucked her tongue and made her hornier and more desirous. She held my cock and started playing with it. She liked my balls very much. As she rubbed my cock I turned on and I put her legs on my shoulder. She was amazed what I was going to do in that style.

I was in a mood to adopt a 'desi' style. I had worn the condom and now I was ready to insert my 7-inch penis in her tight virgin pussy. She was uncontrollable. I put my dick on her clit and rubbed on the light brown hair. This proved to be really gratifying for her.

She had a wail of protest on her face when I was delaying to give her the 'key of paradise'. As I decided to fire, I pushed the 7-inch missile into the chasm and a streak of red blood with a groan of anguish were eminent. She felt a flit of pain for some moment. In the mean time I unloaded my dick from that virgin pussy.

I put my lips on her lips and kissed her long to vanish her pain of 'first time' and to make her hot and ready to take part in the game. This was successful. She turned on again and was ready to accept the 7-inch-long dick in her obviously small pussy which she previously thought not to be so ruthless to let her delicate pussy bleed out.

But it was over and we were ready to take the real enjoyment. I loaded my shaft into her slicker canyon and felt it was a genuine and a tightest stuff I ever found and tasted. I start sliding my shaft in the silky way and with every stroke I put her in a New World of exhilaration.

She was feeling herself on the seventh heaven and I was pushing my shaft deeper and deeper into her pussy which was a hot and spicy one. It lasted for five minutes. I wanted to change the posture. I then made her in doggy style and blew inside her from the back. It was delightful for her, while watching movie on the computer.

I fucked her for 1 hour almost. She liked to continue it forever. But we were too hot to cum. I unloaded my dick from her cunt and adopted a posture while I was over her body kissing her, her both breasts were in my hands and my shaft in her pussy.

At the climax we both were moving fast and she was pushing me from downward and I was stroking fast in response. With sudden bursts I cummed inside her pressing my dick so forcefully as I supposed to enter whole of my torso in her scorching pussy.

She also cummed soon after me and she held my body with her legs so vigorously that I was confined in the prison between her legs. For five minutes we forgot everything in the world. Our bodies merged into each other, our lips sticked and our genitals welded with each other.

When we relaxed it was time to get ready for next session. We took on our dresses and moved to drawing room. Then I requested her to allow me to change her dress. She took me to her room again n then opened her almirah. I selected one for her school dress, which was light blue shirt n navy blue skirt.

She said that this skirt is very small and she don't wear it anymore. But I was rigid on that dress. I opened her jeans again in asked her to insert her legs in skirt. She did so. But she was right. This skirt was too short for her. I could see her panty very clearly. But I still kept myself rigid on wearing that skirt only.

She did so. Then I put her shirt and kept top 3 buttons opened as I was unable to lock them coz her breast was not allowing me to do so. So, I could see her cleavage very clearly. I clicked few photos also with my phone in that dress.

Then we had another session of love. I fucked her many times afterwards. But after her exams were over, she got admitted to Priyadarshini college of engineering, in Nagpur. So, I was able to meet her even after I left tutoring her. I used to bring her to my hostel too and fuck her there too.

Once we went to her friend's room, where her friend was staying as paying guest and I fucked her there too. This carried on till I left Nagpur. But now I don't meet her anymore. I don't have many friends in Delhi. So, I'm thirsty for love.

30. Suja

It is an experience of mine that happened between me and Dr Suja, the Dr who treated my Bhabhi (sister-in-law) during her pregnancy. She was a very charming lady doctor and it was quite normal for her to talk sex with her patients and sometimes with their husbands.

I consider myself indeed very lucky that I got a chance to have an affair with her who till that time had never got involved with any other man than her husband. It was me, who impressed her more.

I used to visit her in her clinic very often along with my Bhabhi (sister-in-law). She would counsel both of us about various things but she used to deliberately cut short her talk while approaching the real subject – intercourse. She would make an eye contact with me then look away.

I just kept my head nodding and acting as an avid listener. I kept smiling in my mind and waited for the right moment, the right time, the time when only we two are there and, and, …… Just fanaticizing about her. Her beautiful face, long hair with curly ends and a glorious figure remained permanently etched in my mind.

Fortunately, the day arrived soon. I received a phone call while I was still in my office from Dr Suja. She asked me to come to her clinic while returning home. She had to give some medicines and advice for my Bhabhi (sister-in-law). I said ok. I reached her clinic at the appointed time.

We were already very friendly as we exchanged the customary hellos. After advising she asked me a question, "Mr. Nayak, how do you keep your wife happy?"

I was surprised but then I thought this is the time. As a matter-of-factly I said, "I don't know really. May be my organ is long enough to satisfy her."

"O really?" she asked, "Let me see."

Without hesitation I stood up from my seat, unzipped my fly and took out my penis which was not fully erect.

"Hmmmm." She put up her fingers on her lips. "Not so big as you think."

"It is now up to you to bring life into it." I challenged her. "You are a Doctor."

She smiled and knew what I was meaning. "I am a woman too."

She came forward from behind her desk and took a step closer to me trying to hold my penis. I stepped backwards. "Yes Suja, you are really a woman first," I said, "Very beautiful and sexy.... you have to bring it to life without touching it."

She understood my challenge. She smiled sexily as I praised her and called her name. She took a step backwards and arched her arms upwards as if to relieve herself of some ache due to a day's work. Her chest flung out revealing her tits. She bent her arms to free her hair from the pins.

Soon her hair had opened and fell on her back. My dick now started to twitch. Seeing this she put up a winning smile on her face. She was making her hair fall loose by slowly shaking her head. At the same time the pallu of her silk saree started to slide across her chest revealing a cream-colored silk blouse underneath.

Soon the pallu had fallen and her tits were visible from her low-cut blouse and probably buttoned up at the back side. Her fair skin between her blouse and petticoat was shining and waiting to be eaten up.

She moved her hands over her tits feeling the silk. Then she turned her back towards me and started trying to unbutton her blouse. Till that time, I could not wait any longer. I rushed towards her and embraced her in my arms from behind. "Oh Suja, you win." I murmured in her ear. I pressed my dick against her firm ass.

She turned her face as I kissed her slowly on her lips and continued sucking her lips while holding her waist between the edge of her blouse and petticoat. I gently caressed her breasts bringing my arms up over her blouse and could feel her nipples become erect through her soft bra and blouse.

We simply stood there together for a long time softly stroking her body from behind as our tongues explored each other's mouths. Then I undid the buttons of her blouse and unhooked her bra from behind but did not remove them. I slowly turned her to face me and again I started kissing her juicy lips.

I moved my hands inside her blouse to feel her warm tits. "Ah lovely, " I murmured. She too heaved a sigh of pleasure. I kept kissing her lips and kneading her breasts. Then I slowly lifted her open blouse over her tits. What a sight it was! I quickly closed my mouth over her erect nipple while still holding and caressing her other breast.

She meanwhile caught hold of my dick which was now in its full form. She could not hold it with both her hands which made her comment, "Yes, very long indeed. Put it in me, my darling."

"Yes, but wait I want to..."

"No," she cut short, "Just put it in me."

Then I lifted her saree along with her petticoat which made a bundle around her waist. Her creamy thighs now uncovered were a sight to behold. But she was growing more and more restless. Her pink panty was soaking wet. I ran my fingers around the edge of her panty to pull it down. Our conditions were now totally out of control.

I just held my dick with my hand and placed it at her cunt's entrance. A gentle push and my dick went inside her. With my dick inside her vagina, I could see her relax and then I resumed devouring her breasts. The more I sucked her breasts the more my dick went inside her cunt. I could feel my dick stroking her inner depths.

Then I could feel my climax building up and as I was about to cum she too shuddered and held me tightly in her arms. Her breasts crushed against my chest. Our mouths joined together with our tongues.

This was our first fuck. She wanted it this way. She told me later. Fully clothed and yet we became one. Without uttering any word, she knew this has brought us closer and for days to come we can have a more lasting session. Both of us knew very well that this is only the beginning. The best is yet to come.

INDIAN LUST STORIES

From Book 1: Indian lust stories are a collection of erotica stories. Wife cheating encounters with her boss, husband friend, Neighbor, Friend's husband. These complete or incomplete short stories will surely want you crave for more. Indian Lust Stories are proud to be able to offer a large and fine selection of erotic sex stories. With each written in erotic literature, we're able to provide you with a beautiful collection of hot, erotic, and tasteful erotic sex stories. We ensure that each and every line and word within each sexy story is packed with beautiful, sensual and erotic lovemaking so we know there's something for absolutely everyone. Take your time to read through our finest and most celebrated works of erotica stories today.

Indian Lust Stories

Indian Lust Stories 2

Indian Lust Stories 3

Indian Lust Stories 4

Indian Lust Stories 5

Indian Lust Stories 6

Indian Lust Stories 8

www.ingramcontent.com/pod-product-compliance
Lightning Source LLC
Chambersburg PA
CBHW072217150726
48002CB00005B/1854